Glimmer of Gold

GLIMMER
OF GOLD

by William Nikkel

jms books

GLIMMER OF GOLD

JMS Books LLC
10286 Staples Mill Rd. #221
Glen Allen, VA 23060
www.jms-books.com

Printed in the United States of America
ISBN: 9781475057287

For my wife Karen and my mother Shirley for their love and support.
And to my writer friends Millie Hast, Dani Brown, Trish Heckman, and Edna Leo
for suffering through early drafts of the story.

Chapter 1

JACK FERRELL NEEDED to breathe. He'd been under water for more than a minute and realized he'd have to surface soon. But if he did, the flash of gold that winked at him from the coral would be lost to him forever.

The tidal surge swept him dangerously close to the jagged reef.

He kicked hard with his fins and avoided the coral's sharp edges.

Again, he caught a glimpse of something small and round—like a golden eye gleaming at him from darkness.

He had to know what it was.

He focused on that one spot in the reef.

The violent surge sucked his body forward and pulled him back. A washing machine of turbulence swept him sideways, threatening to roll him, and pressed him to the bottom.

It was impossible for him to hold his position.

He kicked and clawed against the vicious cross-currents, and again he saw the twinkle of golden light from below.

He reached out with his hand.

The surge sucked him backwards.

His lungs screamed at him to breathe; and he fought the urge to surface.

He wasn't giving up.

Already, he'd resolved to get his hands on whatever was taunting him from this tumultuous hell, even if it turned out to be a cap from a beer bottle or a piece of sea glass.

Another second passed.

If only he could take a breath!

His mind worked as if it were mired in molasses, his thoughts dreamy, detached. He was a visitor here. This was not his world, it belonged to the fish darting around him. For a moment he considered sucking in a little water, just like the fish. Let it slosh around in his mouth. Test it. Spit it out if it didn't feel right.

Damn!

He shook his head to clear away the fog and dry swallowed to buy himself a few extra heartbeats of time.

The dreaminess inside his head faded, and he frantically kicked and clawed at the turbulence to position himself over the hole.

It wasn't working.

There was only one way to get the object: he'd have to make a grab for it.

He prayed nothing else was home to make him wish he hadn't. He'd already seen two large moray eels lurking in crevices in the reef—their powerful jaws opening and closing, as they drew water in over their gills and lured unsuspecting fishes into rows of savage teeth.

There was room for one here, too.

Again the surge sucked him backwards and he fought against its hold.

Precious seconds passed.

The beat of his heart was a loud *thump, thump* in his ears.

Another second ticked by.

His lungs burned and still he made himself stay down.

Then the current swept him forward. This was his chance.

He made a grab for the glimmer of gold and felt something solid in his grasp.

He had it!

The moment Jack's face broke through the surface of the water above the reef, he jerked the snorkel from his mouth and sucked in a lungful of air. He coughed out the breath and quickly took in another, which he exhaled— only more slowly this time. After a couple more deep breaths, the mist cleared from his mind and he swam to his inflatable boat.

"What are you trying to do, kill yourself?" Robert's strong arms and hands reached over the side and hauled Jack up and over the starboard air chamber.

Wet and dripping, Jack plopped onto the seat behind the control console in the center of the eighteen-foot Zodiac.

His chest swelled with each breath as he eyed the object that had almost cost him his life. He rotated it in his fingers for a closer examination and recognized the molded loop of gold for what it was: a class ring, and from the marine growth on it, an old one.

He glanced at his friend and noticed his concerned expression.

"You really do need to be more careful." Robert pointed at Jack's hand. "What'd you find that was so important, anyway?"

Jack dropped the ring into his mesh goodie bag and tossed the sodden nylon sack into the bottom of the boat. The age and location of the ring intrigued him, but he couldn't deny the twinge of disappointment that he hadn't found something more valuable—like a gold Rolex watch, or a three-karat diamond wedding band dropped there by a rich honeymooner.

"Just an old ring," he said. "It doesn't look like much, but who knows?"

"Did you see *A Perfect Storm*?"

"Not another one of your anecdotes?"

"Humor me."

Jack sighed. "Okay, sure I have. What fisherman hasn't? Your point?"

"Those men on the Andrea Gail took a chance they shouldn't have because they wanted more fish. You wanted that ring. Is a few dollars in gold worth drowning for? Because that was where you were headed."

"Why the concern? You've been down longer yourself."

"Because I—" Robert looked his friend in the eyes a moment, then smiled.

"Because Ellery told me to have you back by noon," he said. "If you drowned, she'd have my ass."

"So she's giving you orders too, huh?"

Robert chuckled. "That's 'cause she's gorgeous and rich. It's in her blood to give orders. You might as well get used to it."

"Yeah—maybe."

Robert tossed Jack a towel and used one on himself.

"Come on," he said, tossing his towel aside. "Let's get out of here."

Jack grinned and started the engines. Taking hold of the steering wheel with one hand, he shoved the throttle controls forward with the other.

The inflatable skipped across the surface of the ocean like a flat stone on a millpond. He put the boat on a northerly course, back to the Kihei boat ramp where their vehicles were parked.

Ten miles ahead stood the dramatically eroded, cloud-shrouded West Maui Mountains, a 1.3 million year-old monument to Maui's oldest volcano. Puu Kukui—its tallest peak, fifty-seven hundred and eighty-eight feet above sea level—constantly competed for the title of the rainiest spot on earth.

A hundred yards to starboard lay the sixteenth fairway of Makena Golf Courses' South Course. Fifty-foot-tall coconut palms swayed lazily in the balmy afternoon breeze. And beyond, a sweeping vista of *kiawe* trees, eucalyptus, and redwood trees drew his gaze ten thousand feet upward to the summit of the dormant volcano Haleakala.

Nature's majesty. Lush. Green. Rugged. Magnificent.

It was easy for him to become lost in the beauty of it all. But he was not so naïve as to think it would stay that way.

Man always found a way to leave his mark.

Some good, some bad, the scars were there to stay.

He gazed at the shoreline in front of them. The mega resorts and big-dollar condominium complexes of Wailea and Kihei that lined South Maui's white sand beaches stood out, as a steel and concrete testimonial to the tourist dollar so vital to the island's economy.

In the middle of it all sat the multimillion dollar beach homes of the rich and famous. And the guest house he now called home.

Already his mood was beginning to deteriorate. The sunset cocktail party at Ellery's parent's house was not an evening he was looking forward to. Rubbing elbows with the Seaports' haughty friends was not his idea of a good time.

Why was that?

He liked a good party.

What did those people mean to him, anyway?

He struggled for answers.

He glanced at his divers' watch. He might not have a choice as far as going to the party, but he still had a few hours before he had to be there, and he meant to enjoy every minute of that time. He throttled down to half speed and cranked the wheel, banking the boat into a hundred and eighty degree turn.

"You up for one more dive?" he asked Robert over his shoulder.

Robert gripped the center console to steady himself. "You bet. What ya got in mind?"

"A sunken World War II tank I heard about. Hold on." He shoved the throttle levers forward.

Chapter 2

JACK BACKED THE trailer holding the Zodiac, into its parking spot next to the six-foot high stone wall that marked the edge of the parking area in front of the *ohana* at Ellery's parents' beach home in Wailea. He peered over his left shoulder at the one-bedroom guest house.

Living there was not working out the way it should have.

The cottage fronted the main house, which fronted Keawakapu Beach to the west. He knew he should be happy, living a couple of hundred feet from one of the nicest beaches on Maui. But moving into the *ohana*, it turned out, was one more concession on his part, and an indication of the path his relationship with Ellery was taking.

A move he regretted.

He'd rather Ellery and he live away from her parents, in a place without strings attached.

He slid from behind the steering wheel and stood next to his Jeep, admiring his restoration job on the 1949 Korean War refugee. An indulgence he'd allowed himself.

Ellery used to think it was cute.

Not so much since moving home with her parents.

He grabbed his goodie-bag from inside the Zodiac and stood for a quiet moment, staring through the mesh at the ring inside. What were the odds that something so small and insignificant would be found after all this time? He couldn't help wondering about the man who owned it.

Perhaps this was not simply a lost piece of jewelry to him.

But then maybe it was. The ring looked as though it had been submerged in the reef a long time.

He walked into the *ohana*, and snagged a longneck Corona from the refrigerator on his way through the kitchen. The night's dinner party was only
one of many to come. He'd be expected to attend them all. The cold brew
would help take the edge off of the evening's festivities.

Taking a long draft from the bottle while he walked, he stepped into the
bedroom and laid the mesh goodie-bag on top of his dresser.

The glimmer of gold drew his gaze back to the sack.

He retrieved the ring from the mesh bag, pulled open the top drawer of
his dresser, and stuffed it under his neatly folded boxers. But not before taking a long look at the center stone, and the words and date molded into the
soft yellow metal: West Point, 1941. And the three initials inscribed on the
inside of the band.

An omen? Good, bad…both?

Who is this soldier who lost the ring?

Is he still alive?

Chapter 3

PEOPLE BEGAN ARRIVING at five minutes before six. Jack stood at the door with Ellery and her parents, doing his part to keep up appearances. After a few minutes of nodding and smiling and saying 'nice to meet you,' he excused himself and wandered off in search of a drink.

It was going to be a long evening.

But worth it, if it turned out the way he hoped.

Cocktails were being served on the lanai overlooking the ocean. He walked to the bar set up by the caterers in the far corner, and asked for a beer. The bright orange sun was well on its way toward the cloudless horizon, promising another spectacular Maui sunset.

Nature at her finest.

For the better part of half an hour he nursed a beer, doing his best to stay out of the way of the throng of chattering partygoers. He stood a few feet from the far end of the bar with his back to the railing, watching. Ellery, he noticed, was mingling with the couples wandering the lanai. She seemed to enjoy herself; and that was fine with him.

The party was exactly what he had envisioned. He had nothing in common with any of these people and he found himself thinking about the ring. The initials C. W. M. were clearly visible on the inside of the band, and the West Point emblem was easily recognizable. So were the words *West Point* and date 1941. WW II brought a lot of soldiers to Hawaii, and one of them had lost that ring.

"Jack, come here a minute. I want you to meet some friends."

He glanced in the direction of Ellery's voice and saw her wave him over. She stood next to a middle aged couple. They were all looking at him.

He groaned.

He'd seen the man walk into Seaport's house a number of times during the past few months but had never been formally introduced to him. The guy was a full six inches taller than he was, and a good fifty or sixty pounds of solid muscle heavier.

Big and imposing.

Jack wasn't sure he had seen the woman before tonight.

He pasted on a smile and walked over to Ellery.

She took him by the arm and said, "Jack, darling, this is Russ and Beverly Carter. Russ has done a lot of work for my dad on the mainland and in the islands. They own a zillion-dollar home in Sausalito with an outrageous view of the Golden Gate Bridge, and a fabulous oceanfront condo in Makena, just down the road from here."

Jack smiled at her and said, "How nice."

Carter had the broad shoulders and trim waist of a guy who worked out. He stood a solid six foot six inches tall and weighed in at two-sixty or seventy. The man had a firm, set jaw and the type of smile that instantly puts a person on guard. His wife was nearly six feet tall, trim, and quite beautiful.

Jack got the impression she may have been a model at one time.

He wasn't sure about her husband. He thought he'd seen the man somewhere, besides here at the house.

Ellery gripped his hand and held onto it with both of hers.

"I'm so excited," she said. "Russ and Daddy have big plans and you're going to be part of them, Jack. Isn't that positively wonderful?"

He shot her an if-you-say-so look and shook Carter's massive hand.

He'd seen the man before. But where?

Suddenly it occurred to him: eight months ago, at Ellery's apartment in San Francisco. Carter had shown up at her front door, and the two of them had spent quite a few minutes in the doorway, talking in hushed tones. Afterwards, she had explained only that Carter was her father's business partner. Two weeks later she told him she was moving back to Maui to be near her parents, and that she wanted him to move with her.

She must have forgotten about that prior encounter.

Now he wondered if Carter's visit had played a part in her decision to move. He figured it had.

"Glad to meet you," Jack said, not sure if he really meant what he was saying.

"Mr. Seaport has told me good things about you," Carter said. "It'll be good to have you on board."

"I'm looking forward to the challenge."

"I hope so. Mr. Seaport has put a lot of money into making his projects here in the islands a success."

Jack detected a hint of wariness in the man's voice. His loyalty was being measured, and he knew at once, Carter would not be someone he could warm up to.

"I can handle my end," he said, looking Carter in the eye.

Carter's dark brown eyes locked onto his. He watched the man's mouth spread into a sneer.

"I'm sure you can," Carter said.

Jack held Carter's gaze, but didn't like the game. He felt as though he were being sized up like a prize bull, and knew this wouldn't be the only time. He'd have to constantly prove himself to this man. Russ Carter wasn't—by his estimate—a person to take someone at face value. You needed to demonstrate your ability and loyalty to be on the inside, or you were out. When it came to doing business, there was no *middle-of-the-road* for someone like him. And Carter wanted the people around him to know it. Intimidation was part of his power game, because with it came control.

An ugly word in Jack's mind.

But he wasn't worried. He firmly believed he could handle anything Seaport or Carter threw at him.

Both women stood quietly with blank expressions. He got the feeling they were waiting for him to respond. He would. But it was time to put the conversation on a different tack.

"Tell me, Russ," he said in his most festive party voice, "do you play golf?"

The big man's eyes narrowed into hard slits for an uncomfortable moment. Then his linebacker shoulders visibly relaxed.

"When I have the time," he said.

Jack grinned, flashing Carter a row of even white teeth.

"Good," he said. "We'll have to be sure and make time for a game or two."

Russ Carter didn't comment.

"Well," Ellery said, "hate to run, but I'm off to play hostess."

No one seemed to care, least of all Jack.

He watched her give Beverly Carter a peck on each cheek and rush off to chat with a young woman who had just stepped onto the deck.

He waited for the Carters to make the next move.

Beverly hooked her arm around her husband's and said, "Nice to have finally met you, Jack. I've been looking forward to meeting the lucky man who landed Ellery."

Jack winked.

He said, "We sort of landed each other."

"But of course," she said.

Her lips curled into a thin smile. He waited some more.

She added, "I'm sure we'll be seeing more of you."

"I'm sure you will," he said.

With that, the Carters drifted toward the house, leaving him standing there, alone.

He smiled. The game had started, and he had no intention of letting them win.

Chapter 4

JACK PULLED A second Corona from the portable bar and resumed his post at the railing near the far end. He planted his forearms on the top rail, leaned on them, and watched the waves and the couples strolling along the beach. Sunset was his time of the day.

He intended to enjoy this one.

For about thirty seconds he was able to do just that. Then he heard his name being called.

Ellery, again.

She tottered up to him, sipping a martini. She pressed her breasts against his shoulder, leaned in, and kissed him on the cheek.

"I see you're back in your corner," she said.

A shudder of desire pulled him from the railing. He chugged half of his beer.

"It's quieter over here," he said.

"But you're supposed to be mingling and enjoying the party."

"I am."

"Standing here?"

He pointed with the neck of his beer bottle. The sun hadn't quite yet slipped below the horizon. But already the western sky was an artist's pallet of color. Van Gogh couldn't have done better.

"Look at that sunset," he said. "Remember the time we watched the sun set from the hills above the Golden Gate Bridge? Remember that weekend at Bodega Bay?"

"Jack," she said. "It's important to me that you get to know everyone."

"Just give me a few minutes."

She glanced at the room full of guests.

"Well," she said. "Just so I can find you."

"I'll be right here."

She blew him a parting kiss, and he watched her hurry off to play the socialite. These were her people, not his. But she had been looking forward to this evening, and he would be there for her and do whatever was necessary, because his old man had taught him that was the right thing for a man to do when he loves a woman.

He turned to finish watching the setting sun and caught a lingering scent of Ellery's exotic perfume. He put his back to the railing and took another long look at her. She *was* the reason he was at the party.

Damn she was pretty. Spectacularly gorgeous, really.

Hands down, she was the best looking woman he'd ever been with.

He sucked down the last of his beer as the final golden rays of the day dipped into the ocean. His perseverance was rewarded with the bright green flash locals and vacationers talk about. A reward, indeed.

And there would be more, later.

He had nothing in common with Seaport's guests. But he would put up with their haughtiness and be on his best behavior for Ellery. This pretentious social game was a sure turn on for her.

Some of the hottest sex they'd had occurred after parties like this one.

Chapter 5

JACK AND ELLERY were a moving mass of arms and legs as they stumbled through the doorway into the *ohana*. The hem of her cocktail gown was already above her thighs

She kicked off her heels.

He fumbled with the zipper on the back of her dress and slid it down.

She hooked her fingers behind his belt and tugged on it, undoing the buckle. And one-handed the clasp on his pants.

"The door," she gasped out of breath. "Someone will see us."

He couldn't have cared less. But he reached back with his foot, found the door and kicked it closed.

Off went his shoes.

Her hand went deeper, taking the pant's zipper with it.

His khaki Dockers dropped to his ankles.

He stepped out of his slacks and kicked them aside.

An instant later her dress fell to the floor.

Off went his boxers.

Off went her bra. Small, lacy, black, narrow straps. Barely enough.

His hands found her breasts. Large. Round. Soft. Warm. Areolas constricted. Nipples erect.

He pushed back her hair and kissed her throat.

She nibbled his ear.

He traced the curve of her neck with his tongue. Found her plump ripe lips with his. Kissed some more. Hungry. Passionate.

She grabbed his hand and moved it up the inside of her thigh.

Legs long, smooth, toned. Panties tiny, lacy, black to match her bra.

Garter belt and stockings. She was moist, ready. He was, too.

He guided her toward the hallway leading to their bed. He kissed her mouth, nibbled her bottom lip, her neck, her shoulders.

His back flattened against the wall, and she pressed against him as her nails dug into his shoulders.

She raised her leg and hooked the crook of her knee over his hip as if she were trying to climb him. He lifted her up by her butt and buried his face between her breasts.

Her arms wrapped around his neck and her hands gripped his hair.

They locked in a drunken sex dance.

He turned her back against the wall and moved his hips in rhythm to hers.

She was all over him, and he was all over her.

She moaned. He did, too.

He lifted her and carried her to the bedroom. They stumbled through the doorway and fell on the bed together.

"Fuck me," she said.

Her voice was hot and sexy, not crude. It made him want her even more.

He fumbled to undo her garters and tugged on her thong panties.

"No," she said in that sultry voice. "Tear them off."

The lace tore easily and he tossed them on the floor.

"Yes," she whispered and guided him inside her.

Long and slow.

Her breath caught for a quick second, then she began to move her hips in a steady rhythm to his thrusts.

He pushed himself deep inside her.

She arched her back and pressed her shoulders hard against the mattress.

Almost at once she let out a gasp, and her body shuddered. Then her hips thrust hard against him in one quick motion. Her entire body quivered.

He felt the moistness that signaled her release.

But that was only the first.

He continued, long and slow.

Then deep and hard.

Then faster, harder.

She buried her fingers in the hair on his chest and began moving her hips again, just as eager and hungry.

His eyes were open. So were hers. He felt the room begin to spin.

He was so ready.

Then she was on top of him.

Just as quickly she rolled him over and was under him again.

Then she was on her hands and knees, and he entered her from behind.

Deep and hard. Faster and harder.

Their breathing quickened. And all at once the silence of night was filled with the cries of both of them climaxing.

They collapsed onto the bed, and for several minutes they lay in each other's arms. Neither of them moved.

Their breathing returned to normal. And Ellery began drawing circles in his chest hairs with her fingers.

He closed his eyes, consumed by her touch.

"Jack, honey," she said. "I'm so happy things are working out with you and Daddy. At first I was a little worried you two wouldn't get along. It's such a relief for me, knowing nothing has to change."

"Change," he mumbled. "Change what?"

"You and I—Maui," she said. "Now that you're going to work for Daddy, he'll make sure we have everything we need once we're married. And you'll always have a job and lots of money to keep me happy."

He took a long moment to think about what she had just said. She was right of course.

Too right.

Working for her father was not a problem: he could deal with that part of the arrangement. The part about needing lots of money to keep her happy concerned him. He'd convinced himself marrying a rich, drop-dead gorgeous blonde was a good thing.

But was it, really?

He hadn't come down off the high long enough to consider the consequence of her having so much wealth.

"Money's that important to you?" he asked.

"What else is there?" she said in a voice laced with sleep.

"Try love."

She snuggled against him.

"That, too," she murmured. "Now, you'll be a good boy and do what Daddy says, right?"

He didn't answer. In the next breath he heard her soft coo of sleep.

He wanted her to tell him she loved him. That wasn't going to happen.

Not tonight, anyway—and maybe never.

Did he really care that money was so important to her, and that in their relationship love did not seem as important as wealth?

He thought about that. She had her priorities in life. He had his. They were not necessarily the same. The important part—he reasoned—was that they did love each other. Surely the sex they shared was an expression of that love. He couldn't believe it wasn't. Still, he was troubled by the direction their life together was taking.

Is the sex enough?

He felt Ellery move, settle, let out a gentle humming sound. For a moment he closed his eyes and listened to her breathe—soft, slow, rhythmic breaths.

Contentment.

The answer seemed painfully clear.

He glanced at her lying on her side, curled into a ball.

Beautiful. Childlike.

Only Ellery was all woman—a gorgeous, vibrant, sensual creature, and anything but innocent. Gifted with sexual talents beyond any he'd known before her—an inherent animalistic sexuality that captivated him.

He laced his fingers behind his head and stared at the ceiling. He'd often wondered what it was like to have an addiction.

Now he knew.

The reality of her hold on him settled in, and he realized that was one part of their arrangement he hadn't considered. Good or bad, what he did know was he was enamored with the sex, and that no amount of lovemaking would kill him the way an overdose of heroin or cocaine or any number of other drugs would.

But where that obsession would lead him was a question he couldn't answer.

Not yet.

He felt Ellery's legs twitch against him and heard her murmur something he couldn't quite understand.

He wondered what her dreams were like. And for a moment he pictured his family's black and white cat, remembering how that lethal feline used to twitch her legs in her sleep as though she were chasing a mouse or bird.

Moving in for the kill.

Chapter 6

AT SEVEN THE next morning, Jack met Robert at Makena Golf Courses' clubhouse for their scheduled eighteen holes on the South Course.

Robert won the coin toss and stepped to the first tee. He bent over, shoved a tee into the ground, and balanced a ball on top of it. As he lowered his club and took his stance he gave Jack a sideways glance and caught him yawning.

He asked, "Ellery keep you awake last night?"

Jack gave him a pained look. "Just hit the goddamn ball."

Robert took a practice swing, adjusted his stance, took another swing and drove his ball two hundred and fifty yards straight down the middle.

"How about that one?" he said.

"It'll do."

Jack didn't bother taking a practice swing. He focused, brought his driver back and swung the club, taking out all his frustration on the small white ball sitting on the tee, two inches above the turf. His Slazenger 2 flew straight as an arrow for about a hundred feet before it hooked sharply and crashed into the *Kiawe* trees.

Robert chuckled.

"Nice shot," he said.

"Screw you," Jack said. "It's only a stroke and I'll make that up on the green."

Robert shrugged.

"That's two," he said. "But who's counting?"

Jack said, "You calling that a lost ball?"

"Wouldn't you?"

"Not at all. I know right where that ball is—I just can't get to it."

Robert rolled his eyes and said, "Just hit another one. People are waiting."

Nine holes later Jack was behind by five strokes.

Robert said, "You're playing like shit."

Jack huffed and said, "That's going to change, starting right now."

"Think so?" Robert said, "If you ask me, you'd been better off playing tennis like Ellery wanted you to."

Jack wished he could forget what Ellery had said to him: *If only you could play tennis, then you could work in the pro-shop and I could accept that.* A prospect that sent shivers up his spine. He didn't play tennis, and he sure wasn't going to work in a tennis pro-shop at some resort. But he had quit his job, which he'd realized was what she had wanted in the first place.

"Fucker," he said. "I never should have confided in you."

"But you did," Robert said. "So don't think I'm not going to get some mileage out of a gem like that."

"Go ahead, be an asshole. At least I didn't cave in on that one."

"Yeah, but you quit the Hyatt and agreed to work for her father."

Jack eyeballed the green behind them to see if anyone was waiting to play through. No one was there.

He said, "I've got to admit you and I had a lot of fun working together: parking cars, talking shit, jockeying for the tips."

"I do miss working with you, Jack."

Jack gave his friend a long look.

He said, "It hasn't even been a month. What's really on your mind?"

Robert's gaze dropped to the ball he was holding. He turned it in his hands until the Nike swish faced him. He said, "I'm just not sure you're making the right decision."

"Working for her father isn't going to be that bad."

Robert huffed out a breath and said, "If you like being someone's yes-sir man."

"You're the one who's parking cars, when you were only a couple of years away from a law degree."

"At least I made the choice on my own."

"And your girlfriend didn't have anything to say?"

"Kazuko wasn't exactly happy about it, but she didn't tell me what to do."

Jack's expression hardened. "You can be a real asshole," he said.

Robert grinned and said, "Should be good for at least a couple of strokes, don't you think?"

"Not if I can help it," Jack said. He teed up, sighted down the tenth fairway, and hit his ball, his longest shot of the day. The ball fell just short of the water hazard. A mud hen skittered across the pond.

"Nice shot," Robert said. "Scared hell out of that bird."

"Mud hens are about the dumbest birds I know. And the ugliest."

Robert chuckled. "You know why they don't have feathers on their heads?"

Jack stepped aside and said, "I'm sure you're going to tell me."

Robert positioned himself on the tee box and gazed down at the mud hen. "You know the story of the demi-god Maui and how he raised the Hawaiian Islands with his magical hook?"

"Sure."

Robert shoved a tee in the turf and positioned his ball. "According to legend," he said, "Maui's mother Hina wanted some fish and summoned her sons. Maui and his three brothers rowed their canoe out to sea off of Kaupo." He glanced at Jack and added, "In case you don't know, that's on the south end of the island."

Jack sighed. "I know where Kaupo is. Get on with the story."

Robert smiled. "Once Maui and his brothers reached the fishing grounds, Maui looked toward land and saw smoke from a fire burning on the mountainside. As the story goes, they had been without fire for a long, long time because Haleakala had become extinct and the hot coals they'd kept alive, died.

"So seeing the fire, they decided they'd row ashore and cook their fish. They tossed lines with baited bone hooks into the sea, and when they had the canoe filled with fish, they rushed ashore to get fire. Maui left his brothers behind and raced up the hill toward the pillar of smoke and saw a family of mud hens scratching out the flames. Before he could stop them, they scratched out the last embers and flew away."

"Okay, so the mud hens made fire?" Jack said. "Hit the ball, already."

"Relax," Robert said. "I'll keep the story short."

"I wish you would."

Robert continued. "Maui remained on land, hopeful of getting fire. But to no avail. Finally, he realized the mud hens only made fire when he and his brothers were at sea. To outsmart the hens, he made a dummy out of *Kapa* cloth so it would look like he was in the boat. Then his three brothers rowed out to sea while Maui hid in the bushes near the mud hens haunt.

"The plan worked. But Maui got impatient. When the mud hens started collecting sticks to make fire, he rushed in. And in his anger against the mud hens for having kept fire from them, he snatched one of the birds up by the neck."

Robert paused for breath and Jack said, "This is the short version?"

"It is," Robert said, and continued. "The mud hen cried out: 'If you kill me, the secret of fire will die with me!' Hearing this, Maui told the mud hen he would spare her life, if she gave him the secret of fire. The hen agreed and told him fire came from rubbing sticks together. At last Maui found fire.

"As the flames rose, he said: 'There is one more thing to rub.' He snatched the poor bird by the neck, grabbed a stick, and rubbed the top of the mud hen's head until its head was raw flesh and featherless. Thus the Hawaiian mud hen and her descendants have had bald heads and the Hawaiian's have had fire."

Jack huffed. "Your point?"

"Point?" Robert said. "Just that there is a reason they're bald."

"Don't forget ugly."

"Okay, and ugly. But smarter than you give them credit for. Quite often it's the same with people."

"Being ugly?"

Robert just looked at him.

Jack said, "Ellery isn't ugly."

Robert said, "But she got you to quit a job you liked."

"I'm going to work for her dad."

"Right."

Jack said, "Hit your stupid ball."

Chapter 7

JACK COULDN'T GET his mind to focus on the game. When they got to the sixteenth hole, he was down by eight strokes. The lady on the snack cart came to a stop behind their cart just as they were climbing out to tee up.

She looked directly at him and smiled. "Playing any better?" she asked.

Jack said, "You've been watching."

She smiled.

He said, "Give me two Coronas."

She dug into the cooler and fished out two cans. "That bad, huh?" she said.

Jack gave her a ten dollar bill and said, "Not for long."

She drove away, and Jack handed Robert his beer. For once, he refrained from comment.

Jack opened his can and looked out over the ocean and the reef where he'd found the ring. The usual fleet of dive boats, a similar swarm of tourist snorkeling, the scene was the same.

With all those people diving on that reef day after day, why had I been chosen to find that ring?

He'd spent enough time on the ocean, and hanging out with people who make their living from it, to know its briny depths were a treasure-trove of mystery, and that those deep dark waters did not surrender their secrets easily. The ocean had given up another of its enigmas for a reason.

He was going to find out why.

"Let me show you how it's done," Robert said from the tee box. He adjusted his stance, getting ready to swing.

Robert's voice brought Jack back to the game. "Make it good," he said. "You're going to need it."

Jack pared the sixteenth and seventeenth holes and birdied the eighteenth. He still lost to Robert by six strokes, which cost him another beer that they agreed would be collected at an unspecified time and place.

Robert loaded his clubs into the bed of his pickup and said, "Maybe you need to get away from here for a couple of weeks. I get the feeling this whole wedding thing with Ellery has you second guessing yourself."

"Perhaps you're right," Jack said. "But I'd feel like I was running away from my problem if I did. Besides, I start work tomorrow."

"I think that's the point of getting away. As for the new job, I'm not so sure you want to be part of that group. If I were you, I'd give some serious thought to what you're doing. Ellery might ease up some if she sees her hold on you, slipping."

"It might come to that, but first I'll give the issues some time to sort themselves out."

Robert shrugged and climbed into the cab of his Toyota pickup. He rolled down the window and said, "I've known you what, six months? You're smart. You could have done anything you wanted—and still can. You're far too intelligent to be wasting your time working for a man like Seaport."

"Don't you think it ripped my insides to leave college after only two years when I had a full four-year scholarship? My dad was sick. What was I supposed to do, let my family starve while the bank took everything my dad had worked for? I did what any good son would do. I sacrificed. And because of it, I spent six years doing something I was trying to get away from. If it wasn't for my younger brother taking over the family business, I'd still be up to my elbows in salmon guts."

"Operating your father's fishing boat was something you had to do," Robert said. "But your brother *is* old enough to run the boat now, and your dad's doing a lot better. That's why you got out, remember? You wanted to make something of yourself."

"I thought I was doing that."

Robert looked at him.

"What?" Jack said when Robert didn't answer. "Do you expect me to go back to college? I'm twenty-nine years old, for Christ's sake."

"You could," Robert said. "I plan on picking up where I left off, just as soon as Kazuko finishes her Masters. What I'm getting at, is I'm not sure working for Ellery's father is your solution."

"Come on. I can't believe it'll be that bad working for him. And it seems to make Ellery happy."

"Right—and she buys you presents to show her appreciation."

Damn!

Jack sucked in a sharp breath. Robert had a way of stripping off the pretty outer covering in life, exposing reality. The Zodiac had been Ellery's gift. At the time he had thought the gesture slightly suspect, but decided the money was hers to spend. He hadn't wanted to even think she'd given him such an expensive present for any reason other than an expression of her love.

He said, "There's nothing you like about her, is there?"

"It's not that I don't like her," Robert said. "On the surface, you two make a handsome couple. Inside—well—you guys just don't think alike."

Jack sighed. "Did I ever tell you how we met?"

"You told me you had sex with her that night," Robert said. "And that you thought she was the best thing since canned beer."

"I'm talking about *how* we met," Jack said

"Guess you didn't."

Jack peered into the past and smiled. "I'd done my best to hit every winery in Napa," he said. "I'd already had one too many samples. But hell, I was having a ball. My next stop was the Coppola winery and that's where I noticed her sitting under a tree reading. She'd just graduated from USC and had moved up from LA to live in the Bay Area for a while." He grinned. "Poetry—can you believe it? She was reading poetry."

Robert said, "And she invited you to join her?"

"Not exactly," Jack said. "But I did sit down and start talking with her. One thing led to another and well—you know what happened after that."

"Is that when you were hanging out on your uncle's houseboat?"

"Yeah, *Waterdog*. I liked that old tub. Hell-of-a-barge and hard to navigate in the river, but you could anchor in the backwaters of the delta and stay for a week. Ellery and I did that a couple of times. Looking at her now, you'd never believe she'd ever do something like that."

"Ellery's got you all fucked up, is what I think," Robert said. "Too bad you didn't grow up with an older sister like I did. You might have a more clear understanding of women. Or at least you would have had a better chance of seeing through a woman's pretty exterior. I swear, when a woman affects your golf game, it's time to take a break—from the game, or the woman." Robert started his pickup truck and added, "But who am I to tell you what to do."

Jack watched his friend drive off. Confused, mixed up—that's how he viewed himself. Fucked up was probably a better way of putting it.

There had been truth in what his friend had said—all of it. He could see the wisdom in giving Ellery a dose of reality. He'd always heard absence makes the heart grow fonder.

But deep down was that the solution to his dilemma?

It was obvious to him the answer to that question was not going to come easily.

He glanced at his watch: five after one.

His gaze was drawn to the broad expanse of blue water a half mile away. He peeled his tattered Giants ball cap from his head and raked his fingers though his hair.

Taking a long look at the Pacific, he wondered, *What have I got myself into?*

Chapter 8

JACK SHOWERED AND stretched out nude on the bed, under the coolness of the ceiling fan. He tried closing his eyes, but when he did all he could think about was the ring he'd plucked from the ocean.

He slid his legs over the edge of the mattress, stood up and stepped across the floor to his dresser. Pulling open the top drawer, he found the ring right where he'd left it, stashed beneath his boxers. He picked it up and padded back to his bed.

The ceiling fan twirled above his head, as he lay on his back studying the finely-crafted symbol of achievement for the academy's graduating glass of 1941. It had to have meant so much to the soldier who lost it. The heavy, yellow metal was solid gold—he could just make out the 18kt stamp on the inside of the band. A single, large red jewel graced its center. Glass maybe, but more likely a garnet or possibly a ruby.

Regardless, the big signet ring was worth several hundred dollars or more for the gold in it. But the ring had history.

A value far greater than mere money.

He imagined the young soldier swimming on the reef. What had that part of the island looked like, sixty or seventy years ago? Had the reef changed? Was the coral more vibrant and full of sea life then? Had nitrates, seeping into the water from the golf course over the past thirty years, taken a toll?

He'd heard there were gun emplacements along that stretch of the coast. Even now, there was a bunker on big beach a mile to the south.

Maybe the soldier had been in charge of one of the big guns guarding Maui from attack? Or maybe he was on leave? Maybe the island was just a stopping off point for him on his way to one of the other islands? That awful war took place so long ago....

How old would that soldier be now?

The date on the ring was 1941. The owner was a graduate of West Point. He was sure the man would be well into his late eighties. If he were still alive.

Still alive?

The thought intrigued him, and he couldn't help but wonder. Had the man been killed in a bloody battle, fought against the Japanese on one of the many islands they had occupied in the Pacific during World War II? Or had he gone on to do great and wondrous things after the war?

He tried to remember the names of the men who had raised the American flag on Iwo Jima, thinking the owner of the ring might even have been one of them. Ira Hayes was the only name he could come up with, and that was thanks to an old Johnny Cash song

So many had died....

He heard a car pull into the driveway and doors slam shut. He knew Ellery was home. He waited. A minute later he heard the front door to the *ohana* open and close. Heard her call his name.

He wrapped his fingers around the ring.

"You were supposed to meet us for lunch," she said from the doorway of the bedroom.

"I planned to," he said. "But it was after one when we finished playing the last hole."

"You're lying, Jack."

"All right, I'm lying," he said. "Truth is I didn't feel like discussing wedding plans."

"You don't seem too enthusiastic about the wedding. You're not having second thoughts, are you?"

"Not at all," he said. "I'm just a little tired."

"More bullshit?" she said. "Mom and I have more to talk about. Get dressed and join us in the main house. You can look over the bridal catalogues I brought home. I've marked the pages showing a few of the ideas I have in mind."

She turned and strode out of the *ohana*.

He watched her go. No way was he joining Ellery and her mother to look at bridal stuff—not on an empty stomach and without at least a couple of tequila shots under his belt.

Rachel Seaport—he'd discovered—was one of the few women in the world he couldn't stand to be around for more than five minutes, without wanting to choke the living shit out of her. She had a squeaky voice that reminded him of a cartoon mouse, platinum hair, and she gossiped incessantly. He shuddered to think Ellery would turn out anything like the tight-faced old broad.

He shook his head at the thought.

There was no doubt in his mind Ellery and her mother would do just fine without him.

The big ring bit into his palm and he realized he'd tensed his grip.

His thoughts quickly shifted. He relaxed his fingers and studied the unique piece of jewelry as though it were a portal to the past. The circumstances behind the loss of the ring posed a mystery that pricked at the deepest recesses of his mind, conjuring up a thousand images of what could have happened out there on that reef all those years ago.

Is it really possible the man is still alive?

He wanted to know everything about that young soldier's story and what had happened that fateful day when the heavy ring slipped off his finger.

He pinched the bridge of his nose and held it tight. So much was going on in his life. Even as he lay there, Ellery was waiting for him to join her and her mother to discuss nuptials with him. And in the morning he'd meet with her father to discuss work. That's where his mind should be.

Or should it?

Is that voice inside my head trying to tell me something I don't want to admit?

He released his hold on the bridge of his nose and stroked his chin. The mystery would continue to haunt him, and he knew now, he had to find the owner of that ring.

He tugged on his faded swim trunks and sat down in front of his computer.

Once online, Jack typed in the words *West Point* and hit 'enter.' He got a list of options and selected *US Military Academy*. The academy's home page filled the screen. A column on the left side held a list of choices. Scanning the index, his mind processed the information it offered.

Moving on, he selected *Search/Reference* and again was prompted to type in a name. He only had the initials C. W. M. to work with and feared that would present a problem. He'd get nowhere unless he had a name to match the letters to.

Determined to find the information he needed, he clicked on the search box at the top of the page displayed on the screen, and typed in the words *West Point Class Rings*. An option labeled *Ring Recovery* appeared. He clicked on it and got a link: http://www.west-point.org/wp/ring_recovery.

His first impulse was to select the site. But then he raised the tip of his finger off the mouse button.

This was his quest.

It was personal.

He felt a tad guilty, but as far as he was concerned, he didn't have a choice in the matter. He couldn't explain why, but he *had* to be the one to locate the owner and return the ring.

It was as if he had been chosen.

Chapter 9

JACK LAY ON his side in bed, listening to the hiss of the shower. Dim light from the sun that had yet to rise above Haleakala, shone through the chinks in the two-inch wood blinds on the window.

The scent of lovemaking from the night before lingered in the air. He wanted to prove his long-standing belief that an utterly fantastic first round should be followed up with a just-as-good-or-even-better second round.

The hiss of running water stopped, and a minute later Ellery walked into the bedroom, her white bikini skin standing out in stark contrast to her rich mahogany tan. He propped himself up on his right elbow and ran his gaze down her body.

"Don't, Jack."

"Don't what?"

"I know what you're thinking."

"So?"

"So forget it."

Breathing in, he watched her slide on a pair of lacy, red thong panties. Then he watched her buckle the strap on a matching bra, and lift the lacy cups into position over her magnificent breasts.

He let himself breathe out.

"Forget about wanting to make love to you?" he said. "Never. You drive me crazy."

"Crazy?"

"Can't you tell?"

He reached for her.

She ignored his outstretched hand, and his obvious arousal.

He pulled his hand back and said, "I can't believe you'd rather have breakfast with your parents."

She slid her sundress on over the skimpy underwear and smoothed it into place with her hands.

"Don't be that way," she said. "They're expecting me. And you, if you care to join us."

He fell back on the bed and intertwined his fingers behind his head. His gaze settled on the mirror. Her beauty reflected back as she admired herself.

"Remember when we used to wake up early in the morning and lie in bed in each other's arms?" he said. "We'd play those finger games, and make love while the rest of the world got ready for work?"

She shook her head at the mirror, and sighed.

"Wasn't last night enough for you?" she asked.

He grinned and said, "Nothing wrong with wanting more."

She peered down at the dresser, picked up her diamond rings, and slid them on her fingers. When she had each of them twisted into position, she turned to him.

"I don't want you to be late for your meeting with Daddy."

"Late? It's six-thirty!"

She glanced at her watch. Nodded.

"Then dress and join us for breakfast."

He rolled onto his side so that he was facing her, and propped his head up on his arm. His desire had gone beyond mere sex. He wanted to hold her. To feel the comfort and security of her warmth.

"Come back to bed," he said. "I miss what we had."

Ellery gave her dress a final adjustment in the full-length mirror on the closet door, and walked over to the bed. Her gaze fixed on his. She gently bit her lower lip.

"You know I want the same thing," she said. "And there will be plenty of time for sex later. After you start working for Daddy."

"And if there isn't?"

She kissed him on the forehead and said, "You'll just have to be a dear and be patient."

Jack stood and cupped her breasts with his hands.

"Or you could climb back in this bed with me now," he said. "Just in case."

She slapped his hands away and stepped backwards out of his reach.

"Daddy's doing this for me, Jack—and for you," she said in a firm voice. "I don't want you to disappoint him."

"Disappoint him?"

She gave him a hurt look and said, "He's putting a lot of trust in you. Just do your stuff and make us tons of money."

He slid to the edge of the mattress and sat there looking directly at her. He asked, "What's this money thing?"

"What do you mean?"

"That's all I've been hearing lately."

"Is it?" she said and glanced at herself in the mirror.

"It is," he said. "When we started going together, our relationship was all about us and what we wanted in life. And more importantly, you told me I was the strength you needed to be your own person. You wanted a job in design, and I would continue working at the Mondavi winery until a better opportunity came along."

"Your point?"

He shrugged.

"Simple things made us happy," he said. "Being together, laughing, making love in the middle of the day, sunsets, that sort of thing. It sure wasn't about money. And it definitely didn't include living fifty feet from your parents."

"Don't be so idealistic and naïve, Jack."

She narrowed her eyes. "Money *is* what it's all about. It just took me some time to understand that. And living here with my parents—at least for now—is part of the deal."

"Deal?"

She blew him a kiss over her shoulder and walked out of the room.

He started to follow her out, but thought better of it. He buried his face in his hands, and for a moment held them there. Then he sighed and raked his fingers through his short-cropped hair.

He felt trapped, as though he had been sucked in by design.

Even so, he wanted to believe the current situation would work itself out, and that their relationship would return to the way it was when they first started spending time together.

He'd just have to give her time to adjust.

He stretched out and peered at the ceiling in thought, wondering what their life together would be like. Surely everything would be wonderful.

It had to be…

Still, the picture forming in his mind wasn't a pretty one.

Damn it!

He tucked his hands under his head, unable to shake the feeling Ellery was going through some sort of metamorphosis—as if she'd emerged from a cocoon or fallen victim to someone's cruel experiment—or maybe that her true self was blossoming, having lain dormant until now. The outcome was the same for him. Fall in line with her way of thinking and toe the mark, or be left standing at the gate with the other boyfriends when he no longer served a purpose in her bigger plan.

He thought he had a basic understanding of the users in the world, but Ellery was giving him a quick, hard study on the subject. And he was learning just how unpalatable that kind of life was for him.

A friend of his, back home in Fields Landing, had once told him about a very personal problem he was having with his live-in girlfriend. Nymphomaniac was the term he used to describe her when he broached the trouble between them.

Even now, he remembered recalling the definition of nymphomania and not seeing the condition as being a problem, especially given his own sexual needs. But then his friend had gone on to describe the manipulation and control that went along with such a seemingly wonderful attribute. Something Jack now understood.

Ellery, in his opinion, was much the same.

He feared she was destined to become a user in her Daddy's world, where she would have power and control as well as a satisfied sexual appetite, and maybe that's what life was really all about for her. In that world her sexuality would get her whatever she wanted, in order to live the life she so obviously desired.

The squawk of birds squabbling drew his attention to the window.

He pictured Ellery and her mother chatting away like the cantankerous myna birds.

Making plans for them—*for him!*

He shook off the image. The change in Ellery's behavior was responsible for the unsettled thoughts racing through his head, but he refused to believe she was as wicked as his mind was making her out to be. He rolled out of bed with the hope there was a way to resolve the issues between them.

In the quiet of the early morning Jack could just hear the muted rumble of waves, and could tell from the sound that the tide was out and the waves were not big. He decided a mile or two running on the sand would clear away the tarnish forming on his thoughts.

He'd need a clear head in his meeting with Ellery's father.

He slid on his swimsuit, quietly closed the door to the *ohana*, and crept past the main house. Then he trotted down the steps leading to the beach.

The shoreline was just as he'd imagined it. The tide was out and the lower part of Keawakapu beach was a long flat stretch of hard wet sand, with only a few early risers spreading their towels on the soft granules fronting the neighboring houses.

He ran up and down the beach for thirty minutes straight, followed by ten, grueling fifty-yard sprints. When he finally stopped, he was breathing hard and fell back on his butt to stare at the ocean.

Another day in paradise.

Chapter 10

AT NINE AM sharp, Jack was sitting in one of the expensive chairs reserved for the select few allowed inside Thomas Seaport's office. He put a hand over his mouth to force back a yawn and glanced around, not really sure what to expect, and realizing this was the first time he'd been allowed for more than a few seconds inside Seaport's private sanctum.

The room was quite large and richly decorated, in the classic island motif maintained throughout the house. It was located in the back corner of the main residence off the living room and was separated from the common areas of the home by a solid teak door—a door kept locked whenever Thomas Seaport was not occupying his office. A shuttered four-foot by eight-foot window on the west wall afforded the occupants a view of the ocean.

He'd been given a peek inside the room during his initial tour of the house, but not since. Before today, the conversations he'd had with Seaport about working for him were conducted on the lanai. But that was prior to becoming a member of the team. Once he had agreed to come on board he'd become one of the select few in the inner circle.

Russell Carter was, too.

And he was also here in the room, but that was no surprise. During the past few days Russell Carter and Thomas Seaport had spent a lot of time together in this office, behind closed doors.

Jack watched Seaport as the man stepped to the office door and pulled it shut. Seaport had said little to him, and that left him feeling edgy. He was glad the meeting was getting underway.

"Jack," Seaport said, settling into his chair behind his massive teak desk, "I want to welcome you aboard. You'll soon be part of my family. It's time you got your feet wet."

"I'm ready," Jack said, as if his comment made a difference. He had to say something.

The subtle reference to his upcoming marriage to Ellery made him feel a bit like a charity case. He was anxious for the opportunity to prove himself, and could feel the adrenaline rushing through his body.

Thomas Seaport glanced at Russell Carter. The unspoken words passing between them sent a flutter of nervousness through Jack.

He asked, "What exactly is it I'm going to be doing?"

Seaport's gaze bore into Jack. "Whatever I need you to do, of course."

The man's reply could have been taken as humorous, if it hadn't been for the flinty coldness in his eyes.

Jack didn't smile. "So tell me," he asked, "what exactly might that be?"

Seaport gave him a long look.

Jack waited.

"You know how to run a fishing boat," Seaport said. "For one, I'm going to have you take over the operation of that forty-one foot *Hatteras* of mine. I have clients who like to fish."

"I thought you had a captain for your boat."

Seaport smiled. "I'll also have you doing errands for me and handling issues as they come up. On a few of those assignments—especially in the beginning—you'll be working closely with Russ."

Jack glanced at Russell Carter, then back at Seaport.

"No problem," he said. "Like I told you, I'm ready to get to work."

"That's what I wanted to hear."

"Great. Do I report to you here in your office every morning, or do I check in someplace else?"

Seaport handed Jack a cell phone.

"Keep this with you at all times," Seaport said. "And be sure it's charged and turned on. Check in with me here at eight sharp every morning. Otherwise, I'll call you if I need you. As for how much I'll be paying you—we'll talk about that in a few days. But don't worry. You'll be making a lot more than you did parking cars. And of course you and Ellery will continue to live in the *ohana* rent-free."

Jack looked at the cell phone in his hand. *His leash.* He asked, "Am I to understand that includes weekends?"

"Every day," Seaport said. "But don't worry. You'll have plenty of free time to keep my daughter happy."

"Is there something I can do this morning? I'd like to get started."

"As far as this meeting goes, you're done. But I do need you to take care of a little matter for me."

Chapter 11

JACK WATCHED SEAPORT tear a sheet of paper off a small note pad on his desk. There was writing on it.

Seaport stood and handed him the paper. The writing was an address.

Jack didn't recognize the name of the street.

Seaport said, "The guy you mentioned a minute ago—the Hawaiian who's been the captain of my boat and doing odd jobs around here—fire him."

Jack stared at the paper. Seaport had caught him by surprise. He couldn't have been more gutted if he'd been sliced open by a knife. He peered across the desk at Seaport.

"Fire him, Jack," Seaport said. "He's no use to me anymore."

"Yes sir!"

Jack caught himself too late and swallowed hard. Seaport hadn't given his order a second thought. *His* own "Yes sir!" had come just as easily—*too easily*. He didn't like the way it felt.

He folded the paper and stuffed it into the breast pocket on his aloha shirt. "Anything else?"

Seaport retook his seat behind his desk. He pulled a wad of cash from the center drawer and counted off a sheaf of bills. He held the money out in front of him, in a clear offering to Jack.

"Here's five hundred for expenses," he said. "Keep the phone on."

Jack took the money, recognizing the dismissal when he heard it. But the money didn't change how he felt.

Seaport obviously did not spend time in idle discussion. He was a man of confidence bordering on conceit with an attitude that didn't invite questions. Someone who tells other people what to do and when to do it.

Tolerating that kind of arrogance would be a bitter pill to swallow.

Jack kept his mouth shut and left the office, closing the solid teak door behind him. He let out an exasperated breath. Robert had warned him this was how it was going to be. He'd just become Thomas Seaport's *Yes-Sir Man*.

Swallowing the bile in his throat, he took a step into the living room and stopped. A muffled outburst inside the office drew his ear to the door. The two-inch-thick teak distorted the words making it difficult for him to tell for sure who had raised his voice or what exactly was being discussed. But he believed it was Seaport doing the talking.

Thomas Seaport had always appeared to be in total control of himself at all times, but something had angered the man enough to send him into a tirade. Jack wished he knew what it was.

He pressed his ear to the door.

The voices returned to a garbled mumble. Whatever set Seaport off, it had passed.

Jack didn't linger. He had his own problems to worry about.

Ellery called to him from the back door as he stormed out of the house. He kept his thoughts to himself. A moment later, he heard the slap of her sandals on the walkway behind him.

She followed him into the *ohana* and once they were inside, he turned to face her.

"I can't do it," he said, shaking his head.

"Do what?"

He locked stares with her. "Your dad wants me to fire Kimo Holowai—the man who captains your dad's yacht. I met the guy that day we went fishing. And one other time, when I was at the harbor and saw him doing some work on the boat. In fact I spent quite a bit of time talking to the man. He's nice and seems to take his work seriously. I can't tell the man he's fired and then take his job from him."

"That's what Daddy wants?"

"He says he doesn't need him anymore. I think he's doing it just because he's finding a place for me."

"What's wrong with that?"

"I'm taking the man's job, for Christ's sake—his livelihood! He's got a family to feed."

"So what? If that's what Daddy wants, then do it."

"But what about—?"

"What about nothing," she said, cutting him off. "It's what's good for us that's important."

"Honestly, Ellery, I expected a little more empathy from you."

"Look at it this way, Jack. Do what Daddy says, and you'll be making me happy."

She put her arms around his neck and kissed him passionately on the mouth. When she pulled away, she ran her tongue seductively along her lips.

He was well aware of her intent.

She said, "And you know how I get when I'm happy."

He did know how Ellery could get when she was happy, and he knew he'd fire Kimo because Thomas Seaport ordered him to.

But I don't have to like it.

Chapter 12

JACK CLIMBED BEHIND the steering wheel of his Jeep and jammed the key into the ignition, more than ready to leave Kimo Holowai's house in North Kihei. The news that he'd been fired had initially left Kimo slumped and hollowed. But, just as quickly, the man had straightened and nodded, as if he'd arrived at an understanding.

Jack wondered if the old Hawaiian had decided it was for the better.

He couldn't help thinking that was the case.

He cranked over the vintage flathead four-cylinder and waited for the engine to sputter to life. He'd never robbed a man of his livelihood before, but that's exactly what he'd done.

And all because he had been ordered to.

He needed to pop a few beers and talk about fishing, diving, golf, the high price of gas—anything that would take his mind off Kimo and let him forget the look on the man's face when he learned he'd lost his job.

But the person he most wanted to talk to would side with her father. She'd already done that. There was really only one person he could go to. He palmed the cell phone Seaport had given him and punched his friend's number.

Robert was the one person on the island whom he felt comfortable sharing his problems with.

"You up for a beer?" he asked when Robert answered the call.

"Sure, why not? Besides, it's your turn to buy, and I like free beer."

"Let's meet at the park."

"You got it."

On the way to the beach, Jack made a quick stop at the ABC market and picked up a twelve-pack of Fosters. He was feeling Australian for no particular reason and knew Robert wouldn't care what he drank. He buried the beers under ice in the cooler he kept in the back of his Jeep, and then drove to Kamaole Park III to meet up with Robert.

Robert was standing next to his pickup truck, waiting, when Jack pulled into the lot. He parked in a nearby space and they walked down to the beach. They settled their butts in the sand and popped open a beer each.

"To us, mate," Robert said, holding his bottle up in a toast.

The two of them clinked bottle necks and joked with each other about golf, women, and anything else that came to mind.

"Did I tell you I recently picked a new primary care physician?" Robert asked.

Jack knew his friend was setting him up but played along.

He asked, "How'd it go?"

Robert smirked and said, "Well—after two visits and an exhaustive lab test, he said I was doing pretty good for my age."

"That's not so bad."

"Maybe to you it's not, but I was a little concerned about that comment and couldn't resist asking him if he thought I'd live to be 80."

"What did he say to that?"

"The guy starts asking me all kinds of questions. 'Do you smoke tobacco or drink beer or wine?' he asked. 'Oh no,' I said, 'I've never done any of those.' Then the man asked, 'Do you eat rib-eye steaks and barbecued ribs?' I shook my head at the man and told him I'd heard that all red meat is very unhealthy. Then he asked, 'Do you spend a lot of time in the sun—like playing golf, motorcycling, sailing, or rock climbing?' I told him, 'No, I don't.' Well, he wasn't done yet and asked, 'Do you gamble, drive fast cars, or sexually fool around?' Again I shook my head and told him, 'No, I've never done any of those things.'"

He looked Jack squarely in the eye, straight faced, and said, "I have to admit, by then I was getting a little nervous. That's when the doctor gives me one of those furrowed-brow looks and says, 'Then why do you give a shit if you live to be 80?'"

Jack laughed and twisted the caps off two more beers.

"I swear," he said. "You're full of shit. But you keep me laughing and I like you for it." He handed Robert his bottle.

"So, Jack, what's eating you?" Robert asked.

Chapter 13

JACK SAT LOOKING at his friend. "Obvious?" he said.

"Duh!"

"Okay," Jack said. "Stupid question." He dug his toes deep into the sand and said, "Had to fire a man today."

"Your new job?" Robert asked.

Jack forced a wry smile.

He said, "Nice, huh?"

"If you like firing people."

"Made me feel like shit."

"So?"

"So Seaport told me—among other things—he was giving me a job captaining his boat. Then he tells me I have to fire the guy who's been running it."

"Ouch!"

"That's putting it mildly."

"You could try finding the guy another job."

"Not exactly easy there days. I was going to ask you to keep your eyes and ears open."

"Be happy to."

They both fell quiet.

"And the other part?" Robert asked a few long seconds later.

Jack sighed and leaned back in the sand, supporting himself on his elbows. He peered wistfully at the ocean.

"Maybe I do need to get away from here for a few days," he said.

"Take a little walkabout?"

"Geez," Jack said. "I never should have brought Foster's."

"Be glad you didn't bring Corona. You know how bad my Spanish is."

Jack shook his head and said, "Next time I'm bringing Budweiser."

Robert grinned. "I'll brush up on my Clydesdale?"

They both laughed.

Robert took a long pull on his beer and wiped his mouth with the back of his hand.

"Speaking of Ellery," he said. "What's new with her?"

"Who was talking about Ellery?"

"Why else would you need to get away from Maui for a few days?"

Jack shrugged.

Robert asked, "So how are things going?"

"She's still spending money like there's no tomorrow. I think she's got a natural talent for it."

"That's what rich women do, Jack. Get used to it. The wedding's still on, I take it?"

"The end of next month. Just like the announcement says."

"You don't exactly sound happy about it."

Jack chugged down his beer, set his empty bottle on the sand next to him, and opened them another.

"I don't know," he said. "I should be, but I'm not."

Robert glanced from the Foster's Jack had just handed him, to the half-empty beer he held in his other hand. He set the full bottle aside and took a swig from the one he was working on. "That houseboat of your uncle's," he said. "Looking pretty good to you about now, is it?"

Jack shot Robert a look and fell quiet. Robert didn't push the point.

"Something's happening," Jack said a moment later. "I still love Ellery a lot. She's pretty, and Lord knows she's great in bed. But I don't know. It's like she's not the person she was when I met her."

Robert made a sucking sound with his cheek and asked, "Did I ever tell you the story about that friend of mine from high school?"

Jack shrugged. "I'm sure you're going to tell me anyway," he said.

"Derrick Martin and I were buds all through high school," Robert began. "I owned a Datsun King-Cab pickup and he drove a Toyota 4x4. Each one of those old trucks had over a hundred thousand miles on the engine, and we never had to do anything to them but change the oil, replace the battery, and put on a new set of tires. Then, as a graduation present, Derrick's parents gave him his choice of brand new cars. He chose a flashy looking Audi."

"That wouldn't be my choice."

Robert shook his head at Jack and said, "You going to let me finish my story or what?"

"Sorry."

Robert continued, "The new Audi looked wonderful and it drove like a dream. But after about a year, the car started giving him all sorts of problems. He'd take it in to the dealer and they would fix whatever the problem was and he'd drive it another month or so and then have to put it right back in the shop. This went on for about a year. Finally he figured it out. The car looked great and was a dream to drive when it was running, but it was a lemon and nothing would change that. He ended up trading the Audi in for another Toyota pickup. Last time I talked to him he was still driving it."

Jack looked at Robert. After a beat, he said, "You're saying Ellery's a lemon?"

"I'm not saying anything, Jack. It's only a story."

"Right." Again Jack gazed at the ocean, weighing Robert's words. He said, "That could very well be the problem. Maybe Ellery's all flashy paint and custom interior, and I'm only just now seeing her for the person she really is."

"Could be. Or you're just all fucked up."

Jack laughed and shoved Robert sideways onto the sand.

"Easy, mate," Robert said with a grin. "You'll make me spill my beers."

"Back on the Australian thing, are we?"

Robert held up both his bottles and eyed the labels. "I don't know," he said. "Surely there are worse places in the world to be?"

"And better, I'm sure."

"Beauty's in the eye of the beholder."

Jack grinned. "You're quite the philosopher this afternoon."

Robert swallowed the remainder of his first beer and smiled. "What can I say?" he said. "You bring out the best in me."

"I do, huh?" Jack scoffed. "Tell me, then. Do you know why women are like hurricanes?"

"I don't know," Robert said. "Because they're full of air?"

"It's because they come in all wet and wild and leave with your house and car."

Robert laughed and said, "It's good to have you back among the living, Jack."

Jack arched a brow at his friend. "Am I?" he asked. "There's still tonight."

Chapter 14

THAT NIGHT JACK and Ellery walked the fifty feet to her parents' house for dinner. His time on the beach with Robert had taken some of the edge off his having to fire Kimo, but not much.

For a long moment he eyed his pasta, not sure he could eat. When he finally forked a bite and glanced up from his plate, he saw Thomas Seaport looking directly at him.

Seaport pointed his fork and said, "Jack, I'm sending you to San Francisco with Russ Carter. This is an important trip and I want you to pay attention to how Russ handles business."

Jack dropped his fork on his plate and his jaw practically fell open.

"San Francisco?" he said. "When?"

Seaport took a bite of salad, chewed it, and chased it down with a swallow of Pinot Noir.

"Couple of days," he said. "But don't jump to any conclusions. You'll strictly be Russ's shadow on the trip."

"Then—" Jack was silenced by a raised hand from Seaport.

"I know what you're going to say," Seaport said. "Forget it. It's a done deal. If you're going to be part of this family, I want you to know how we do business."

Jack lowered his forkful of pasta to his plate.

Fuck!

He couldn't believe the shitty day he was having. First he was told to fire Kimo when the guy didn't have it coming, now this. He had no desire to travel with Russell Carter and couldn't imagine having to spend time with the man in San Francisco, or anywhere else for that matter.

Ellery reached over and touched Jack's arm. The sparkle in her eyes spoke before she did. "Isn't this exciting, honey?" she said. "It's exactly what we wanted."

We wanted?

Jack looked from Ellery to Thomas Seaport, then back at Ellery. He was being put on the fast-track to learning the family business and wondered how much of what was happening had to do with Ellery and how much had to do with her father's confidence in him. He figured her father's decision to send him to San Francisco with Carter had everything to do with what Ellery wanted.

He forced a smile: not that he was happy.

He said, "I can't wait."

TWO DAYS LATER Jack sat in first class on Hawaiian Airlines flight 678, en route to Oakland airport across the bay from San Francisco. All he knew about the trip was that he was there to tag along while Carter contacted a few of Seaport Enterprise's suppliers, and several key investors dumping huge sums of money into Seaport's latest projects.

He wondered if his being ordered to fire Kimo had been a test more than a necessity. He believed it was, and felt this trip was yet another test in a series intended to probe his willingness to do whatever Seaport told him. If that was the case, how would Carter react to having *him* for a shadow?

The absurdity of the situation was almost laughable.

They tolerated each other only because they had to. Besides, how was he supposed to do a job when he had no real understanding of what that job was?

Do what he was told, that's how.

Flight 678 landed in Oakland, California five hours and thirty-seven minutes after takeoff. Their limousine driver stood waiting for them when they exited through the doors of the baggage claim area and promptly escorted them to a black stretch Lincoln sitting at the curb. Russ Carter led the way and Jack played his role of shadow.

He might as well get used to it.

The limousine ride into San Francisco was slow, due to a backup on the Bay Bridge. Jack was thankful he wasn't behind the wheel.

He settled into his seat and stared out of the side window at the people in the cars around him.

But his mind was somewhere else.

His thoughts were on the ring.

The driver eased the limo to a stop in front of the Fairmont. A gray sky and a cool breeze greeted Jack when he jumped out, eager to get settled into his room. He shrugged off the chill and scanned the outside of the hotel. He'd lived in Northern California most of his life, but had never stayed at the Fairmont.

He planned to make the most of it.

A pretty woman whom Jack guessed to be in her fifties, stepped out of the hotel and cast an engaging nod his way as she walked to a waiting cab. He smiled back, and arched a brow.

"It's a shame you're not staying here," he said to Carter, nodding at the cab as it sped away. "Even you might get lucky."

Carter threw him a hard look and said, "I'll be staying at my house across the bay. You have the number and my e-mail address, so keep in touch. And take it easy on Mr. Seaport's expense account."

Jack grinned at Carter's concern. First-class seating on the flight, a limo ride from the airport, a room at the Fairmont—the man made it too easy to push his buttons.

"Nothing more than a few bottles of French champagne." Jack winked. "And a lobster dinner or two."

He grabbed his bag and walked inside the hotel, leaving Carter glaring at him from the curb.

Fifteen minutes later he was unpacking in a spacious room with a view of the building next door. Twenty minutes after that, he had showered and was on his way to the bar for a beer—courtesy of Thomas Seaport.

The trip might turn out better than he expected.

Chapter 15

THAT NEXT AFTERNOON Jack plopped into the cushioned chair in his room. One day of sitting on his ass, playing Carter's shadow was enough to drive him crazy. Even so, the day's events had been an education. He couldn't deny that.

His job description was still a bit of a mystery, but at least he had a better understanding of what the trip was about. He'd sat through four closed-door discussions and paid close attention to the negotiations: investors willing to put millions into Seaport's latest and apparently most grandiose venture yet. Carter had referred to them as *The Big Four*.

They were venture capitalists, or VCs for short. Jack had first heard the term during the limo ride to their 9 AM appointment. Carter used the expression when referring to the businessmen they were meeting with.

An explanation hadn't been necessary. These men were powerful entrepreneurs with money to invest in projects calculated to give them a large return.

Thinking back, he recalled overhearing a phone conversation where Seaport mentioned working with the Hawaiian people to build a casino on the island of Kahoolawe, across the channel from Maui. For years, the Hawaiians had pushed for sovereignty which—among other things—opened the door for them to build a casino on native land just as the American Indians had. Apparently that project was on its way to becoming a reality.

For a moment he envisioned the stack of money it would take to complete such a monumental project.

All at investors' expense.

Now he understood why Carter had been sent to make absolutely sure the venture went according to plan. The casino deal would net Seaport millions.

Rich men getting richer.

It didn't take a business degree for Jack to grasp the financial game: money to make money. He also understood the delicate balance in play there. And the temptation for greed.

He didn't like the game, but the venture would mean jobs for people living in Hawaii. That was the upside. Residents there had been hit especially hard by the floundering job market.

But what was the long-term cost?

With the next meeting scheduled on Monday morning, he had a three-day weekend ahead of him. He mulled over his options. There was nothing keeping him in the city, and he had no real desire to hang out there. Home was just a few hours up the coast in Fields Landing. And there was his uncle's houseboat *Water-dog* to consider. It was berthed at Crawdads Marina on the Sacramento River, an hour away if he got on the road before commuter traffic jammed the highways.

Both good choices.

Or he could spend the time locating the owner of the ring.

This trip was the perfect opportunity for him to continue his quest. He had brought the ring with him as an afterthought: for some reason he'd not felt comfortable leaving it behind.

Now he was glad he hadn't.

The owner—if he were still alive—lived on the mainland. Jack was convinced of that. The man could have settled in Hawaii or some far away point on the globe, but he thought that possibility remote.

He pulled his butt from the soft chair and stepped over to his laptop on the desk.

Returning the ring was the easy part. First he had to find out the soldier's name and address. When he checked his e-mail the night before, there was still no answer from the West Point Library regarding the request he'd sent, for information on the academy's class ring and a roster of the class of 1941.

He needed that list of cadets.

With his finger paused an inch above the *Start* button, he stared at the blank screen. His quest could begin or end with the pressing of that switch.

Where will it take me?

He fired up his laptop and pulled a Budweiser from the refrigerator in the mini bar. Screwing off the cap, he took a seat in the hard-backed desk chair.

A column of icons lined the left side of the computer screen and he clicked on *E-mail*. When his home-page appeared, he perused the list of messages—ignoring one from Ellery, a forwarded joke from Robert, and two from Russell Carter titled: *Important*.

There was only one message he was interested in.

The message was from a Suzanne Emhoff entitled *Information Request*. He clicked on the subject line and the response filled the screen.

West Point actually invented the concept of class rings. The library here at West Point has a collection, one from every year. The class of '41 had 424 graduates. You can find their names and information about them in the current Register of Graduates, published annually.

If you are interested, some information on the history of the class ring at the U.S. Military Academy is included on our website: http://digitallibrary.usma.edu/collections/photographs/classrings/

You will also find a roster of the Class of 1941 beginning on page 25 (27 in the electronic facsimile) of the 1941 edition of the Official Register of the Officers and Cadets, which is available in its entirety on our website: http://www.library.usma.edu/archives/content/oroc/v1941.pdf

Although we will attempt to answer specific questions, detailed research on this topic will require you to make a research appointment.

Suzanne Emhoff
Associate Director for Special Collections and Archives
USMA Library

"Yes!" Jack shouted, unable to contain his excitement.

He wanted to hurry and match a name to the initials on the ring. But he was also intrigued to learn West Point had invented the concept of class rings. He still had his class ring from high school, but the question of how or when the tradition began never entered his mind.

Till now.

He clicked the link to the historical information on the academy's class ring, and read down the page. The tradition of class rings, he discovered, was believed to have originated at West Point when the class of 1835 designed rings which were made to individual order and purchased at private expense. The class of 1836 chose not to have a class ring, but in 1837 the custom was resumed and had been consistently observed ever since.

Now he understood why West Point laid claim to the concept.

Continuing down the page, he learned that in 1881 the class rings began to show uniformity of design. And that prior to 1897, what would eventually evolve into a center stone was not a jewel like the one in the ring he'd found. Instead, it was a signet engraved with the class motto. It wasn't until 1897 that the engraved seal gave way to an ornamental stone.

The article went on to say that that in 1898, the Academy motto *Duty, Honor, Country* was the only motto allowed to be placed on the ring. By 1917 the custom was to place a class crest on one side of the ring and the Academy crest on the other, so that individual preference was limited to the stone in the middle, which is selected by the owner.

The information about the ring fascinated him, and he thought it would be interesting to take a trip to the Academy's library, if for no reason other than to see the rings from three of the Academy's most famous graduates: Douglas MacArthur, Dwight D. Eisenhower, and Omar N. Bradley.

After his history lesson, he selected the link to the class roster. When the *Official Register of the Officers and Cadets* for the academic year ending June 30, 1941 appeared on the screen, he scrolled forward to the list of names on page 27. The names, he discovered, were in order of academic standing at the time of graduation.

He started down the names of the graduates. It took a moment, but he finally found a name that matched the initials on the ring. Careful to go over the list once more, to make sure he hadn't overlooked any other possibilities, he was then positive he had the right man. C. W. M. stood for C. W. McIntyre—Cadet 161 in the class of 1941.

With the hope of putting an address and phone number to the man's name, he accessed the West Point home page and navigated his way through the sites he'd already visited.

But again, he was disappointed.

Frustrated, he knew he could go to the site titled *Ring Recovery* and put the matter into the hands of personnel at the Academy. He may yet. But he felt he'd found the ring for a reason and wasn't ready to hand it over to someone else to return.

Not until he'd exhausted every available resource.

He clicked on the e-mail address at the bottom of the *Military Records* site and typed a message. In the note, he said that his father—who was in failing health—had served in WWII with a soldier named Charles McIntyre. His father had recently been reminiscing about the war, and his friend from so long ago, wondering if he was still alive. He concluded by saying McIntyre was a graduate of the class of 1941, and that he was requesting McIntyre's current address, if known.

When Jack read over what he'd just typed, he couldn't help but think the staff at West Point must have received similar notes from people whose fathers really were dying and wished to reconnect with their old war buddies.

At least, he hoped that was the case.

He reread the note and pressed *Send*. He still had Friday to receive an answer. And if all went well, that left him the weekend to make his quest to find the owner of the ring a reality.

Chapter 16

WHEN JACK RETURNED to his room after breakfast on Friday, the message light on the phone by the bed was blinking. He picked up the receiver, pressed the button for retrieving messages, and listened. He could hear Russ Carter's boisterous voice demanding a call back on his cell.

The voice on the line wasn't the voice Jack wanted to hear.

He hung up the phone and stared at it. He had hoped to avoid having to explain his plans for the next couple of days. It seemed that was not going to happen. The ball was in play, and his strings were being pulled.

It's Howdy Doody Time.

He picked up the phone and tapped in Carter's number. The phone rang twice.

"It's Jack," he said when he heard Carter say hello.

"About damned time!"

Jack wasn't going to let himself be intimidated by the irritation in Carter's voice. The guy was just being an asshole. Nothing new there.

"So what's the scoop?" Jack asked.

"I've talked to Tom and he's pleased with how our first round of meetings with *The Big Four* went. He wants me to push hard during our meetings on Monday to get a few million up front: ten at least, more if I can. Without that money the casino project will stall and quite possibly fall apart all together. And, Jack, whatever you do, be careful what you say to these men. The last thing we want now is for one of the VC's to pull out on the deal before the venture has a chance to get started."

Jack couldn't help but wonder why the concern? He was only a tag-along on the trip and hadn't said more than half a dozen words to any of the VC's.

Unless…

What an asshole.

Believing Carter to be a back-stabbing sonofabitch who'd protect his own butt before anyone else's, Jack could think of only one reason the man made a special point of putting him on notice.

The fucker.

Jack knew *he* would take the fall if something went wrong with the deal!

The muscles in his jaw tightened. He said, "You don't have to worry about me, Carter."

"There's a lot on the line," Carter said. "You need to understand that."

"I'm not stupid."

"That remains to be seen."

Jack swallowed his welling anger. "Do you really think you can push these guys to move forward with this the way you want them to? They're obviously smart, powerful men who know the financial game."

"So are we, Jack. And I don't need to remind you that Seaport doesn't like excuses."

Jack noticed that Carter had stopped referring to Thomas Seaport as "Tom." He'd called him "Seaport," as though the man's last name was supposed to bring fear at the mere mention of it.

Screw 'm both!

He wasn't going to be pushed around by Seaport or Carter. Ellery might have him by the balls, but they didn't. He planned to keep it that way. "What excuses?" he demanded. "I thought Seaport was pleased with the way the meetings were going?"

"For your sake, I hope it stays that way. If there is even one aspect of this deal that these investors don't like, they could take their millions somewhere else and drop us like a stone. I don't need to tell you what that would mean."

Jack had been right about Carter. "I assure you, if something does go wrong it won't be because of something *I* said." He dropped the phone's receiver onto its cradle without saying good-bye and plopped onto the bed.

Carter definitely got under his skin. He'd have to work at not letting that happen.

He rolled to the edge of the bed and sat up. He'd play the game with Thomas Seaport because he had to. Russell Carter was another story. He wasn't going to be able to tolerate that man's shit for long. But at least he hadn't had to explain his plans for the weekend.

He'd been thinking about the ring all night and the idea of putting his mind to work on his quest to find its owner, as opposed to spending even a second more worrying about Seaport or Carter, looked better and better to him. He walked over to the desk and switched on his laptop.

The message he hoped to find was there, along with another forwarded joke from Robert and a note from Ellery.

Ellery...

He'd been trying hard not to think about her. It wasn't working. He opened the note from Ellery.

The message wasn't quite the steamy proposition he was looking for, but she told him how much she missed him and that she'd make it worth his while when he returned.

In his mind, that meant there would be a heart-felt *I love you* from her as well as a night of hot unadulterated sex. Now he could only hope that was the case.

He skipped over the forwarded joke from Robert and opened the reply from the *National Personnel Records Center*. The note was from a Scott Linton. It read:

> *I am saddened to hear about your father's poor health. It is not the Record Center's policy to give out address information without written permission from the veteran or their family. In this case, however, I have personally made an exception to the policy because of the immediacy posed by your father's failing condition. And a sincere interest on our part to help two old soldiers reunite after so many years. According to our records, Mr. Charles William McIntyre's last known address is 112 Riverbend Lane, Boise Idaho. I hope this information helps your father reconnect with his wartime buddy from WWII.*
>
> *Sincerely, Scott Linton*

He scribbled McIntyre's address on the hotel note pad angled on the desk in front of him. For a moment he stared in disbelief at what he'd written.

Here was all the information he needed to complete his quest!

He picked up the phone and dialed the concierge to have a rental car brought around.

Now nothing could keep him from returning the ring.

Chapter 17

TWENTY MINUTES LATER, Jack was sitting behind the wheel of his rental car steering toward the Bay Bridge. The mid-morning traffic out of town was relatively light, and he made it across the bridge and to Vallejo in record time. He wanted to get through the Sacramento congestion before noon. If he avoided the lunchtime traffic there, he'd have clear sailing all the way to Boise.

And plenty of time for him to think about what he was doing.

At eight-thirty that night, he pulled into the parking lot of the Double-tree Riverside Hotel in downtown Boise. Even though he was road weary and sorely in need of rest, he was excited about finding and talking with Charles William McIntyre, and couldn't imagine settling into a room and going to sleep.

Not after driving across two states to find the man.

He checked in, picked up a complimentary Auto Club city map from the concierge, and carried it upstairs to his room. He only planned on being in town one night, so he didn't bother unpacking his duffel. Instead, he just dropped the bag on the floor. Then he stripped off his clothes, climbed into the shower, and let the hot water run over his head.

Ten minutes later he was sitting on his bed, a copy of the local phone book open on his lap. He had McIntyre's address, but not a phone number. Something he should have addressed in San Francisco.

But he hadn't.

He was now, though. It was only polite for him to call ahead rather than show up unannounced at the guy's front door. He ran his finger down the column of McIntyres looking for a listing under the name of Charles.

Nothing...

It occurred to him the man might go by his middle name. But he didn't find a listing under William, Willie, or Willy either. As much as he had wanted to avoid dropping in on the old guy without advance notice, he had no choice. He'd have to drive to the house to find out if McIntyre still lived there.

Or if he was even alive.

So many WW II veterans had died. The former soldier would most likely be in his late eighties or maybe even his nineties. There was a good possibility he was one of the vets who'd passed on. Either way, it was too late at night to be knocking on McIntyre's door without prior notice

He decided to drive by the address. At least he would know where to go in the morning. And it beat sitting in his room, wondering.

The Doubletree Riverside Hotel, he discovered, was on the same side of town and not all that far from the street where he hoped McIntyre still lived.

With the map open on the seat next to him, he leaned forward and studied the street sign. Maui was a world away. Yet a simple glimmer of gold had led him to a lost ring, and that ring was about to bring him together with the soldier who'd lost it.

The moment he made a right turn onto Riverbend Lane he started looking for the address. To his left he saw a one-story building with a small parking lot and a sign in front with *Ridgeview* written across it in gold two-foot tall bold script. Directly under that—in gold letters half the size—was the slogan: *Assisted Living for the Golden Years.* A foot below that were the numbers: *112.*

McIntyre's address.

His gut told him there was no mistake. But he needed to be sure. He steered into the parking lot, stopped, and compared the numbers on the sign to the address he'd written down.

They matched.

His fingers tightened around the sheet of paper as he strained his eyes to see through the large, curtained window facing the street. He could make out partial silhouettes: heads above furniture, blue glow of TV, nothing else. The three cars sitting in the lot must belong to employees.

He had acknowledged that Charles McIntyre would be pushing ninety or more, or even be dead. But he hadn't considered the possibility that the old guy was confined to a nursing home. A shell of his former self.

The fear that McIntyre had died there settled like a vast emptiness in the pit of Jack's stomach.

He took a deep breath and blew it out.

But the sick feeling remained.

He couldn't imagine discovering he'd found the ring's owner, only to learn the man had passed away the day before, or that his mind was gone, leaving him with no memory of his class ring.

He shook off the dread, convinced he'd find McIntyre alive and well. No other scenario would work.

During the drive back to his hotel, he imagined how it would feel to return the ring and have his search come to an end.

He stepped into his room not sure how he felt: excited, disappointed, or both. He switched the light off and opened the sheer curtains, pulled tight across his window. The night sky filled the room.

Basking in the darkness, he stood staring at a lighted window across the way. The drapes were open. A moment later a well-dressed woman stepped into view. From the look of her outfit, he figured she had attended a late-running business meeting, or even a seminar here at the hotel.

As he watched her, he noticed she was looking down and calmly moving her arms about. Her hands were below the windowsill, but he could tell by the way her arms moved she was fussing with something. Possibly she had just checked in and was unpacking.

He stepped away from the window then stopped. Turning, he continued to stare at the woman without really knowing why. After a couple of seconds her arms went up and she tugged her blouse over her head. Then she unhooked her black lace bra, exposing her breasts.

He couldn't make himself turn his head, even knowing how embarrassed he'd be if she caught him watching her.

The woman arched her back and massaged her breasts—not in a seductive manner, but as though she was relieved to have them out of the confines of the bra. Then she pulled on an old oversized white sweatshirt and fluffed out her shoulder length dark hair.

She had let go of her day by slipping off her work clothes and pulling on something casual.

He felt slightly ashamed of having witnessed such a private ritual.

He could only imagine life being that simple: it wasn't that way for him.

He picked up the cordless phone from the bedside table and dialed room service to order a turkey sandwich. Returning the receiver to its cradle, he walked back to his window hoping to catch a glimpse of the woman. But the lights in her room were dimmed, and she was gone from view.

An unexpected twinge, of disappointment laced with expectation, kept his gaze focused on the darkened window.

Are our lives all that different?

He wondered.

Are anybody's…?

Chapter 18

THE DIGITAL CLOCK sitting on the bedside table read eight o'clock. Jack couldn't believe he had slept this late, even if it were five o'clock Hawaii time. He rolled out of bed, anxious to meet Charles McIntyre.

He climbed into the shower and stood there, hands against the wall, with the hot spray beating down on his head and neck. The cobwebs of sleep cleared from the recesses of his mind, replaced by thoughts of that day on the reef when he'd plucked the molded gold symbol of *Duty, Honor, Country* from its watery tomb.

The years it had lain in the coral undiscovered, the hundreds of people who snorkel there every year—he knew then, he'd been chosen to find the ring for a reason. But he never dreamed he'd be in Boise, Idaho, a week later, reuniting the long lost relic with its rightful owner.

What would the man say? How would he react?

There would be gratitude of course. But more importantly, he'd be told the story of how that ring had become lost on the reef.

And then he could put his quest to rest.

On the way out of the hotel he stopped at the café in the lobby and snagged a breakfast croissant and coffee to go. Then he stepped outside and glanced at the sky.

Only a few puffy cotton-ball clouds floated overhead in a sea of brilliant blue, but there was a chill to the air that made him thankful he'd brought his windbreaker with him. It promised to be a beautiful fall day.

He climbed into his rental car and drove out of the hotel parking lot. When he arrived at Ridgeview fifteen minutes later, he took a few seconds to quiet the nervous flutter in his gut. Even having rehearsed what he was going to say to McIntyre, he was more nervous than he had been following Russell Carter from meeting to meeting.

That thought made him chuckle. He took one more look at the ring, got out of his car, and went inside.

He spied a reception counter and staff work area off to his left. A tall, red-headed woman, in a pale yellow uniform with a floral print, smiled a greeting and asked if she could help him.

"You can," he said with a smile of his own, and stepped to the counter. "I'm here to see Mr. Charles McIntyre,"

"Are you family or friend?"

"Friend."

"Let me check with the duty nurse to make sure it's all right for you to see him."

He was alive.

But what kind of life did he have here?

Jack looked around while the receptionist checked with the nurse. He appeared to be in a lounge of sorts: a place for the residents to gather and socialize. The wall at the far end was a massive stone fireplace with a raised hearth, stacked high with crackling logs that warmed the room. To the right of that, a hallway led deeper into the building. The wall across from him had a sixty-inch, flat-screen TV mounted on it. Two codgers played checkers at a table next to a large window in the wall facing the parking lot. Others sat on sofas, reading newspapers. A few thumbed through magazines. The walls were clean and painted a bright white, and hung with large paintings of meadows filled with wildflowers, streams, and snowcapped mountains.

Assisted living at its best.

"You can see him. He's in room eighteen," the woman said, pointing to her left. "Just down that hallway and to the right."

He left the lounge and followed a white corridor of light gray tile flecked with gold. The hallway led to rooms on both sides of it. Most of the doors stood open. Some were occupied. A couple weren't.

When he walked into McIntyre's room toward the far end of the building, he found the old man sitting up in bed and staring out of the window. He was thin and had a few strands of gray hair adorning his otherwise bald head. The television was on low, and from the doorway he looked like anyone's grandfather.

McIntyre glanced in Jack's direction, then resumed his vigil at the window. "You're new here," he said.

Jack put on his friendliest face and stepped to McIntyre's bedside.

"Good morning Mr. McIntyre," he said, and offered his hand. "My name is Jack Ferrell. I have something that I believe belongs to you."

McIntyre's eyes widened as he turned and faced Jack.

He said, "Something of mine?"

"I believe so, yes."

The old man's forehead creased with confusion. He wrapped a large hand around Jack's and pumped it.

Jack was surprised at the strength of the old guy's grip. He dug the ring from his pocket and held it out, pinched between his thumb and forefinger.

"My ring!" McIntyre said.

He plucked it from Jack's fingers and held it close in front of his face. His lips curled up at the corners in a way that could only be interpreted as immense joy.

There was nothing Jack needed to say. He just stood and watched the man's reaction, noticing a sparkle in the codger's eyes that hadn't been there a moment ago. He was glad he'd kept his quest, personal.

McIntyre held the ring up as though he was showing it to Jack for the first time. "I got this the day I graduated from West Point," he said. "God, what a group of know-it-alls…"

Jack's lips spread into a grin.

He said, "I found your ring on a reef in Maui."

Again, McIntyre frowned.

"Maui?" he asked.

"Off shore from Makena beach," Jack said. "Were you stationed there during the war?"

Jack watched McIntyre's eyes narrow. There was no mistaking the look on the man's face; the old guy was searching his memory.

"I was in Pearl for a few days," McIntyre said. "But I don't believe I've ever been to Maui."

Chapter 19

JACK FOUND IT difficult not to badger the old guy. He'd driven a long way to find McIntyre—to hear the story behind the loss of the ring. When McIntyre finally spoke, Jack noticed a wistful tone to the guy's voice.

"A bunch of wet-nosed Lieutenants itching to get into the battle in Europe, is what we were," McIntyre began. "But the United States hadn't officially entered the war yet. It wasn't until December 7th of that year—three days before my twenty-second birthday—that the Japanese bombed Pearl Harbor. A lot of us did go to Europe, but I ended up in the Pacific."

Jack slid a chair under him and sat facing the bed. McIntyre watched with interest. The thought occurred to Jack that the guy didn't receive many visitors.

He rested his forearms on his knees and said, "Those were definitely bad and bloody days."

McIntyre sighed and his attention wandered toward the window. After a long moment he said, "They were at that."

Jack followed McIntyre's gaze. He saw a couple of people milling about the lawn outside and the mountains in the distance, but got the feeling that this soldier of long ago was not looking at those sights. He was seeing into that ugly period of history when war took so many people's lives.

"Saipan," Jack said, recalling his knowledge of World War II, "was some kind of turning point for the US forces wasn't it?"

McIntyre turned his head, held Jack's gaze, and explained, "It was right after the battle of Saipan that Tinian and Guam fell. That left the Japanese mainland vulnerable to air and sea attacks. Hell, it was eight days after the fall of Saipan that Premier Tojo and his entire cabinet resigned. It makes me feel good to know I helped make that happen."

McIntyre eyeballed the ring and said, "The battle of Saipan began in the early hours of June 15th, 1944. For two days prior to the invasion, some twenty-four hundred 16-inch shells were fired to soften up the enemy." He peered at Jack and said, "That's a sound you don't forget. Kind of like a boxcar swishing by overhead."

Jack shook his head in disbelief. "That must have been hell on the Japanese?"

"Not as much as we would have liked. Because of possible mining in the water along the coast, the firing had to be done from six miles off shore, and the spotters had problems pinpointing the dug-in gun pits."

"Six miles! It's a wonder they could hit anything from that far away. What happened after that?"

McIntyre gave the ring a long look, his mind clearly resurrecting the events that followed. "At sunrise," he went on, "Six hundred ships became visible to the enemy. Admiral Spruance had amassed over a dozen battleships, two dozen carriers and carrier escorts, a couple of dozen cruisers, a hundred and forty odd destroyers, and countless transports to carry out his vengeance on the Jap bastards. All of us were hoping the Japanese officers—especially Admiral Nagumo, who had hit us at Pearl and was reportedly on the island—were watching the attack through their binoculars, believing the ghosts of Pearl Harbor had returned to haunt them.

"Anyway, the Japanese defense strategy had been simple: destroy the Marine landing force at the beachhead. But we were determined to fight it out, and at 0542 hours the orders came. There were four miles of beaches attacked by the 2nd and the 4th Marine Divisions.

"Being Army, I wasn't part of that initial landing. I was assigned to the 27th Army division as an advisor and came ashore later. By about 0800 hours, seven hundred and nineteen assault amphibian tractors, called AM-TRACKs, loaded with Marines, began circling at the line of departure four thousand yards off shore. At the same time light gunboats were firing four-and-a-half-inch rockets, and 40mm canon were sweeping the beach. For good measure, a half-dozen fighters strafed the beachhead, and a dozen bombers dropped hundred pound bombs to soften the landing for our guys.

"Twenty minutes later, eight thousand Marines were under fire on the beaches. By nightfall twenty thousand Marines were dug in there." McIntyre sighed and took a deep breath.

Jack waited.

McIntyre continued. "The Marines suffered two thousand casualties—a tenth of their entire force—taking that beach, and the fighting wasn't even close to over. I went ashore the next day with the 27th Army Division. The final, major battle took place on the night of July 6th and 7th when three thousand Japanese, made a *banzai* charge down Paradise Valley and Harakiri Gulch, armed with rifles, spears and some with nothing at all. The Japanese forces were decimated, but we lost four hundred and six men in that charge."

Jack, who had moved to the edge of his chair during the telling of the story, leaned back. "I just can't imagine fighting like that," he said

McIntyre smiled. "Did you know Lee Marvin got shot in the ass on Saipan?"

Jack chuckled. "I'll bet that hurt?" But he knew there was nothing at all funny about getting shot—in the butt or anywhere else.

"Like a sonofabitch," McIntyre said soberly. He added, "You know, that wasn't as uncommon an injury as you might think. All of us crawling around on our bellies the way we were, with those Jap bullets whizzing over our heads."

"Were you with him when he was shot?"

"I was assigned to a different unit, but I was there when it happened. At the time he was just another wounded Marine. It wasn't until after the war, when Lee Marvin became a popular actor, that I found out he'd been shot during that battle."

The door opened and a nurse entered. She walked to the side of the bed, carrying a tray of tiny plastic cups.

"Time for your medicine," she announced loudly enough for everyone in the place to hear.

"Is that my breakfast?" McIntyre smiled. "I'm starving."

"You've already had your breakfast," she assured him. "It's time for your pills."

Jack rose to his feet, scooted his chair back, and watched while she handed McIntyre his meds and a glass of water. He noticed McIntyre close his hand around the ring and slide it under the covers.

He asked, "Mr. McIntyre wanted to know if you brought his breakfast. He's already eaten?"

"Just before you got here," the nurse said. "Sharp as a tack when it comes to remembering things that happened twenty, thirty years ago. It's his short-term memory that gives him problems."

Once McIntyre had swallowed his pills along with half a glass of water, she patted him on the arm and walked out. A moment later Jack heard her call out the same loud greeting to a patient in the next room. He shook his head at the volume of the woman's voice.

When he refocused on McIntyre, the man had the ring out from under the covers and in his hand.

He said, "Your nurse seems nice. A little loud, but nice."

McIntyre slowly looked up at Jack. "Were we talking about something?"

"The battle for Saipan," Jack said. "You were telling me that was where Lee Marvin got shot in the butt. I'd still like to know how you lost your ring on the reef. You said you don't remember going to Maui. But you must have. Maybe you went there on leave or something? It was a long time ago."

McIntyre closed his fist around the ring as if he were afraid Jack would take it from him. The sparkle was gone from his eyes.

"Where...?" he asked.

"Maui—surely you haven't forgotten?"

McIntyre closed his eyes and scooted down in his bed. He settled his head onto the pillow and pulled the covers tightly around his neck. "I'm tired now," he said. "I think I'll go to sleep."

Jack wanted to keep talking and get the old guy to remember. But he didn't see how that was going to happen, not now anyway. McIntyre had already faded out on him. He got up from his chair and stepped to the bed. McIntyre's eyes were closed, and he was clutching the ring.

It seemed to Jack the old guy was smiling.

The man's ramblings about his experience in Saipan touched Jack in a way he'd never expected. They should have been able to talk more.

He opened the drawer in the bedside table looking for a pad of paper and a pen. He found both and not much else. Hoping for the best, he wrote down his name, cell phone number, and a short note asking McIntyre to call him so they could talk more.

He left the note sitting on the table where McIntyre could see it. Then he stepped into the hall and closed the door behind him.

He doubted he'd ever get a call from the old guy, but hoped he was wrong.

He stared at the door, then turned and walked out of the building the same way he had come in.

He may never know how the ring had come to be lost on that reef.

Chapter 20

MIDWAY INTO HIS flight home on Tuesday morning, Jack reclined his seat-back and stared at the panel overhead. He hadn't received a call from McIntyre and didn't figure he would. The ring had brought a glimmer of happiness to the man's tired eyes. But how it had been lost on the reef in Maui remained a mystery. The old guy simply had no recollection of ever having been there.

But his nurse had commented on his keen long-term memory.

He would have remembered.

But he didn't.

Jack glanced at Russell Carter, who sat in the aisle seat next to him eyeballing the blond stewardess like a vigilant guard dog. He'd been trying to figure out whom Carter reminded him of. Finally, it dawned on him that the big man looked like a taller and heavier Clint Eastwood in the movie Heartbreak Ridge—buzz cut and all.

But the similarity between Carter and the veteran actor ended there. He could never picture Carter leading a troop of men into battle, but he sure could see him sneaking around behind the lines, torturing handcuffed prisoners to get information—or just for the fun of it.

Nothing the man had said or done on the trip convinced Jack otherwise.

He reached into the magazine pocket on the back of the seat in front of him and removed the copy of James Rollins' *Deep Fathom* he had snagged from the used book shelf at the Fairmont. He'd spend the rest of the flight lost in the story.

A couple of hours later, they walked out of the baggage claim area and onto the sidewalk fronting the Kahului airport. Beverly Carter pulled to the curb in her black Mercedes sedan and parked. The trunk popped open, and they loaded their bags. Russell Carter slammed the lid shut and climbed in on the driver's side, forcing his wife to slide over the center console and onto the passenger's seat. Jack sat in the back and promptly fastened his seatbelt.

Ellery wasn't in the car. He had thought she would have ridden along to meet him.

He asked, "Ellery couldn't make it?"

Beverly Carter twisted sideways in her seat and smiled.

Strained. A little forced. Jack thought she beamed a bit more broadly and a beat too long.

She said, "Her and Rachel are out playing. I'm afraid you two handsome men are stuck with me."

Russell Carter shot his wife a sideways glance.

He said, "Aren't we the lucky ones?"

Jack couldn't believe Russell Carter's rudeness. He gave Beverly Carter a half smile. Not strained, and not forced.

"It really was nice of you to pick us up," he said. "Thanks."

He mentally shrugged and gazed out of the side window at the Iao Valley in the distance.

Ellery should have been there to welcome him home, but she'd been too busy running around with her mother.

Thirty minutes later Jack was inside his *ohana* unpacking. Ellery still had not made an appearance to welcome him home. She could have easily called him on her Blackberry. Now he wasn't sure he cared. But when his cell phone trilled a couple of minutes later he found himself hoping it was her.

"It's about time," he said, pressing the phone to his ear. "I was beginning to think you didn't love me anymore."

"Now, you know better than that," Robert said.

"Oh, hell! I thought you were Ellery."

"No shit. How was the trip?"

"I found him."

"Found who?"

"Charles McIntyre, the guy who owned the ring. I found him."

"Holy shit."

"Right."

"Let's grab a beer. You can tell me about it."

Jack glanced at his watch.

"That beer will have to wait," he said. "Seaport wants me in his office when Russell Carter briefs him on the trip."

"You're the man, huh?"

"Can't see how. I didn't do shit but sit with my thumb up my ass."

"Obviously Seaport has big plans for you."

Jack snorted and said, "Sure hope so. I hate thumb sitting."

Robert said, "Seaport doesn't strike me as a man who does anything without a good reason."

"No, he doesn't. And I guess I'll find out shortly what he's up to. One thing's for sure. I definitely got an education as to how he does business."

"And?"

"No comment."

"Give me a buzz when you're ready for that beer."

"Just as soon as I'm done."

Chapter 21

JACK HUNG UP the phone and headed for Seaport's house. He didn't bother knocking. Ellery and her mother were still gone, and Thomas Seaport and Russ Carter would for sure be sitting in Seaport's office waiting on him. He walked into the house and up to the teak door of Seaport's inner sanctum. As usual the door was closed.

Or so he thought.

When he lifted his hand to knock, he noticed the door hanging slightly ajar. He heard Thomas Seaport raise his voice. He and Russell Carter were having a heated discussion about something.

Jack decided to wait until the tempest passed. He couldn't imagine he was the source of Seaport's anger and sure didn't want to step into the middle of whatever it was that had the man so upset.

But he was curious as to what had set Seaport off.

Seaport lowered his voice, but there was enough venom in his words for Jack to know the man was not happy about something. He listened.

From what he could make out, Seaport was complaining that he had already paid enough money to ensure his casino project would move forward as planned, and that Gordon Kaeha was just being greedy.

Greedy? Greedy about what?

Jack pressed his ear to the door, hoping to hear more, but Seaport's voice dropped to a low grumble. Then he heard Seaport say, "Take care of this guy personally, and see that this doesn't happen again."

Russell Carter's reply carried the same venom. "Consider it done."

Working as a salmon fisherman on the family boat in Fields Landing Jack had seen enough under-the-table dealings to recognize one when he heard it. And even though he didn't really know Russell Carter, he knew enough about him to believe the man when he said *Consider it done.*

Once Seaport's office fell quiet, Jack counted to ten then knocked. Carter opened the door for him, and he walked into the room. There was no mistaking the tension hanging in the air.

"Take a seat, Jack," Seaport said from his chair behind his desk. "It'll be a minute."

"Yessir."

Jack winced at how quickly the words flew from his mouth. He swallowed back the bitter taste that went with them.

He took a seat in the same chair as on the day he was told to fire Kimo Holowai. He saw Seaport pick up several note-book sized sheets of paper, tap them into alignment, paper clip them together, set the sheaf of paperwork aside, and repeat the process with several more sheets. He figured the man was taking the time to regain his composure.

A long, silent minute later, Seaport stopped shuffling papers and asked, "Tell me about San Francisco."

Jack settled into his seat. This wasn't his show.

Carter spoke up. For the next fifteen minutes, he briefed Seaport on the discussions with *The Big Four* and reassured him his current suppliers would continue to meet his demands.

Jack listened. There was nothing for him to add or say that Carter wasn't already saying. Still, he was being made to sit through the meeting.

More grooming, he supposed.

And a taste of what was to come.

He could only wonder when and what his role in it all would be.

Carter finished talking, and Seaport's gaze settled on Jack.

"We're done here," he said. "But before you do anything else, I want you to make sure the boat is fueled and ready. Tomorrow morning, you're taking some associates of mine out fishing. Nothing fancy, just troll around for a few hours and see if you can hook a mahi mahi or an ono—something big."

"Consider it done," Jack said. He resisted smiling at his choice of words.

Carter shot him a hard look, but didn't say anything.

"Good," Seaport said. "You can go now."

Jack walked outside and looked at his watch. It was a little after two. Ellery wasn't back yet, and he needed to get to the boat. He tossed around his options. Not all that complicated: call her on her cell or go right to the boat and get done what he needed to do.

Why call? She'd blown him off at the airport and hadn't bothered to even give him a buzz to welcome him home.

Dammit! She thought she had him pegged. She was wrong.

Chapter 22

JACK FLIPPED OPEN his cell phone, navigated to Robert's number, and hit *Send*. He should think about upgrading to a Blackberry. But he wasn't there, yet.

He pressed the phone to his ear.

The boat was pretty much ready to go. That's how Kimo Holowai kept it. But Jack knew there were always last minute checks to make. Robert could meet him there, and they could talk.

And have that beer.

So far he wasn't all that happy to be back on the island. He hoped that would change.

"Hello," Robert mumbled in a voice thick with sleep.

"What are you doing asleep? Jack asked. "I just talked to you an hour ago."

"You sound a tad upset. Ellery piss you off again?"

Jack exhaled an audible *humph*.

"Like always," he said.

Robert groaned. "I think I want a new friend."

"Relax," Jack said. "You told me you wanted to hear about the ring."

"I do."

"Well then drag your lazy ass off the couch and meet me at Seaport's boat at Maalaea Harbor. It's about halfway down the first dock you come to—named *Ellery Queen*. I'll buy the beer."

"Damn right you will," Robert said. "Give me twenty minutes."

Jack switched off his cellular. He really needed to talk to his friend, and not just about McIntyre and the ring.

Damn!

His life should have been getting better, but it was all fucked up.

At least that's how he felt.

He wondered if he were making a big deal out of nothing. Maybe he was being cynical as a result of wanting to believe Ellery's father was a bad man, because he was her father—Thomas Seaport, Mister Pillar-of-the-Community Seaport—and his money was responsible for Ellery's rapacious attitude.

Or was she just that way?

But is she using her finely honed sexual talents as a form of control over me? Are her kisses laced with poison that will eventually transform me into someone exactly like her father?

He couldn't imagine being one of *them*.

He rubbed his scalp with his hand, feeling for the small curved horns he was sure would be there if he had begun the transformation.

Not even a bump.

How long does it take for the points to appear once you've been infected?

Chapter 23

ROBERT POPPED THE cap from a bottle of Foster's Lager. He took a seat in the teak and chrome fighting chair bolted to the stern deck, and listened to Jack talk while readying the reels for the next day's fishing.

"So what's the old guy's story?" Robert asked when Jack told him how he'd located McIntyre and driven to Boise to meet him. "He lose the ring during the war or what?"

"Don't know. He talked a lot about the battle of Saipan and how Lee Marvin got shot in the ass there, but he never did tell me how he lost the ring."

"And you didn't ask?"

"Of course I did, more than once. McIntyre was sharp as a tack when he was talking about Saipan, but he didn't remember being on Maui. And when I tried to press him about it, the old guy just kind of zoned out on me."

"What you mean *zoned out?*"

"He couldn't remember shit. His short term memory is shot."

"Damned sad," Robert said. "Something tells me it's an interesting story."

"That's the feeling I had the moment I left him lying there in bed. I'm even thinking about flying back to find out what did happen."

They both fell quiet.

"And the other part?" Robert asked, breaking the silence between them.

Jack sighed and leaned against the bulkhead. "You're talking about San Francisco?"

"Of course I am."

Jack huffed. "I didn't do shit."

"So?"

"Seaport's happy as a clam in mud with the outcome of the meetings and pushing hard to make his casino venture fly."

Robert leaned forward, and picked up a green and yellow skirted marlin lure from the deck in front of him. He eyeballed the monster and tested the sharpness of the barbed hook with the tip of his index finger.

He winced at a spot of blood that formed. "I have to tell you," he said. "A while back, when you told me Seaport talked about a casino project he was putting together, I didn't say much. But I'm not sure that's a good thing—the casino on Kahoolawe I mean."

"I don't know," Jack said. He stared wistfully at Kahoolawe in the distance and added, "From the way Seaport and Carter talk, the Hawaiians want it."

"At what cost?" Robert asked. "Hawaii needs the jobs, there's no denying that. But Makena's a treasure-trove of ancient villages and shrines. The out-of-control development that comes with a venture like that would destroy the irreplaceable Hawaiian history in that part of the island. And we certainly don't need any more boats harassing the whales."

Jack harbored the same concerns. He'd tried to convince himself otherwise. "Doesn't sound good when you put it that way."

"It's not," Robert said. "Locals have fought against development in Makena for years. Doesn't seem likely their feelings would change that easily."

"But it's possible?"

"Or someone wants people to believe that's what's happened."

Jack eyed the fishing reel in his hand but his thoughts were focused on what Robert had just said. He hadn't even stopped to consider the possibility that Thomas Seaport had pioneered the project in the name of the Hawaiians just so he could get the multi-million-dollar contract to build the casino. He should've realized the venture was Seaport's idea from the beginning. "Do you know a man by the name of Gordon Kaeha?"

"I don't think so," Robert said, and asked, "Why?"

"Just curious," Jack said. "Forget I asked."

"Come on, buddy. Out with it."

Jack stepped to the rod locker and stowed the pole and reel. He'd ignored the bottom line of his concern. Robert knew what it was and wouldn't let up on him. "Out with what?"

Robert said, "I think Ellery and this whole money thing has you all fucked up."

"I think you're right."

"*Duh*! And Gordon Kaeha, what's up with him?"

Jack picked up his beer. He drained it, set the bottle on the gunnel and faced his friend. No reason to play games. "This afternoon I overheard Seaport and Carter talking in Seaport's office—quite heatedly, I might add. From what I could make out from the other side of the door, I got the impression Seaport is paying this Gordon Kaeha guy a lot of cash under the table for something. It might not be anything, but my gut tells me different."

Robert gazed toward the ocean, and for a few seconds there was only the sound of the mooring lines creaking.

Jack quietly waited.

"I think payoffs have been a part of Hawaiian politics since day one," Robert said. "And I'm afraid they will be for a long time to come."

"Why is that?" Jack asked. He knew his friend, knew he had more to say.

Robert held his answer a breath and said, "Third-world cultural influences have a lot to do with it, no doubt. But I believe there are other reasons as well. Like a propensity for people to be motivated by personal greed rather than the good of the whole. And because people seem to buy into the practice of payoffs."

"How's that?" Jack asked. Robert had his attention.

"By demonstrating a willingness to lay out whatever money it takes to get them what they want," Robert said. "It's not that way with everyone in local government. But it's that way with enough of them, that the very concept of having to line a crooked bureaucrat's pockets with money to get a job done has become an accepted part of doing business here." He sighed. "I'm not saying it's right. I'm only saying that's the way it is."

Jack nodded. "Can't say I don't agree. But I'm inclined to believe payoffs aren't necessarily bad if the end product is inherently good for the whole. In a situation like that, the good far outweighs the bad. The issue becomes a matter of morality, nothing else. And that may be the case here. I don't know."

"And if it is only a matter of morality?" Robert asked. "That makes feeding some bureaucrat's greed okay?"

"Not necessarily okay, just easier to accept."

Robert took in a deep breath and let it out slowly. He bounced the heavy lure in the palm of his hand.

Jack watched.

"Shit, I don't know," Robert said. "Somehow I have a problem with the whole concept."

Jack took the lure from his friend's hand and laid the twelve-inch monster in the tackle box with several others of different size and colors. His arsenal for the next morning's fishing. All lined up like artillery shells in an ammo box.

He straightened and said, "And I'm just kidding myself thinking graft and corruption in any form could ever lead to something good. I guess that's why I'm here talking to you about this shit."

"We'd all like an ideal world," Robert said. "Where nothing crooked goes on. But whenever you have a venture of this magnitude, there are always those who step forward to capitalize on the project any way they can. Largely, that's the way the game is played. But not necessarily to the extent anyone's hurt by the end result. From what you told me, I'd say Thomas Seaport is paying off some of the key players in his casino deal so that he can make sure the project goes through without any hitches."

"That's the impression I got."

"And you're worried about where all this will lead."

"You said it yourself: *At what cost?* In the long run, the Thomas Seaports of the world aren't the ones who suffer. I might not be able to do anything to stop that kind of graft from happening, but I'd sure like to know if that's what's going on here."

"Who knows," Robert said. "Maybe there *is* something you can do?"

Jack shrugged.

Robert opened him and Jack another beer. He handed Jack his.

"The Hawaiian people have a word for what you're doing," Robert said; and explained, "Returning the ring—acting on your concerns about Seaport's casino venture, and the long-term effect it'll have on the island and the Hawaiians. It's called *ho`oponopono*."

Jack gulped down a quarter of his beer and wiped his mouth with the back of his hand.

"*Pono, pono?*" he asked.

"*Ho`oponopono*. It means correctness. You want to set things right."

"That's me, for sure. A regular knight in shining armor."

Robert chuckled and said, "Let's finish these beers and walk up the hill to the aquarium and talk to Kazuko. She's politically better connected than I am. And I know she'd love to put the hook to someone collecting bribes."

Chapter 24

JACK AND ROBERT walked into the parking lot fronting the aquarium and stood looking at the building. There were a dozen or so cars and pickups parked in the spaces near the entrance and a tour bus was edged in next to the curb. A couple of dozen visitors milled around, squeezing into a line of people that extended fifty feet out the glass doors.

"You really think Kazuko will help?" Jack asked. He was only recently truly getting to know Robert's girlfriend.

"She hates the crooked shit running rampant throughout the islands," Robert said. "Development along our creeks and shorelines is sending tons of chemicals into the ocean every time it rains or someone turns on a sprinkler. She says the runoff is poison to the reefs—primarily pesticides and nitrate fertilizers. And that the toxins are killing off the coral, and ultimately the sea life that depends on it for survival."

Jack huffed and said, "I'm really getting to hate this shit."

Robert glanced at a noisy delivery truck bouncing along the dock on the street below the aquarium, and made a sound resembling a grunt of dissatisfaction.

Jack ignored the truck and waited for Robert to explain.

"Been going on a long time," Robert said, when the truck noise lowered to a distant rumble. "It seems everyone doing business on Maui is in someone's pocket one way or another. And the developers—hell, they're the worst if you ask me. Especially the last few years—over building changed Maui and probably most of Hawaii. I'm not sure it was for the best."

The tourists crowding the sidewalk outside the entrance finally settled into a single line. Jack slapped Robert on the back and said, "Let's hear what

Kazuko has to say."

Robert led the way to the counter, flashed a smile at the clerk and said, "Hi Lani. I need to talk to Kazuko if she's free."

Lani smiled back, but her eyes were fixed on Jack.

He met her gaze. She was dark haired and pretty. He let her talk.

"I don't think I've met your friend," she said.

"Lani, this is Jack. Jack this is Lani," Robert said. "Now, if Kazuko is free, I'd like to talk to her."

"Let me check."

She picked up the phone and pushed a couple of buttons. She mumbled something Jack didn't catch, then nodded as though the person on the other end could see her and returned the receiver to its cradle.

"Kazuko's at the jellyfish exhibit," she said to Robert. She pointed at the double doors leading into the aquarium. "Go on through."

They found Robert's girlfriend standing next to the acrylic jellyfish habitat: a tall cylindrical tank brightly lit from the inside and filled with a hundred graceful jellies of different sizes, undulating like miniature parachutes drifting through a liquid sky.

Even standing ten feet away in the darkened room, Jack could see Kazuko clearly. Her face glowed in the soft blue-white light from the tank. Her long, dark hair shimmered like threads of black silk. Her almond-shaped eyes were pools of oil that reflected the iridescent water. And her flawless brown skin—a tribute to her island heritage—stood out in betrayal to her father's fair-skinned Japanese ancestry. Her full lips curved into a permanent smile as she peered at nature's beauty. Soft music flowed from speakers in the ceiling. Viewers lined the bench along the wall while others hovered around the tank, pointing, whispering.

He'd had long conversations with her on numerous occasions and knew how smart she was, and he'd always thought she was pretty. In the light from the tank she looked like an angel. It became very clear to him why Robert had chosen to stay with her on Maui.

Kazuko turned as Robert and Jack approached and widened her smile. "Hi, babe," she said. "What's up?"

Robert's grin matched hers. He took her hand in his and said, "Jack needs to talk to you a minute. Can you take a break?"

She glanced from Robert to Jack and back to Robert. Her smile slipped slightly. "Sure. Let's go outside."

She led them out of the building and over to a patch of shade next to the hammerhead shark exhibit. She leaned against the railing with her back to the tank. Robert leaned against the railing next to her, and Jack stood in front of them.

"So, Jack, what's on your mind?" Kazuko asked.

Jack considered for a moment that he shouldn't involve Kazuko. But then it had been Robert's idea for them to come here and talk to her. "Robert thought you might know a man by the name of Gordon Kaeha. I think he's some kind of county or state official."

His question narrowed her eyes.

"I know you and Robert talk," he went on. "No doubt he's told you about the casino Ellery's father is planning to build?"

"The casino on Kahoolawe?" she confirmed, crossing her arms in front of her in obvious disgust.

"That's the one."

He saw her look at Robert and get a nod back from him.

She refocused and said, "Be careful who you talk to about this."

He glanced at her, then Robert, and back at her again. "Why's that?"

"People go missing on this island."

"And you think that might happen to me?"

"I'm only saying be careful."

"Understood," he said. "Now what about this Gordon Kaeha guy? I have a sneaky feeling Thomas Seaport is paying him big money under the table for some reason."

"A bribe!" She practically spit out the words.

"That's what I'm thinking. Or some kind of kickback."

She shook her head. "Those fuckers!"

Profanity didn't normally suit her. Jack believed it did in this case.

Robert took her by the hand and asked, "Do you have any idea who Gordon Kaeha is?"

She looked at Robert but didn't answer.

"Kazuko," he prompted after a couple of beats.

She pursed her lips, then relaxed. "The island's full of guys like him," she said to Jack. "They're the same ones who turn their backs on the damage being done to the reefs and sea life around the island. The lousy crooked assholes…"

Jack had never heard Kazuko swear before and she'd now done it twice in less than a minute. He figured she had to be really pissed.

Robert sighed. "But do you know him?" he asked.

She shook her head slowly from side to side. "The name sounds familiar. But I can't place it right now."

"Can you do some checking?" Robert asked. "Maybe one of your co-workers knows who he is."

"Sure, Stephanie might know him, or even Stan. They handle most of the regulatory issues that come up around here. But they're at a conference on Oahu and won't be back until sometime tomorrow."

"Thanks," Jack said. "Would you let me know, one way or the other?"

"You bet I will," she said.

She walked with them as far as the exit. There, she gave Robert a peck on the cheek and said good-bye.

He looked at her with concern. "Do what you can," he said. "But be careful."

Chapter 25

JACK FINISHED READYING the boat and was in his Jeep driving back to the *ohana* by five that afternoon. He hadn't heard from Ellery, so he called her. She said she was at Tommy Bahamas having a martini with her mother. She'd leave as soon as she finished her drink. Five minutes, tops. There was no mention of the trip or how much she missed him.

He didn't press the issue.

When he arrived at the cottage thirty minutes later, Ellery wasn't there.

He glanced at his watch.

Big drink!

It took him fifteen minutes to shower, shave, and dress for dinner.

He was ready for a couple more beers with Ellery, but most of all he wanted to stop thinking about Gordon Kaeha.

He thought he had. Apparently not.

But he wasn't going to let his thoughts about the guy ruin his evening. Nothing was going to keep him from having a good time out with Ellery and a great night afterwards.

He really was hooked.

When Ellery finally sauntered into the room, Jack quickly tossed aside the copy of *Dive Magazine* he'd been perusing to keep his mind from running amuck and gave her a good long look. One word came to mind, and he found himself muttering it under his breath.

Gorgeous!

He'd told her on the phone he was starving. Seeing her in her new Verducchi dress with the low-cut bodice made up for the forty-five minute wait.

An hour wouldn't have been too long.

"You ready?" he asked.

"In a minute," she grumbled and disappeared into the bathroom.

Twenty minutes later she strolled past him, picked up her purse, and walked out of the *ohana*, leaving the door standing open. He followed half a dozen steps behind her. When he got outside he saw her standing by the passenger side of her BMW, waiting for him.

Her mood confused him. "I feel like the bastard child, here," he said. "What's up?"

"Figure it out," she said. "My dress—I bought it for you."

"It's beautiful. *You're* beautiful. Didn't you see my jaw drop when you walked into the room?"

She handed him the keys. "Next time, tell me."

He continued to stand there. "I thought a picture was worth a thousand words?"

"It's not," she said. "Can we go?"

"Absolutely." He opened the passenger door for her, held it while she slid onto the leather seat, and pushed it closed. The car was a perfect fit for her. He enjoyed driving it. But his Jeep was more his style.

The BMW started on the first turn of the ignition. Music blared from the CD player. Before he could reach to turn down the volume, she'd ejected the CD and inserted another.

He'd have preferred conversation.

The music filled the silence between them. The volume was still up, but the tune was easier on the ears. He turned it down a few notches, eased the car out of the driveway, and drove in the direction of the Outback Steak House.

"I'm thinking steak," he said. He was still feeling Australian.

"I'm thinking French would be better." She was, studying her face in the vanity mirror on the sun visor.

"Maybe," Jack said. "But only if you plan on carrying the theme right on through the night."

He caught a look from her that told him she was in no mood to joke around, even if he was half-serious. And he was. He'd been anxious to get home to her. That was changing.

The reunion hadn't gone the way he imagined.

"Sorry," he said. "I have my heart set on a thick, juicy rib-eye hot off the grill. And dinner *is* on me."

"If you insist," she said. "But that's not what I want."

He shot her a toothy grin.

When they walked into the Outback Steak House fifteen minutes later, the hostess seated them in a booth next to a window without making them wait. Two male waiters rushed up to the table. One waiter poured them glasses of water while the other just stood there. They both stared at Ellery's tits, and Jack tried not to let it bother him. It wasn't easy.

Observing the customers seated at the tables near them, he noticed the heads of the men were turned toward Ellery. She had that effect on the male population wherever she went.

The price of being engaged to a drop-dead gorgeous blonde.

He cleared his throat to interrupt the men's ogling and ordered a 20-ounce glass of Foster's Lager. It took a couple of deep breaths, but the waiter closest to the table finally wrote it down.

Jack glanced questioningly at Ellery.

"Order me a Sauvignon Blanc," she told him before he asked.

"We just have Chardonnay." The waiter with the order pad finally spoke up.

Ellery rolled her eyes. "Figures."

Jack glanced at the waiter. "That'll be fine."

The two young waiters hovered around Ellery a moment longer then scurried away.

Jack raised the menu and scanned his choices, even though he already knew what he wanted.

"You'd better order a steak," Ellery said. "That's what we came to this place for."

"I plan to. I just like perusing my options."

Ellery pushed her menu aside without looking at it. "I'll just have a dinner salad."

"We've got to have a Bloomin' Onion," he said. "And I can't eat an entire one by myself."

"If you say so. I still would have preferred French tonight."

Jack grinned. "That's for later, remember?"

Ellery's stoical expression didn't change. "Where did you go this afternoon?"

"You know where," he said. "Your dad wanted me to get the *Ellery Queen* ready for tomorrow. I'm taking some associates of his out fishing in it in the morning."

"But where were you? I dropped by the boat to surprise you, but you weren't there."

"I met Robert and we had a couple of beers. Then we went to the aquarium to see Kazuko."

"If you were done doing whatever it was you had to do to the boat, don't you think you should have come back here to be with me?"

"You were out with your mother," he said. "Besides, Robert's my best friend. We had some catching up to do."

"Makes no difference," she said.

Her gaze dropped to her left hand. She fingered the half-carat diamond engagement ring and frowned.

He saw her scowl, and regretted not having been able to buy her a bigger diamond.

She said, "At times, I think the two of you spend too much time together."

"Let's not go there," he said. "You were busy doing whatever you were doing. Robert called wanting to get together for a beer. Your dad wanted me to get the boat ready, which is exactly what I did. Robert met me there. But it didn't take me that long to do what I needed to do, so we walked over to the aquarium for a few minutes to talk to Kazuko. There was no offense intended against you. So get off it, already. Jesus, what's with you lately?"

Ellery's gaze met his, then she peered down at her hands again. In a pouty little-girl voice she said, "I wanted to give you something." She flashed a quick, thin smile and added, "You know, a thank you, for the way you're getting along with Daddy."

He took a deep breath. He kicked himself for losing his cool.

"You didn't have to get me anything," he said.

"I know," she said. "But it's something you need."

Chapter 26

ELLERY REACHED INTO her purse, pulled out a wrapped gift in the shape of a small box, and handed it to Jack.

From the size and shape of the package, Jack guessed she'd gotten him a wristwatch. He was sure it was nice, and expensive, but he liked his old Seiko dive watch a lot and couldn't imagine not wearing it.

She knows that.

He tore the wrapping off the box and opened the lid. He sighed to himself. It was a Rolex sports watch: very nice, and very expensive.

"It's beautiful." He leaned over and kissed her on the corner of the mouth. "But you shouldn't have, really. It's too much."

She beamed. "I want my man to look good."

Jack liked the watch. Still, it wasn't his Seiko.

"Put it on," she said.

He removed his relic, slipped it into his pocket, and strapped on the Rolex. "It's wonderful," he said. "Thank you."

The waiter brought their drinks. He lingered a moment before walking away.

Ellery picked up her wineglass and took a sip of chardonnay. "So tell me about the trip."

Jack took a gulp of beer, and held onto his glass. "You're really interested in what went on in those meetings?"

"You bet I am." She returned her glass to the table. "You talked money, didn't you?"

Money—the bottom line.

"We did." He described the meetings with the Venture Capitalists. But she was so enamored with the big-dollar aspect of those closed-door conferences, that he didn't bother telling her he had found the rightful owner of the class ring and returned it to him. He doubted she'd be interested in hearing about the old man, or what it was like to see his eyes sparkle at the ring's return.

Ellery rested her arms on the tabletop in front of her and leaned in close. Her eyes remained fixed on his, and there was gleam in them that hadn't been there a second before.

The corners of her mouth curled into a cruel smile. "How'd it feel? You know, to get all that money?"

"I didn't get anything," he said. "Your father will, I guess. But not me. You make it sound as though we were a school of sharks going in for the kill."

"That's kind of how it is, isn't it?" Her smile was still there, as was the gleam in her eyes.

He watched her fidget with excitement and said, "It's just business. And to be honest, all I did was sit on my ass and watch Russell Carter put on his dog and pony show."

Ellery pursed her lips in that same pouty expression. "But that's not any fun," she said. "You should have been the one going in for the kill."

"I wouldn't even know how to," he said. "But it's interesting you put it like that. I would never have looked at securing an investor's money as: *Going in for the kill.*"

"You size them up and then move in close to take something from them, don't you?" she said, her eyes narrowed slightly. "Sounds like going in for the kill to me."

He could practically feel the chill in her gaze. "And you think that's fun?"

"Don't you?"

"Not hardly." He didn't like the direction their conversation was taking. It appeared money was all that interested her. Perhaps it was time to tell her about Charles William McIntyre.

"Remember that ring I found?" he asked.

"You sold it, didn't you?"

"That's what you wanted me to do; it's not what I wanted. I decided to see if I could find the man who lost it. And I did. Charles McIntyre—the old guy's alive and living in a retirement home in Boise, Idaho. I drove there over the weekend and returned the ring to him."

She pulled her hand away. "And you're only just now telling me?" Her gaze was still cold, and as deadly as the venom in her voice.

He'd hoped she would be happy for him. Obviously, he'd guessed wrong. "I'm sorry, I didn't think you'd be interested."

"I'm interested in everything you do that concerns money."

"The right thing to do was return the ring to its owner."

"You need to tell me what you're up to, Jack."

Control, that's what this was all about. *And money*—he couldn't forget that. Aloud, he said, "Now I wish I had."

Her expression softened a little, and she patted the back of his hand.

"Next time," she said.

"Of course," he said. "I'm sorry."

He'd said *I'm sorry*, one too many times. But the apology had been made. He launched into an abridged version of his encounter with Charles McIntyre, focusing on the part about Lee Marvin having been shot in the butt during the battle of Saipan. He was happy when that part of the story got a chuckle from her.

"I never knew he was shot," she said.

"Yup, in the butt."

His comment turned her chuckle into a laugh. He joined in. And before he knew it, they were poking fun at Lee Marvin's unfortunate encounter with a bullet in the butt. This was the evening he'd looked forward to. Several of Robert's best jokes kept the mood alive, and Ellery seemed to enjoy hearing the jokes as much as he enjoyed telling them. She even told a couple of her own.

He liked that.

The evening had started badly, but they had progressed beyond that rocky beginning. Over the din of the other patrons' dinner conversations and the clatter of plates of food being served, they talked about things old, new, and yet to come.

And they laughed a lot.

Late that night when the world outside the *ohana* was dark and quiet, Ellery lay cradled in the cook of his arm. Her breathing was a gentle rhythm of soft whispery breaths that told him she was asleep. Her blond tresses spilled across his shoulder in a spray of gold; her arm was draped at an angle on his chest, her fingers entangled in his dark mat of hair.

The long day, and even longer past few days, had worn him out. But even so, he was awake, his eyes open and staring at the ceiling. Their lovemaking had been almost mechanical. More like a union, as if sex had been expected. Not fiery passion fueled by desire and heightened by their love for one another.

It shouldn't be that way.

He thought about Ellery's obsession with money. And he thought about the Rolex watch she had given him. As he drifted into sleep, he dreamed he was driving a yellow car shaped like a lemon.

Chapter 27

JACK LAY NAKED at an angle across the bed. His head was perched precariously on the edge of the mattress, his left arm dangled to below the box springs. The sheet and bedspread had spilled into a heap on the floor next to him. His leaden eyelids told him it was way too early to get up.

With one eye pried open, he peered at the clock on his bedside table: 6:27 AM.

Shit!

He frowned in the direction of the bathroom. The hiss of the shower hummed inside his brain, making his head hurt.

With a sigh, he sat up on the side of the bed and rubbed his face with both hands. This was not how he had wanted to start the day. He'd hoped to awaken and find Ellery snuggled tight against him, not find that she had left their bed. She hadn't said a thing. And there was no good reason he could come up with as to why she was up so early.

He stretched, fell back on the mattress, and pulled his pillow tight against his ears until the noise stopped.

Peace and quiet at last.

He was beginning to doze off when he felt fingers tickle him on the bottom of his foot. He pulled the pillow from his head and saw Ellery standing at the side of the bed. She was smiling, naked and beautiful. Instantly he became aroused and there was no hiding his desire.

He made a grab for her arm. She jerked it away and just as quickly, stepped backwards out of reach.

"Oh no, you don't!" She smiled. "Don't even go there. Mom and I are playing tennis this morning at eight and I have to have myself pulled together by the time she's ready to leave. Besides aren't you taking Daddy's friends out on the boat this morning?"

"Not until after nine," Jack said. "Don't know what kind of fishing trip that is, but it's their choice. So we've got time."

"Is that all you think about?" she asked.

"Tell me something," he said. "Do women fantasize about sex as often as men?"

"Some," she said.

"And you?"

"Of course."

He grinned.

ELLERY FINALLY SLIPPED out the front door of the *ohana* at seven-thirty.

Jack stood in the doorway, listening to her complain as she trotted to join her mother inside the main house. She was frantic about the time and concerned that her mother might be able to look at her and know she had been delayed because she was having sex.

It was ridiculous for her to think their impromptu romp had left a mark on her that said: *I'm a bad girl. See what I've done.*

What prevented him from laughing openly at the absurdity of the situation was that she had stolen out like a thief in the night. He'd be glad when she no longer felt concerned about what her parents thought about their sleeping together.

Mommy and daddy had accepted the idea when they offered their *ohana*. Nothing had changed.

He shrugged off the moment and climbed into his old Jeep. He had plenty to do to keep his mind off Ellery and the game she was playing with her parents—*and him*.

He drove along South Kihei Road trying to occupy his mind with the day of fishing ahead of him. It wasn't working. When he first met Ellery, she had as much as told him her insouciant behavior was a rebellion against her father and the life he had so carefully planned for her.

A rebellion he now suspected was carefully orchestrated to ensure that her father went along with everything she wanted. Her moving back to Maui was a re-alliance with him, meant to secure the life of wealth and power she had always known was important to her.

What Jack didn't understand was where he fit into all of it.

He had obviously been part of the distraction. And being such, she should have discarded him as quickly and easily as she had the plastic life she lived in San Francisco. But she had asked him to move to Maui with her.

Was he someone she loved for all the right reasons, or was he a game piece in her personal version of Monopoly?

And the sex—was that just one more of her tools?

He was sure she used her carnal talents to keep him on the hook. But now that they were engaged, where did that leave him? He had the uncomfortable feeling he was the worm dangling at the end of the fishing line, waiting to be bitten in half.

Money and power—that's what the game was about, for Ellery *and* her father.

Jack took a deep breath then exhaled. One fact remained. If he was going to be part of their world, he would have to become one of them. He wasn't sure he could do that.

Kimo Holowai and Gordon Kaeha were ugly reminders of how Seaport did business.

He wasn't about to pretend to be even half the entrepreneur Seaport had proved himself to be. Catching and selling salmon were simple in comparison to building a casino or a community of multi-million dollar homes. But he *did* know how a venture of that magnitude would play out. Everyone remotely connected to the casino project would line up for their piece of the pie: Thomas Seaport getting the biggest slice.

And what an enormous pie that was—and what a huge slice for Seaport Enterprises.

He could easily see Seaport's motivation for approaching representatives of the Hawaiian Nation and selling them on the casino project.

He formed a mental list of people who would flock like locusts to capitalize on the endeavor: investors to bankroll the project, manufacturers to produce the materials, suppliers to make the material available to Seaport Enterprises, and shipping companies to bring it all to the building location. And while that was happening, engineers, heavy equipment operators, and laborers would be brought in. Next, the ironworkers, carpenters, plasterers, and stone masons would come to assemble the pieces. Then the painters and decorators would arrive, and finally the staff to run the casino. The project would become a reality. And from beginning to end, teams of accountants and lawyers would watch over the process, to keep everything in order.

Everyone a person could imagine would be involved, each of them in line to get at least something.

He could see the benefit for the whole.

But, as Robert said, was it worth the price?

With Kahoolawe selected as the location for the casino, the Hawaiian people were starting from scratch on an island with no infrastructure and few natural resources. Jack knew the many challenges this presented and realized there were bound to be a lot of strings attached. And with graft and corruption rampant in local and state agencies, at least one key player in local government would be standing in that line with his hand out.

Jack was only just now getting to know Thomas Seaport. But he was sure the man wouldn't hesitate a second to pay off one or more of these governmental officials. He would do whatever it took to ensure the multi-million dollar casino venture went through.

Jack knew he had to get to the bottom of what was going on with Gordon Kaeha, or he'd never feel comfortable working for Ellery's father.

Chapter 28

AT THREE O'CLOCK that afternoon Jack backed *Ellery Queen* into her slip and cut the engines. The fishing trip had been a sham as far as he was concerned. Russell Carter had acted as first mate and bartender. Seaport's four guests did the heavy drinking.

Jack fished and drove the boat.

From bits and pieces of conversations he'd overheard during the day, he gathered that the two men had been central figures in a housing development Seaport had underway in North Kihei. They might have been able to fish, but Jack doubted they even knew how to rig a pole. Partying seemed to be more their style.

The men had spent as much or more time in the cabin with the women than they had above deck where the rods and reels were. It wasn't that Jack minded the parlor games, it was their charter. But they were supposed to be fishing. So that's what he did. And in spite of their tomfoolery, he hooked one of the men up with a forty pound dorado, which the guy managed to reel in amid laughter and cheering from the other three guests, who stood looking on.

Jack included. So he'd gaffed the fish and hauled it aboard.

The guests went back to drinking, and the fish was in the cooler for him to clean. His dinner if he was lucky.

"Take care of the boat," Carter said as he hopped onto the dock.

"You'd better hurry," Jack said, nodding in the direction of the four departing fishing guests, who were already twenty feet up the dock. "Your girlfriends are leaving without you."

Carter glanced toward the group. Then he turned and gave Jack a hard, angry look. "You'd be wise to keep your comments to yourself."

Jack grinned at the big man and bent down to the task of cleaning the boat and fishing tackle. A minute later he turned and saw that Carter had caught up with his fishing party. The group was at the stairs leading up to Buss's Wharf.

For a moment he watched them climb the wooden steps. A day of drinking and fishing onboard *Ellery Queen* for the men, a few rounds of cocktails at the bar afterwards. More laughs, and more parlor games.

Were the women Seaport's doing as well?

He figured they were part of the deal. Ladies for hire—female entertainment bought and paid for by Seaport to show his appreciation for the men's continued cooperation.

Had Gordon Kaeha been wined and dined courtesy of Thomas Seaport and Seaport Enterprises? Had he been out on *Ellery Queen*? Had he been provided a young piece of ass?

Jack could only wonder.

He went back to cleaning the boat and stowing fishing gear. And while he worked, he tried to make sense out of his overwhelming need to pursue the issue of Gordon Kaeha. He had nothing to gain from it and, if anything, a lot to lose. He was being paid big bucks to do his job, whatever that might entail. He should be happy with that. And he should be happy he was engaged to a rich, beautiful debutant with all the right woman talents.

But he wasn't.

So what was spurring his need to climb onto a soapbox and pound his chest and sound the trumpets? His reputation, his ego? And what about the good of the Hawaiian people? Was he looking to expose Gordon Kaeha for them? Or was he doing it simply because that was the right thing to do?

He'd let a college scholarship slip through his fingers so that he could stay home and help his ailing father run the family salmon boat, because it had been the right thing to do. Now this.

Ho`oponopono—Robert had said—correctness. A desire to set things right.

Jack wondered.

He'd cast out his line: now he would just have to wait and see if he hooked something.

Chapter 29

JACK WALKED INSIDE the *ohana* not expecting to find Ellery there. She was sitting on the sofa looking at his latest copy of *Dive Magazine*. Since she hated SCUBA diving, she must be mad about something.

Jack set the fish fillets in the refrigerator. They'd keep, for now.

"A change of heart?" he asked.

"Diving?" She tossed the magazine on the table. "Hardly."

"So what's up?"

"What did you do, Jack?"

"What are you talking about?"

"What did you do to make Daddy mad?"

Jack stiffened. "Mad? I took his friends out fishing—if that's what you want to call it. What's there for him to be mad about?"

"Daddy is paying you to do what he asks, not to backtalk Russ Carter."

The first stab of the knife.

Jack bit back his anger. He hadn't thought his comment to Carter at the boat was such a big deal. Evidently it was. Still, he couldn't see any reason for Carter to put the mouth on him to Seaport. And there was certainly no reason for Ellery to be in the middle of a pissing contest between him and Carter. Russell Carter was proving to be a real asshole.

And Ellery wasn't helping.

He stripped off his sweaty shirt, gripped it tight, and said, "You needn't concern yourself with the work I'm doing."

"Is that right?" She arched an eyebrow. "After last night, and this morning, you stand there and tell me not to concern myself with what you're doing?"

He didn't answer.

She narrowed her eyes, stood, and marched past him to the front door.

He watched her go.

With her hand poised on the doorknob, she faced him and said, "Daddy wants to talk to you."

He didn't respond or try to stop her. She opened the door, stepped outside, and closed it hard behind her. He gave her a minute, then pulled on a clean T-shirt and walked to the front house.

He marched straight to Thomas Seaport's office and found him sitting at his desk. Russell Carter wasn't in the room.

"You wanted to see me?" Jack asked from the doorway.

Thomas Seaport brought his gaze up from the stack of papers in front of him and said, "Close the door, Jack."

Jack turned and pulled the door shut. He could see no reason not to. Then he took a seat in the chair in front of Seaport's desk. He was pissed and growing more and more irritated, but kept his mouth shut and let Seaport do the talking.

This was Seaport's show, and Jack planned to let him set the tone of the conversation.

"You're a grown man, Jack," Seaport said without hesitation. "I'm going to give it to you straight. You've barely gotten your feet wet working for me, so that makes you the new kid on the block.

"You have absolutely no right to smart off to Russell Carter, or anyone else in my organization. So keep your adolescent comments to yourself. And bear in mind, the only reason you're here at all is because of my daughter. Is that clear?"

"Very, Sir," Jack swallowed back the bile rising in his throat.

Seaport stared unwaveringly at Jack. The man obviously had more to say.

Jake waited. One breath, then two—the air seemed to have been sucked from the room.

Seaport said, "When Ellery informed me you were moving over here with her, I went along with her wishes because this is where she belongs. She thinks she's in love with you, and I guess that's all right if you keep her happy.

"But know this; my daughter could just as easily have a change of heart if she tires of the game. And that just might happen. Now I don't know what you and her do on your own time and I don't really care, but I can't have whatever it is that's going on between you two affect your work."

Jack considered Seaport's words. "I'm sure it isn't."

Seaport gave him a long appraising look that left him uncomfortable in his seat. He'd gotten the message and was ready to be out of there.

"You don't get along with Russ, do you?" Seaport pressed.

Jack said, "I don't think he likes me."

"That's not the point," Seaport said. "I don't care if he likes you or if you like him. The bottom line is you two do have to work together. So figure out a way to get along."

"And him?"

"Worry about yourself. Now do what I asked."

Jack had heard enough. He didn't know if he should be mad, or if he should apologize. Either way, the dick measuring contest between him and Russ Carter was over with.

He said, "Are we done, Sir?"

Seaport nodded and said, "Just mind what I asked."

Jack walked out of Seaport's office and noticed Ellery flash a questioning glance at him from the sofa in the living room. He had no desire to explain. She could find out from her father.

He marched past her without saying a word.

She kept whatever was on her mind to herself.

When he reached the *ohana*, he walked directly into the bathroom and took a hot shower. And when he stepped into the bedroom ten minutes later, Ellery was sitting on the edge of the bed waiting for him.

"Just try and get along with Russ," she said. "He and Daddy are friends. It'll make it easier for you if you do."

"Your *Daddy* already told me that."

He pulled on the T-shirt and a clean pair of cargo shorts. He grabbed his wallet and keys from the top of the dresser and slid the wallet into his rear pocket.

Ellery quietly watched.

"I'm going to stay on the boat tonight." He held her gaze. "That way we can both sleep on it."

"You believe that will fix the problem?"

"No," he said. "But it'll keep me from saying something I might regret." He turned and walked out of the room.

"Jack!" she called after him.

"I'll be at the boat," he said from the front door. "There's a lot for me to think about."

He couldn't shift the gears in his Jeep fast enough.

Chapter 30

JACK PULLED A glass from the cupboard in *Ellery Queen's* galley, grabbed the half bottle of whiskey left behind by the fishing party earlier that day, and carried them topside to the fly bridge. He took a seat behind the controls and propped his feet on the dashboard.

After a few minutes of peering into the western sky, he flipped open his cell phone and called Robert.

"So what did Ellery do now?" Robert asked.

"Are you saying that's the only time I call you?"

"Well?"

"Guess it seems that way, doesn't it?"

"What's wrong, Jack?"

Jack sighed into the phone. "I'm not sure I'm cut out to work for someone who does the type of work Seaport does. I mean, shit, I see all the construction that went on and think that building homes for people should be a good thing. But then I think about all the foreclosures and it makes me sad. Where's going to stop?"

"I hear what you're saying," Robert said. "And it bothers me to know there is nothing I can do to change what's happening. I'm afraid Maui—like the rest of Hawaii—will never fully get hold of the problems brought on by over-expansion."

"Rich men getting richer."

"And Thomas Seaport is one of them. That's what bothers you."

"It's not so much the money. It's the insatiable hunger for power and control that goes with it. Why couldn't she have inherited her money from a dead uncle three times removed?"

"So this *is* about Ellery."

"Same old shit," Jack said. "We spend a wonderful night together, and all's fine. Then today at the boat I had words with that asshole Russell Carter, who in turn talks shit about me to Seaport. I can deal with that. But then Ellery has to get in the middle of it. That woman's so afraid her father will cut off her allowance, or disinherit her, that she can't side with me on anything without worrying what her old man will think or how it'll affect her pocketbook."

"So it's that sex thing again, huh?"

"What, no! The sex is great. It's the other stuff I can't handle."

"Like her being the daughter of a rich, controlling developer?"

"It's that asshole Carter, I can't stand the man. He's definitely got a bur up his ass and I'm not sure Seaport's any different."

"And you're saying this whatever-it-is that's going on with you has nothing to do with Ellery being rich?"

Jack sighed. "I'm not sure what I'm saying."

"We're talking about you having problems with the fact Ellery's rich."

"It's not that she's rich, or even that she's controlling, it's that having a lot of money means everything to her. I don't think she's stopped spending long enough to appreciate any of the things she's bought. I have a real problem with that. But it's more than just her propensity for spending money that has me pissed. I'm having a real problem with Thomas Seaport, the way the man does business—Russell Carter, Ellery, the whole damn game."

"Is the sex worth putting up with a little materialism?"

"A little?" Jack scoffed.

"Okay, a lot."

Jack pondered the question. "Maybe at first," he said, slowly. "Now I'm not so sure."

"Have you talked to her about it?"

"I've tried. But then we end up in bed and so much for that."

"Sounds like you're hooked."

"Yeah, and she's working the rod and reel."

"Not a good place to be, Jack. I wish we could meet and talk this out, but I'm at work."

"That's okay. This is something I need to sort out myself."

"Watch your ass."

"Count on it."

Chapter 31

JACK HAD SPENT the evening attempting to sort out his feelings. It wasn't an easy task, and now the sun was slipping below the horizon and the sky was turning from a palette of colors to darkness.

His sentiments were fitting into separate columns: those involving Ellery went into one column and those involving her father went in another. As the list grew, he noticed a third column emerging: the overlap between the two.

Ellery was doing her best to be just like her dad.

Jack concluded that he would eventually learn the truth about what was going on with Gordon Kaeha. And when he did, it would be a rather simple matter of deciding whether or not he would continue working for Thomas Seaport. If he decided to remain onboard—and if he and Seaport kept their business relationship strictly professional—he'd toe the line and do his best to make sure there were few, if any, emotional entanglements to complicate the situation.

Then there was Ellery to consider.

Her increasingly disdainful attitude concerned him, and he was flip-flopping from one emotion to another. Most important, he was second-guessing their wedding plans. And it wasn't the first time.

He wondered if it might be best to just cut his losses and run before he got in any deeper.

At the moment he felt like running.

He poured himself another drink and set the bottle aside. Slouched low in his seat, he closed his eyes. The *Ellery Queen* wasn't the *Waterdog*, but it was close enough. He'd done a lot of soul searching on that old barge-of-a-houseboat: a fancy forty-one foot *Hatteras* would work just as well.

When his cell phone rang, he figured it was Robert, his buddy, being the concerned friend he was.

"What's up?" he asked in a casual tone.

"I was thinking about you." It was Ellery's voice, laced with regret.

He dropped his feet to the deck and sat up. Alert. His heart felt the tug of desire. "I'm glad you called," he said. "I was just thinking about you."

The line went quiet. "I'm sorry," Ellery said after a breath. "But—"

"I'm sorry too," Jack said without letting her finish. "I don't ever want to disappoint you."

"It's nice you say that. But Daddy's the one you're disappointing, Jack. If we're going to be married, you're going to have to do your part and more. You need to keep that in mind when you're around his friends."

"By that you mean Russell Carter."

"Especially Russ Carter."

He swallowed the burn in his throat. He wanted to keep the conversation about them. She was dragging her father and Russell Carter into it. "*If?* What do you mean: *If we're going to be married?*"

"You know what I'm saying. So please…"

"Maybe I don't."

"Jack, I called to say I was sorry, not to argue."

He filled his lungs and let the breath out slowly. "You're right. And I'm happy you called."

Once again the line went quiet.

He waited.

"I wish you were here with me," she said, her voice sultry. "I've got that itch only you can scratch."

"You can come here," he said. "I'd be happy to scratch it for you."

"I could, but I don't think so. You know where to find me if you change your mind."

"Good night," he said and clicked off his cellular.

He wanted to believe she'd called out of sincere concern and wondered if he was judging her too harshly. She had a right to be who she was. If money made her happy, and she had it to spend, who was he to say whether she should or not? And so what if she didn't want to stay the night with him there on the boat? He certainly wasn't sex-starved. And soon they would be married, and he would be in a better position to have a little more say-so in their relationship.

But she had used that word: *If.*

Exactly how he'd been feeling. Still, she'd been the first to actually say the word. He wondered if it had simply been a poor word choice on her part, or if it had been a slip of the tongue as to how she truly felt.

And she *had* brought up good old Daddy again, and Russell Carter.

Would he and Ellery ever have a life of their own?

Jack felt he'd only made excuses for Ellery's behavior. He'd been truly glad she called to say she was sorry, but she was wrong for putting her father in the middle of their relationship, and getting involved in the riff with Russell Carter. That just wasn't right.

His good feeling about her call was already gone. He was regretting his involvement with Thomas Seaport, and he certainly regretted having overheard the conversation about Gordon Kaeha.

But he *was* involved.

And he still had no idea who Gordon Kaeha was or what was going on with him. There was the slight possibility he was wrong about Ellery's father, and wanted to believe he was keeping an open mind.

But was he, or could he?

He knew too much about Seaport's business ethics and at the same time not enough. He was sure they were far from aboveboard, but he needed concrete proof to say he was right.

Chapter 32

JACK WAS BACK at the *ohana* at seven the next morning. He fixed Ellery breakfast, partly to soothe difficulties between them—but mostly it was because he was hungry. The mood remained subdued, tense and they ate in silence. He cleaned up, and Ellery went into the bedroom and closed the door.

Apparently he was supposed to have come running home when she called him at the boat.

But he hadn't and now she was making him pay.

"I don't need this shit," he muttered to himself.

At eight o'clock he checked in with Thomas Seaport. Ellery's father didn't have a lot to say to him, either. No new assignments. He got the distinct feeling the Seaport family was not happy with him.

Ellery's mother glared at him from across the living room when he walked out of her husband's office. He smiled his best smile at her even though he didn't feel like it. "Good morning!"

She didn't answer, and she didn't smile.

The silent treatment. Even from Rachel, who gabbed incessantly. That did it for him. Now he knew he was in deep shit with the Seaports.

He spent the rest of the day on *Ellery Queen* doing routine maintenance. The boat wasn't in need of any real repair, but from experience he knew where to look for those little things that normally go unnoticed until it's too late. There was always chrome to be polished, oxidation to be cleaned from wear points on hinge plates, the airing out of storage lockers and the organization of equipment inside, checking life preservers, scraping algae from the hull.

Around noon, he thought about calling Robert and asking him to drop by for lunch, then changed his mind. He opened a can of Spam and a box of soda crackers, popped the tab on a beer, and ate alone. He was taking full advantage of the time away from Ellery. She hadn't called him, and he had made his mind up he wasn't going to call her. He couldn't—in clear conscience—act as though nothing had happened.

Their disagreement had become a war of wills he intended to win.

By one o'clock that afternoon, the trade winds were kicking up more aggressively than the usual mild hurricane that roared through that part of the island on a daily basis. *Ellery Queen* bobbed and tugged at her mooring lines. This was making it difficult for him to work topside, so he left the hatches open, to funnel cooler air through the cabin, and stretched out on the bunk in the forward stateroom.

This was not the first time he had spent quiet hours alone on a boat. Nor would it be his last.

He propped his shoulders against the bulkhead and thumbed through a three-month-old fishing magazine. Ten minutes later his cell phone chirped. He answered it.

"Jack, we shouldn't—"

He could hear Ellery's voice quaver with uncertainty.

"Shouldn't what?" he asked.

"You know what I'm trying to say."

He did know. In her own awkward way she was trying to say she was sorry. He wanted to hear her say the words. "Do I?"

"Jack, I called to say we shouldn't argue. You need to come home and be with me. We need to talk."

"Is it so hard to say the words?"

"What words?"

"How about, *I'm sorry*. Why couldn't you just say you were sorry?"

"I did."

"No you didn't."

"Would it change anything?"

Even though he still wanted to hear her say she was sorry. he realized that wasn't going to happen. She had come as close to saying *I'm sorry* as she would get. "I'm done here for the day," he said. "Let's go somewhere nice for dinner. We can talk then."

ON FRIDAY MORNING, Jack sensed a definite awkwardness between Ellery and himself. Their dialogue at dinner the night before had been strained and sterile, their lovemaking afterwards, mechanical. Breakfast together was simple—coffee, toast with butter and mango jam, a bowl of dry cereal, glass of guava juice—and void of any meaningful conversation.

Ellery left not long afterwards for a hair appointment. He did the dishes and put in a load of clothes to wash. Whatever it was she had wanted to talk about was yet to be discussed. But they were at least talking to each other. That made him feel better, but not as good as he'd thought he would. He still believed Ellery was wrong for being so quick to side with her father.

He doubted that would change.

By noon he was back aboard *Ellery Queen* with a can of polish in one hand and a rag in the other. When he left the *ohana* at a quarter to twelve, Ellery still hadn't returned home. She obviously had more on her calendar of activities for the day than her hair appointment. He'd left a note letting her know he was at the boat. There's always something that needs to be done to a boat.

He'd just finished polishing one of the fishing reels and set it aside, when his cell phone chirped. He hoped it wasn't Ellery wanting him to shop or talk wedding plans.

He checked the number on the cellular's display. Not Ellery. He breathed a sigh of relief and flipped it open. "Hello?"

"Is this Mr. Jack Ferrell?" a woman asked. The voice wasn't familiar. Neither was the number or the area code. The last thing he wanted was to engage in a conversation with a telemarketer.

"Depends," he said.

"My name is Mary Kate McIntyre. You left your number."

Chapter 33

JACK HAD NO problem connecting the name. "I did," he said. "With Charles McIntyre—you're related, I take it?"

"My grandfather."

"Interesting man," he said. "I was hoping to hear back from him."

"The greatest," she said. "And I'm certainly glad you thought to leave your phone number."

"I figured the ring meant a lot to him and since, well—"

"There's no way you could have known how important that ring is," she said, before he could say more. "Tell me, where did you find it?"

"On a reef here in Maui, that's where I live. That's what made the ring so interesting. I thought maybe the owner had lost it there during the war."

"My God, it's true," she said, her voice little more than a whisper. "After all this time—"

"True? What's true?"

"Your finding that ring. It proves my father was telling the truth."

"Pardon me." He couldn't help sounding confused. He was. "What are you talking about—proof? Proof of what?"

"Didn't Grandpa tell you? It's proof Dad's innocent. *He didn't kill my mother.*"

Jack furrowed his brow. A momentary blankness washed over him, a kind of dopey gray confusion. He couldn't think, couldn't put the pieces together.

He asked, "You're saying your dad killed your mother?"

"He's in prison for killing her," she said. "He swore he was in Maui when she died. But he couldn't prove it. So don't you see? The ring is the proof. He swore he lost the ring diving, but since there was no way of finding it in the ocean, his attorney couldn't prove he was telling the truth."

Jack didn't say anything for a while, as the gravity of what she had just told him settled in. Finally he said, "Ms—"

"Mary Kate McIntyre," she interjected. "Call me Katie."

"Very well, Katie. Pardon me for saying this, but I find it hard to believe your father wasn't able to prove he was on Maui. Airlines, hotels, car rentals, they keep all kinds of records."

"It's quite complicated, really. Trust me, that ring is his only hope."

"If that's the case, you need to take the information to the police."

"I could go to the police, and probably should," she said. "But I think it'd be best if I take the ring directly to his attorney."

The line went silent a beat.

He waited.

She said, "Mr. Ferrell—"

"It's Jack," he insisted. "Please call me Jack."

Again there was a moment of silence. He got the feeling she was building up to something. He figured she would eventually get around to whatever was on her mind.

"I know it's a lot to ask," she finally said. "But I...uh...wonder if you'd consider coming here as a witness? You know, to give the ring credibility."

Jack didn't need to hear more. "I'll book a flight to Boise today."

"Make that Las Vegas," she said. "That's where I live. Henderson, actually. My dad's attorney's office is there in town."

"Okay, Las Vegas," he agreed. "But you mentioned you found the note I left your grandfather. You're in Boise?"

"I am, but I'll be back in Henderson in plenty of time to meet you at the airport."

He had a million questions for her. They'd wait. "As soon as I hang up with you I'll make some calls," he said. "Hopefully I can get a flight out tomorrow. I'll call you back with the details."

"You have my cell number."

"On my phone. I'll be in touch as soon as I have a flight." He switched off his cell and sat a moment, thinking he might have been quick to jump for the wrong reasons. But he didn't think so.

He peered through the cabin window at the harbor. A squall moved in off the ocean and darkened the sky overhead. Drops began to fall, then came in a deluge. He watched the rain and tried to picture the young woman on the phone. He thought about Charles McIntyre lying in his bed staring out the window at the trees. He thought about the ring. And about murder.

A daughter believing in her father's innocence.

He'd seen enough cop shows to know how a killer is put in prison. And he'd seen enough attorney shows to know how the falsely accused are kept from going to prison. He was being asked to help free a convicted murderer who was already doing time in prison.

Different game, but the same.

He could only wonder what he was getting himself into.

Chapter 34

JACK STOOD HIS ground. He was doing the right thing and no amount of complaining by Ellery would convince him otherwise.

"What do you mean you're flying to Las Vegas tomorrow?" she said, both hands planted firmly on her hips. "You get a call from some strange girl, and at the drop of a hat you're flying off to be with her."

He let out a deep sigh of frustration.

"Not to be with her," he said, "to help get her father out of prison. The ring I found is the evidence her father's attorney needs to get his murder conviction overturned. But the ring means nothing without a statement from me to give it credibility."

She shook her head and said, "It's way too expensive to fly last minute like this."

"What's a man's life worth, Ellery?"

"I'll go with you, then. You can take me to a show."

"No," he said. "You're not going. I'm doing this alone."

He saw her features harden beneath her fine layer of expensive makeup.

She said, "Daddy's paying you to work for him here, not for you to run off to Las Vegas because some girl called about that silly ring. What do you care if her father killed her mother or not? It has nothing to do with us."

"You don't care about anybody or anything but yourself, do you? If what she says is correct, her father's in prison for a murder he didn't commit. He deserves to be free. That's enough for me—and I don't care what your dad has to say about it."

She stomped her foot and said, "What about me, us? We have wedding plans to make."

"A man's life is more important, don't you think? Besides, you and your mother have been handling the wedding just fine without me."

She took a breath, swelling her breast, and moved close enough for him to feel the heat of her skin. Then she wrapped her arms around his neck and parted her lips just so. In a soft voice she said, "What about that itch of mine?"

He peeled her arms from around his neck and took a step backward. The shallowness of her pleas made her appear almost childlike. For a tenth of a second he came within a fraction of an inch of feeling sorry for her.

Almost.

But she would never understand the meaning of compassion. Her concern was her figure, her clothes, and her jewelry. She liked being looked at and doted on, enjoyed sex completely: liked pleasing men and liked to be pleased. And then there was that not-at-all-childlike part of her that reveled in the power her sexual prowess gave her over men.

"Nice try," he said.

LATE THE NEXT morning Jack was sitting in the terminal at the Kahului airport waiting for his 12:25 flight to Las Vegas on Hawaiian Airlines. It had only taken a few minutes of discussing the matter with Ellery for him to realize he was glad he'd gotten the call from Katie McIntyre. It gave him a good reason to get away from Ellery and her father and Russell Carter for a few days without it looking as if they were the reason he was leaving.

Though that was partly the case.

At five minutes till twelve he boarded the Boeing 757 and made his way to his window seat overlooking the left wing. He wedged himself in, buckled the lap belt and pulled the strap tight. A middle-aged man and woman dressed in matching aloha outfits settled into the two seats next to him.

He flashed them a quick smile, then watched the ant-like activity on the tarmac below through the window.

A few minutes later the roar of the engines increased and the plane started to move. The flight attendant at the front of the plane began her preflight speech. He listened, but continued to gaze through the window at the terminal beyond as the plane taxied onto the runway. There was an unexpected strangeness in the way he felt. It was as though he had only been a visitor on the island and was leaving with no plans to return anytime in the near future.

Maybe that's how it was supposed to be.

Once the plane reached cruising altitude, a flight attendant made her way down the aisle pushing her beverage cart. He ordered a double Scotch.

She had a pasted-on smile—pleasant enough, but no real warmth. She moved on to serve the passengers in the row behind him.

He watched her go, her smile unchanging. It was as plastic as the cup in his hand.

There had to be more to life.

He sipped his drink and looked out the window, even though the plane was flying too high for him to see anything but a blue-gray slate of water below. He thought about Thomas Seaport, and he thought about Ellery. They'd been on his mind all night, and all morning, but not with anxiety about whatever fetid notions swirled in their minds. He cared less and less how Ellery felt about him going to Vegas and even less what her old man might think about it.

At the moment, neither of them was high on his list of concerns.

And they could stay that way.

For the next twenty minutes, he tried to read an article in a magazine he'd pulled from the pocket on the back of the seat in front of him. But all he could think about was what lay ahead for him.

There was nothing plastic about what he was doing.

He liked Charles McIntyre, and figured that if Katie McIntyre took after her grandfather even a little, he'd like her, too. And now that he knew the secret behind the ring, he was eager to help her get her father out of prison.

He was no knight in shining armor, but he wouldn't be able to live with himself if he just stood by and did nothing.

Again, he tried to picture Katie McIntyre—her age, what kind of person she was, what she would look like. He remembered watching Charles McIntyre stare out the window in his room, and thinking how lonely the old guy was. Now he realized the man had been gazing into the past—his piece of reality—and that he did have loved ones who visited him.

It had been years since Jack had thought about his own grandfather, Hugh Ferrell. Like McIntyre, he'd been a WW II vet. And he, too, had been in a rest home like McIntyre's. Only he had died alone.

Jack felt bad knowing it had taken a commonality like his Grandpa Hugh Ferrell and Charles McIntyre being veterans of WW II to make him think about his grandfather, especially now that it was too late to matter. He would never get the chance to talk to his grandfather about the war or anything else. He hadn't seen or spoken to his Grandpa Ferrell in twenty years, and would never see or talk to him again because he'd been dead for two years.

Jack was bothered by the fact he'd never been told the story behind what had happened so long ago. All he knew was his dad had had a falling out with *his* dad, over something that was never discussed in front of him. And that at the age of seven, he'd stood in the yard in front of his parent's house and watched Grandpa Ferrell drive away, never to be talked about again.

It especially bothered him that he could only vaguely remember what his grandfather Ferrell looked like. Over the years his recollections of the man had faded, and in time he forgot about him altogether—until the day he learned Grandpa Ferrell died.

The grandfather he had known and grown up with had been his Grandpa Kline, his mother's father. WW II was not something Grandpa Kline ever talked about. And now it was too late because he'd been dead ten years.

Looking back, Jack realized his life was filled with '*too lates.*' It was too late for Grandpa Ferrell, who died alone in an old folk's home. It was too late for his mother, who had died of skin cancer when he was twenty. It was too late for him to make use of his college scholarship, and it was too late to change the hard feelings between his dad and himself.

As far as he was concerned, his dad's holier-than-thou attitude had driven a wedge between them, just as it had with his father.

And now that he was thinking back on his life, he couldn't help but wonder if his interest in Charles McIntyre was a subconscious compensation for how things had turned out with Grandpa Ferrell. Perhaps he was seeing Charles McIntyre as the Grandpa Ferrell he never had the opportunity to know.

He thought about that a moment, then nodded to himself. For once he had a chance to rectify a situation before it became another *too late*—for him, and for Katie and *her* father.

Ho`oponopono. There was that word of Robert's again.

Chapter 35

HAWAIIAN FLIGHT 482 landed in Las Vegas at 10:10 PM Saturday night. Katie had said she'd be waiting outside the baggage claim area, wearing a red sweater. Jack had told her she would recognize him by his lime green aloha shirt with grass-skirted hula dancers on it.

They figured they'd find each other.

He pulled his bag from the luggage carousel and carried it outside, where he spotted a woman wearing a red sweater. She was as described: five-foot-seven, with shoulder length brown hair. Her face was turned toward a group of people walking past her so she hadn't seen him. But he could see enough of her profile to know she was close to his age, perhaps two or three years younger—twenty-six or twenty-seven. And she was quite pretty.

He knew at once the woman was Katie McIntyre.

"Pardon me," he said, when he was close enough for her to hear. "My name is Jack Ferrell."

The woman didn't answer, but looked him up and down.

"The man who found your grandfather's ring," he said. "You called me." He extended his hand.

"I did," she said, and took his hand in hers. "It's hard to believe you agreed to come here and help me."

Jack smiled. "There was no way I could refuse."

Katie beamed. "I can't tell you how wonderful you are for doing this," she said.

She had yet to let go of his hand. He thought maybe she was worried he'd slip away.

"This is something I wanted to do," he said. "Really."

She glanced at her hand. Turning a shade of red, she let his fingers slip from her grasp. "On the phone," she said in a strained tone, "you didn't mention where you'd want to stay. You'll prefer a room on the Vegas strip, of course?"

He shook his head. "I thought it might be better if I stayed in Henderson," he said. "A hotel close to where you live. Nothing fancy, a room with clean sheets and a fresh set of towels will do."

"If you're sure that's what you want?" The tension had disappeared from her voice.

"I think it would work out best."

"Perfect," she said. "I can think of a couple places that should be comfortable enough. I'll be happy to drop you off if you like."

He could see no reason not to ride along. The time together in her car would give them a chance to talk. "That'd be great. I'll pick up a rental car in the morning."

It only took a minute or two for them to walk over to Katie's parked car, a white three-year-old Toyota Camry. The car was clean and well kept; no dents. He believed a person's ride said a lot about their character.

She popped the trunk and he tossed his bag inside. After he'd closed the lid, he let himself in on the passenger's side.

"So, you like living here?" he asked once they were moving.

"You're talking about Vegas, the casinos?" she said, her gaze fixed on the road ahead. "Gambling doesn't excite me."

He peered through the windshield at the panorama of bright lights and magnificent theme-hotels.

"Probably a good thing," he said.

She chuckled. "The town of Henderson where I live isn't at all like this place. And the desert grows on you."

"So how long have you lived here?"

"Twenty years, since I was six. I don't know why, but I still live in the house where my mother and father and I lived together as a family."

She fell quiet, and wiped the corner of her eye with the tip of her finger. He waited.

After a moment she said, "It's strange. I guess I've stayed in the house hoping one day Mom and Dad will walk through the front door together, and everything will have only been a bad dream."

He wanted to hear how her father ended up going to prison for her mother's murder and she appeared ready to talk.

"The food on the plane wasn't much," he said. "Would you mind stopping for a quick bite? A 24 hour coffee shop or something? My treat."

She shot him a quick look. "Sure. Then I'll explain what happened."

Chapter 36

KATIE PICKED A Denny's restaurant in Henderson.

Jack sat across the table from her, finding it difficult to concentrate. He couldn't decide if he should look at her dazzling emerald green eyes or her mouth with those fantastic, full lips or her wonderful all-woman body.

She was much prettier than he'd imagined.

"Run that by me again," he said, his gaze settling on her hair. "My mind was somewhere else."

She smiled. "I was telling you about my dad."

He'd seen her watching him watch her, and wondered if she thought he was going to flirt with her. He couldn't help smiling back. But this was no time to play dating games. "You said his name is Michael. And that this mess all started here in Vegas?"

"In Henderson. Dad's name is Michael Sean McIntyre, after his father. My mother's name was Angela."

Tears welled in the corners of her eyes, and she dabbed at them with her napkin. He could see it was difficult for her to talk about what happened, even now. But he wanted to know the details. He rested his forearm on the tabletop and leaned toward her, fighting the urge to reach across and hold her hand. "Tell me what happened," he said in a soft voice. "You told me your mother was killed. How'd your father wind up going to prison for her murder, if he's innocent?"

Katie sighed. "I've asked myself that a thousand times. All I can say is it happened. Everything in our lives seemed to be going great. *High Desert Security*—the security systems business my father owned, along with his friend Brian Wesley—was really doing well. Vegas, Henderson, Boulder—the entire area was growing like crazy. Everyone wanted a home security system—so did the new companies that flocked here to avoid high California taxes. Dad and mom didn't have to worry about money. And that allowed me to have the things I thought were important."

Her eyes glazed over, fogged by time and memories. She stopped talking, and slowly shook her head from side to side. It was as if she still couldn't understand how her life had changed.

He gave her a moment.

"I had the coolest clothes," she continued, "and all the electronic gadgets kids like. Which was important to me back then, because I was starting high school—even had a shot at being a cheerleader. You know how it is at that age."

He nodded.

"Anyway," she said, "mom was working three to four days a week doing office work for Dad's security business and playing golf with her friends two days a week—barbecues and parties on weekends. It was the best."

Her clasped hands rested on the tabletop in front of her. She peered down at them "What's ironic is Dad has spent the past six years behind bars inside High Desert State Prison in Indian Springs. Who'd have thought he'd wind up in a prison with the same name as his old company? *High Desert*. Jesus, what a name that turned out to be! Before that, Dad spent a little over five years inside a prison up in Ely."

Jack leaned back in his chair and waited for her to collect herself. Two stints in prison: one in Ely, one in Indian Springs. "So your dad's been in prison what, eleven, twelve years?" he asked.

"Eleven and a few months, yes."

"If life was good back then, what happened?"

She gripped her cup with both hands and tipped it, peering at the coffee as though the answer were there.

He watched, and waited.

"Life was good," she said. "But not as good as I thought. It turned out Mom and Dad had problems I wasn't aware of, until the life I'd thought was so wonderful fell apart. Dad admitted to me later that he'd suspected Mom of cheating on him for months."

She looked into his eyes for a long moment.

He winced at what she had to be thinking.

She continued, "A couple of nights before my mother was killed—Valentine's Day to be exact—Mom and Dad were in their bedroom getting ready to go out for dinner. Dad was excited about giving her a diamond tennis bracelet she'd been eyeing for months. The next thing I knew, they were screaming at each other. I hid in my room trying not to listen. That's when I heard Dad accusing Mom of cheating on him. He kept at her, and she finally admitted it. But she wouldn't tell him who she was seeing or how long the affair had been going on. It was right after the argument that everything happened. That's where the ring you found comes in."

She pulled the ring out of her pocket, and held it in front of her. It looked oddly large in her slender fingers. He didn't say anything.

"I read the note you left Grandpa," she said. "I found the ring where he'd hidden it inside a sock in his dresser drawer."

"I'm surprised you didn't have to pry it out of your grandfather's hand, the way he gripped it the day I gave it to him," he said. "So, how'd your dad get the ring from your grandfather?"

"Grandpa gave the ring to him a long time ago. To my knowledge Dad never took it off. That's what made the missing ring so important to his defense. It supported his alibi that he was in Maui. I swore in court there wasn't a time I could remember not seeing the ring on his hand, but obviously that didn't mean much to the jury. The cops, the prosecutor, everyone on the jury, and maybe even my father's attorney, believed he just tossed the ring somewhere in the desert. There was no way to prove otherwise."

Jack planted his forearms on the tabletop and frowned. He was having a hard time with this whole alibi issue. "I don't understand. If your father was in Maui at the time of the murder, why couldn't he prove it, ring or no ring? Like I said on the phone, there was a plane ticket, room reservations, a rental car, something to prove he'd been there."

"And I told you it was complicated."

"You did. But still…"

She let out a deep breath. "That's where the whole mess gets crazy. The mood in the house was extremely tense. I could hear Dad pacing the floors, not saying much, and Mom crying. I remember hearing her swear over and over she was ending the affair and that she didn't want to break up the family. But Dad was so angry he couldn't just pretend nothing had happened. I was mad at her, too. After a while, Dad told her he was going to spend some time away so he could think. That's when he stormed out the door, saying he was going to stay the night in a hotel."

"And he flew to Maui?"

"The next day."

"I still don't understand why he couldn't prove he was on the island."

"Dad did something really dumb," she said. "He purchased his plane ticket and room reservation under a false name and paid cash so mom wouldn't be able to find out where he'd flown to. He was afraid she'd follow him."

"Even smart people do dumb things," he said.

Her lips curled into a thin smile. "He admitted using a false name was stupid," she went on. "But he explained he wasn't thinking straight at the time. His attorney sent an investigator to check out his story but none of the hotel employees could recognize him from a picture. And since everything was paid for in cash, the only written record was a hastily scribbled signature that didn't look anything like his handwriting."

Jack nodded, putting the pieces together. "And that was before airports amped up security. You didn't even need to show a driver's license to board a plane, back then."

"Exactly! And that's what makes this ring so important.

Chapter 37

JACK TOOK A deep breath and let it out. She was grasping at straws, but he couldn't blame her.

"I understand that the ring substantiates your dad's claim he was on Maui," he said. "The court might not see it that way, but I do. One question, though. Why Maui, of all places?"

"Because Maui is where he and Mom honeymooned. He thought spending some time in the places they visited together when they were first married would help him decide if he still loved her. I guess the island worked its magic, because he admitted to me being there made him realize just how much she meant to him. And that he had planned to forgive her and come back home."

Jack leaned back. He curled his fingers into a tight ball, and pressed the side of his fist to his lips in contemplation. Everything that could backfire on her father had. Hard to believe that could happen, but it had.

He said, "And your mother was killed while your father was in Maui?"

"Two days after my dad walked out of the house, the police showed up at the door looking for him. That's when the officer told me my mother had been murdered."

"And you were there alone in the house at the time?" He could immediately picture the horrific scene and shook his head in disbelief. "You must have been terrified."

"Of course I was scared. But I refused to believe Mom was dead and held on to the idea she and Dad were together somewhere, working things out."

"Hope you don't mind me asking, but how'd your mother die?"

She looked down at her hands and picked at her thumbnail. "Mom had been beaten to death." She swallowed hard. "Her body was found inside our houseboat on Lake Mead. The boat was smashed up on some rocks."

Jack remembered a classmate in college who had been severely beaten and robbed. His injuries had put him in hospital, but he had lived. Still, his face was cut and swollen black and blue. Katie's mother had been beaten to death. He could picture what *her* bloodied body must have looked like. He shuddered at the thought.

"Don't worry," he said. "We'll get your dad out of prison."

The waitress brought more coffee, and Jack ordered each of them a piece of berry pie. They'd been there half an hour and he didn't want their time together to end.

"What happened to your father's security systems business?" he asked, when the waitress walked away with his order. "Did you end up taking over for him or did the attorney get your dad's share?"

"Mr. Wesley bought him out. The attorney's fees took a sizable portion of that. The rest went into a trust fund I get when I turn thirty. That's a month and three years away."

"A Christmas baby?"

"Close enough…December tenth. Same as Grandpa Charlie's."

"Your Grandpa Charlie's?"

Katie smiled. "Only he's older."

That made Jack chuckle.

Over forkfuls of pie and sips of coffee, he got to know more about Katie. Not only was she pretty—beautiful, actually—she appeared to have grown into a sweet young woman. He was more than curious about how things had turned out for her after her mother's death and her father's imprisonment.

"It's hard to imagine how tough it must have been for you after your father was arrested."

She sighed, staring at the cup in her hand. She tilted it and peered into the dark rich coffee the way she had a few minutes earlier. "I spent a little over a week in the custody of Clark County Child Protective Services," she said. "That scared me, but my Aunt Regina, on my mother's side, came to live with me in my parents' house as my guardian. She was divorced at the time and had sold her house, so she didn't have a problem moving in. But taking care of me was tough on my aunt—with her own problems and all. A few months later Grandpa McIntyre rented out his home in Boise so he could move into an apartment here in Henderson to help out. I realize now how hard it was for him to leave the house he had lived in for fifty years."

"I can tell you love him."

"I really do. If it weren't for him and my aunt Regina, who knows how I would have turned out?"

"I'm glad they were there for you."

"Me, too. Aunt Regina lived with me in the house until I was twenty and old enough and responsible enough to take care of myself. By then she was engaged to be married and moved in with her fiancé. Grandpa kept his apartment here until age began to get the better of him. When he couldn't take care of himself any more, I moved him into Ridgeview, because Boise had always been his true home and the retirement center was next to the river he loved so much. Still, it was a sad day for us both. He's been living in Ridgeview for four months, and I drive up there every other week to visit him."

Jack liked listening to her talk. She was passionate about life, but at the same time had a calm resolve that comes with an awareness of reality. He felt he could talk to her without the need to apologize for his take on how he wanted to live—something he often did with Ellery.

"So what do you do for work?" he asked. "The casinos must hire a lot of people."

"A ton," she said. "But I work in a couple of dental offices not too far from my house. I'm a dental hygienist and divide my time between the two. Maybe I'm one of the few, but I actually enjoy what I do for a living, and I like the people I work with."

"I take it you're single? What about boyfriends?"

She met his grin with her own. "Guess I've been too busy for a serious relationship. And since I avoid the nightclub scene, I tend to hang out at the house. Or I drive to Boise to spend time with Grandpa."

He couldn't help comparing Katie to Ellery. They were beautiful women, but the similarity stopped there. And *that* was a breath of fresh air.

"What about you?" she asked.

He shrugged and said, "I'm just glad to be here with you."

"You're not married then," she said. "When I asked you to come here and help I didn't even stop to think you could have a wife and kids and a home and a job you couldn't just up and leave."

He gave careful thought to his response.

"No," he said. "I'm not married. And I'm not sure I even have a job."

For a few beats, they just looked at each other. All at once he felt the long day crash in on him and yawned. "Are you ready to go?" he asked, hoping he didn't sound like he was avoiding the topic of marriage. "I'm afraid I'm whipped."

She looked at him for a second longer and nodded. "Any time you're ready."

He paid the tab, and she drove him to a Holiday Inn two blocks away. When they got there, she waited for him in the lobby while he checked in.

"Room 210," he said, walking over to where she was sitting.

She stood and said apologetically, "We won't be able to meet with my father's attorney until Monday. Are you going to be okay until then?"

"Sure," he said. "Do you have plans for tomorrow?"

"I thought perhaps we could get together and have dinner or something."

"I'll probably pick up a rental in the morning and do some exploring," he said. "Dinner sounds great."

"Seven o'clock okay?" she asked.

"Dinner at seven. Perfect."

"I'll drive," she said. "Pick you up here at six thirty. Casual dress."

Casual—he liked that and gave her his best toothy grin. "At six thirty then."

He walked her to her Camry, and held the driver's door open for her as she slid behind the steering wheel. A part of him didn't want her to leave—the part that didn't give in to caution. He stood in the empty parking space and watched her drive away. They had only just met, yet already there was so much about the woman he liked.

And so much more about her he wanted to know.

Maui, Ellery, Thomas Seaport—that part of his life seemed so far away and insignificant compared to what he'd landed himself into here.

Chapter 38

JACK LOWERED HIS menu and watched the redheaded waitress in her quaint cowgirl outfit set down his mug of beer and Katie's glass of red wine in front of them. He peered at her nametag and flashed her a smile.

Bonnie, the name fit. "Thank you," he said. "I'll need another minute or two to decide."

She returned his smile. "Take your time, honey."

The redheaded cowgirl stepped to a nearby table of four and he watched her launch into her routine. Then he glanced at the other patrons and finally, the dining room itself. The rough-cut wood-planked walls were adorned with old picks and shovels and framed photographs from the 1930's and 40's—when the town was in its infancy.

American cuisine at its finest.

That's how he saw it: a simple steakhouse with high-backed wooden booths, thick wooden tables with red checkered tablecloths, and three kinds of draft beer. The wine list was simple: two kinds—red or white. And they flowed from a spigot as well. He liked this place. He even got a kick out of Bonnie. Ellery would never have suggested a restaurant like this.

Katie had told him to dress casually, and he had. But his aloha shirt, khaki Dockers, and brown leather deck shoes didn't really fit the décor. Not like her outfit. Her faded blue jeans, Willie Nelson T-shirt, and cowboy boots were perfect for the place.

"What do you recommend?" he asked, his gaze settling on his menu. "It all looks good."

"And it is," she said. "Are you a steak man?"

"Absolutely."

"Try the fourteen ounce rib eye."

"I think I will. You going for the *Double Deuce*?"

She straightened in her seat. "Do I look like I could eat a 22-ounce sirloin?"

He grinned.

"Not really," he said.

She smiled back. "Actually I have, on more than one occasion. You'd be surprised how much I can eat when I'm hungry."

"And drink?"

"Put you under the table."

He raised his draft in a toast. "We'll see about that," he said.

She clinked her wineglass against his mug. She laughed. "As soon as Dad's out of prison."

Bonnie returned to their table, pad in hand.

"We're ready," Jack said, and nodded at Katie. "Ladies first."

She ordered the grilled chicken breast with baked potato and salad. Jack considered the *Double Deuce*, but stayed with the 14-ounce rib eye, cooked medium rare, and went with the baked potato and salad as well.

When the redheaded cowgirl waitress walked away with their order, he took a sip of beer and let his gaze wander over Katie's body and settle on her face.

He found it exceedingly difficult not to stare at her. Even while perusing the menu he kept trying to catch a look at her over the top of the page. Something about this young woman unnerved him, and he couldn't figure out what.

He held the handle of his beer mug as though it gave him balance and made it easier for him to talk. He wanted to talk, wanted her to talk.

But this was not a romantic tryst.

"So what's the plan?" he asked.

"I took the week off," she said. "I'll call Dad's attorney in the morning. Hopefully she'll meet with us right away."

"I can't believe she wouldn't."

"With you here as a witness willing to testify, I'm almost certain she will."

He picked up on a hint of exasperation in her response. Clearly, Katie and the attorney were not on the best of terms. He grinned. "Pissed her off, have you?"

She took a deep breath and exhaled in a obvious sigh of frustration. "I've been more than a tad persistent in my effort to prove my dad innocent," she said. "It'll be nice to finally produce the hard evidence she has repeatedly told me we needed."

"Perhaps she'll be more receptive if I do the talking—at first anyway—since I found the ring, and that's what the meeting is about."

"Sure, if you think so."

He got the impression she'd only half heard him.

He watched and waited.

She dug the ring out of her purse and held it up. "I haven't let that ring out of my possession since I got it from Grandpa," she said. "And I can assure you I'm not about to. No one believed Dad's story. I'm not even sure his attorney did. And I have to admit, there were times I wasn't so sure I did. I guess now everyone will have to believe him."

"And I'll be the one who will convince them," he told her.

Her expression softened.

"I'm counting on that, Jack," she said. "This ring means everything."

He reached across the table and gently gripped her arm. Robert had said it best. "*Ho`oponopono,*" Jack said. "That's the word the Hawaiians use: correctness—setting things right. We'll make things right for your father. I promise."

Chapter 39

KATIE SNIFFLED AND her mouth curled into a shaky smile. A nod was all she could manage.

Jack gave her a minute to compose herself. He wanted to offer his shoulder for her to lean on, but they were only just getting to know each other.

He stared into his beer instead.

"Here you go, fresh off the range." Bonnie's voice broke the silence at the table. "And a nice plump chicken breast for you, honey."

Jack noticed Bonnie looking at Katie, who had tears welling in the corners of her eyes. One broke loose and streaked her cheek and Katie wiped it away with her hand.

"Are you all right?" Bonnie asked. "Is there anything I can do for you?"

Katie forced a thin smile. "I'm fine, thanks. The food looks wonderful."

Bonnie narrowed her eyes at Jack and walked away.

He caught the look from Bonnie and figured she'd decided he was some kind of cad. He shot her a hard look of his own, and refocused on Katie.

She sat staring at the ring, her eyes appeared pinned on the inscription: *Duty, Honor, Country*.

"I called him," she said. "Before I picked you up, I called him at his house."

"Called who, Katie?"

"I called Brian Wesley and told him about the ring—that I was going to get my father out of prison. He sounded surprised, Jack."

"And you think it's odd he was surprised?"

She frowned. "Of course not. I just thought he would've been happier to hear the news. Maybe I even hoped he'd offer to let my dad buy back into the business—a limited partnership or something."

"It's been how long, Katie, eleven years? Maybe the man just needs a little time to let the reality of what's happening, sink in."

She shrugged. "Maybe you're right. And I guess it's not realistic for me to expect him to just up and jump at the opportunity to sell dad back part of the business."

Jack could see Katie's mind was working overtime. He decided it was time to lighten the mood.

"Why don't we eat?" he said. "My steak looks great, and it's getting cold."

She glanced at her plate of food and then the ring.

"I suppose you're right," she said.

"Did you hear the one about the Blind Man in a Blonde Bar?" he asked between bites.

She dropped the ring back into her purse. "I don't think so."

He grinned and said:

A blind man enters a Ladies Bar by mistake. He finds his way to a bar stool and orders a drink. After sitting there for a while, he yells to the bartender, "Hey, you wanna hear a blonde joke?"

The bar immediately falls absolutely quiet. In a very deep, husky, voice, the woman next to him says, "Before you tell that joke, sir, you should know five things:

1. The bartender is a blonde girl.
2. The bouncer is a blonde gal.
3. I'm a 6-foot tall, 200-pound blonde woman with a black belt in karate.
4. The woman sitting next to me is blonde and is a professional weight lifter.
5. The lady to your right is a blonde and is a professional wrestler.

Now think about it seriously, Mister. Do you still wanna tell that joke?"

The blind man thinks for a second, shakes his head, and declares, "Nah, not if I'm gonna have to explain it five times."

Katie rolled her eyes and gave a little head shake. But the corners of her mouth sneaked up to betray her sense of humor. "I'm glad I'm not blonde," she said.

"Me too," he said and grinned.

His joke brought one from her and another one from him. They were eating, talking, and laughing. Exactly what he wanted.

He enjoyed talking with her, liked watching her lips form the words, liked her laugh; and he liked seeing her emerald green eyes open wide and sparkle when she was excited about something. And then there was the way her hands moved when she talked…and that tender side of hers.

It was twenty to ten when she put her hand over her mouth and stifled a yawn. Their plates were gone. So was her wine and all but a couple of the other patrons.

"I think it's time I get home," she said.

He could have sat and talked with her all night. "I hate for the evening to end. But I suppose you're right."

"We'll get together in the morning, then?" she asked.

"Breakfast is on me."

"Nine-thirty alright? I want to call the attorney when her office opens at nine. If she's not in, I'll leave a message for her to call me back on my cell."

"I'll be ready and raring to go."

She chuckled and said, "One meal in this place and you're already sounding like a cowboy."

He grinned. *"Yeee ha!"*

Chapter 40

BY TEN FIFTEEN Jack was lying on the bed in his room, staring into the dark. He was trying to figure out what it was about Katie that intrigued him so. He closed his eyes and replayed her laugh, her mannerisms. He pictured each feature of her face and that's when it hit him: her eyebrows—those wonderfully thick, carefully shaped eyebrows.

He firmly believed every male over the age of thirteen has a thing about the opposite sex that turns him on. In his case he had several. The one that stuck with him from adolescence was a thick muff of pubic hair. Brazilian was not his preference.

He remembered his first look at a nudie magazine. Eighth grade—his friend Ralph Edwards brought a Playboy to school for him to see. He and several other boys crowded together to look at the foldout. A gorgeous blond with the biggest pair of breasts he could imagine.

Thinking back on it, he was sure his good old Dad was far too self-righteous to have any X-rated trash like that lying around the house for him to find. But his friends' dads did. And his friends had shared those magazines with him.

He'd smuggled them into the house in his backpack. Late at night in his bedroom he had spent countless, restless hours looking at page after page of naked women. It didn't take long for him to realize thick eyebrows were a dead giveaway to a dense pubic patch.

He formed a mental image of her on a page in one of the girlie magazines he'd looked at as a kid.

The perfect pinup.

His cell phone trilled, dashing the vision from his head.

Shit!

He sighed, checked the number, and flipped it open. "Miss me already."

"Jack, someone broke into my house."

He sat straight up in bed. "Did you call the police?"

"I did. They're here now."

"Any ideas who did it?"

"Druggies," she said. "That's the way it looks. The TV is gone, my laptop, and some change I had in a jar on the coffee table. But the worst part is, they trashed the place. The jerks even dumped the food from the kitchen cupboards and the refrigerator onto the floor."

"How about the alarm? Your dad owned a security business; surely the house is alarmed?"

"There is an alarm, but the system was shut off. I must have forgotten to turn it on when I left the house to meet you for dinner."

"Would you like me to come over?"

"That's okay. My neighbors will be over in a few to help me clean up. Ethel next door said I could stay with them tonight. I just wanted you know what happened. I'll see you in the morning, around nine-thirty."

"You sure?" he asked.

"I'm sure."

"Nine-thirty it is."

He clicked off his phone and tried to resurrect the vision of Katie that had been so clear only a minute ago. But all he could picture was a trashed living room and a kitchen floor strewn with food.

He thought about Katie alone in her house with the knowledge that thieves had violated her space. And he thought about Ellery safe in Maui with her parents. Two motivated women determined to get what they're after.

He shook his head.

Two women so different from each other, yet the same. It didn't make sense—or did it?

He wondered.

Shrugging off the thought, he poured himself two fingers of bourbon from the bottle he'd purchased earlier in the day. He downed half the drink and freshened it with another splash from the bottle. As he swirled the liquor around in the glass he knew that sleep would not come easily.

For him, or for Katie.

Her house had just been burglarized.

One tough girl.

He carried his whiskey over to the bed and sat down with his back to the headboard. For a long moment he stared at the blank screen of his television, trying to decide if he should turn it on or leave it off.

He grabbed his laptop instead.

Katie had been a distraction from his issues with Ellery. But Ellery was in his thoughts. They hadn't made up and that bothered him. He believed he should have tried harder and felt terrible for having left Maui with so much anger between them.

This should never happen when two people love each other.

His laptop came to life, and he checked his e-mail. Nothing from Ellery. But the forwarded joke Robert had sent a week earlier was still there, along with a new one from him. He opened Robert's most recent message. It read:

Subject: Forward: An Irish Story…

> *One day an Irishman who had been stranded on a deserted island for over ten years, saw a speck on the horizon. He thought to himself, "It's certainly not a ship."*
>
> *As the speck got closer and closer, he began to rule out the possibilities of a small boat or raft.*
>
> *Suddenly there emerged from the surf a wet-suited black clad figure. Putting aside the scuba gear and the hood of the wet suit, there stood a drop-dead gorgeous blonde!*
>
> *The glamorous blonde strode up to the stunned Irishman and said, "Tell me, how long has it been since you've had a cigarette?"*
>
> *"Ten years," replied the amazed Irishman.*
>
> *With that, she reached over and unzipped a waterproofed pocket on the left sleeve of her wet suit, and pulled out a fresh pack of cigarettes.*
>
> *He takes one, lights it, and takes a long drag. "Faith and begorrah," said the man, "that is so good I'd almost forgotten how great a smoke can be!"*
>
> *"And how long has it been since you've had a drop of good Irish whiskey?" asked the blonde.*
>
> *Trembling, the castaway replied, "Ten years."*
>
> *Hearing that, the blonde reaches over to her right sleeve, unzips a pocket and removes a flask and hands it to him.*
>
> *He opened the flask and took a long drink. "'Tis nectar of the gods!" stated the Irishman. "'Tis truly fantastic…!"*
>
> *At this point the gorgeous blonde started to slowly unzip the long front of her wet suit, right down the middle. She peered seductively at the trembling man and asked, "And how long has it been since you played around?"*
>
> *With tears in his eyes, the Irishman fell to his knees and sobbed, "Sweet Jesus! Don't tell me that you've got golf clubs in there too!"*

Jack grinned to himself and clicked on *Reply*. He typed: "I'm guessing the moral of the story is to always take your golf clubs when you travel? That way you won't be befuddled when a drop-dead gorgeous blonde asks you how long it's been since you've played around. Gotta love those Irish…"

Robert did make him smile.

He pressed *Send*, and slid his laptop onto the mattress, next to him.

A great joke but not the message he'd hoped to see. He sighed, thinking he should send Ellery a note saying he was sorry.

But was it up to him to apologize?

Ho`oponopono.

He was making things right for Katie's father. Obviously Ellery didn't see it that way. It appeared to him correctness extended beyond what was right for Michael Sean McIntyre.

An e-mail prompt drew his attention to the screen on his laptop. He'd received a message from Robert. He was online.

Jack checked the subject line—a single word.

Important.

He clicked on the e-mail. The note read: *Have some information for you. Give me a call. I'm off work tonight.*

He reached for his cell phone and dialed Robert's number. It rang three times.

"What's up?' he asked when Robert answered.

"Maybe a lot," Robert said. "In fact, you could open a real Pandora's box here if you did some digging."

"How's that?"

"You asked about Gordon Kaeha?"

"Yeah."

"Kazuko got your answer. According to Kathy Ellis—a naturalist there at the aquarium—he works for The Department of Land and Natural Resources. And that's not all. He's on the Kahoolawe Island Reserve Commission. Without the KIRC's blessing, this whole casino deal would fall apart before the project has a chance to get off the ground."

"Aren't DLNR Officers those guys that patrol the beaches? What's this commission all about?"

"The Department of Land and Natural Resources isn't a department full of beach cops. They're pretty much the watchdogs for the Hawaiian Islands. The commission was created to manage the Kahoolawe Island Reserve while it's being held in trust for a Native Hawaiian sovereign entity."

"So what the KIRC says, goes?"

"That's about it."

"And this Gordon Kaeha guy has the influence to get the board to go one way or the other?"

"Apparently so. From what we've been told, he's done this type of thing in the past."

"He can be bought?"

"That's what we hear."

Jack gave a low whistle.

Dammit!

"I'd like to know how these dirty politicians keep their jobs!" he said. "You'd think the people would get wise and vote them out."

"You'd think so. And maybe they do," Robert told him. "Perhaps it's just that the old bad politicians are replaced with new bad politicians. So tell me, where are you going with this?"

"Good question."

"That's what I thought. Well, whatever you do, watch your back."

"You got it. And Robert, thanks."

Jack clicked off, not really knowing what to do with the information. What he did know was Gordon Kaeha was dirty, and Thomas Seaport was paying him a lot of money not to interfere with the casino project.

Which left one big question unanswered. If the KIRC had been created to manage the Kahoolawe Island Reserve, and the native Hawaiians wanted the casino, why the payoff?

There was turning out not to be any part of Thomas Seaport's operation he liked, and he certainly didn't like being a part of that group. But what could he do about it?

Chapter 41

JACK SAT UP on the edge of his mattress and buried his face in his hands. Having rubbed the sleep from his eyes, he looked around. His bedspread, blanket, and extra pillows lay in a pile on the floor. The sheets were a tangled mess on the mattress. And even though the temperature inside the room was cool, he was drenched in sweat. Sleep had brought the nightmare of all that was bad in his life.

He stroked back his hair and sighed. He was ready to think about other things, anything but Ellery and her father.

His gaze wandered to the window. On the other side of the glass, the early morning was turning steel gray. In another hour the sun would rise above the mountains and it would be a beautiful November day, no fog, no rain, just plenty of sunshine and clear skies—a real Indian summer.

Perfect weather for making things right for Katie's father.

At a quarter after nine he sat nursing a steaming cup of black coffee in the same Denny's restaurant he and Katie had stopped at his first night in town. He had on wrinkled khaki Dockers, deck shoes, and a red aloha shirt with a parrot design on it. His old Ray-Bans hung from a strap around his neck.

Katie arrived ten minutes later. She was wearing a navy blue skirt, a short-sleeve white silk blouse and glossy, white leather sandals. Persol sunglasses fashioned in a tortoiseshell design, sat propped at an angle on top of her head. Attire for a visit with the attorney.

He felt awkwardly underdressed.

As she slid into the booth across the table from him, he waived to their waitress, holding up his cup in a gesture for more coffee.

"You look nice," he said to Katie. "You managed to get some sleep?"

"A couple of hours," she said. "But the house is back in order."

"Still no idea who broke in?"

"No."

The waitress stopped by and splashed coffee into their cups. They ordered breakfast and waited for her to step away.

He was looking at Katie again—had been since the moment she walked in and sat down. A real lady in every respect. He felt a bit guilty for having pictured her in a full-page layout on the centerfold of a girlie magazine. But those wonderfully thick eyebrows were dragging back those same thoughts.

He took a sip of his coffee and slugged down half of his glass of water to force his mind back on track.

"You called the attorney?"

"Left a message."

"So now we sit back and wait for her to call back, right?"

"That's about it." She sighed. "Unless you think there's something else we should be doing?"

He smiled.

"This has to work," she said. "If it doesn't, Dad will die in that prison for a horrible crime he didn't commit."

The confidence she'd worn like a suit of armor, had cracked, letting her desperation show through. He wanted to tell her to believe in the system, that justice would prevail. But he couldn't do that with a straight face. That kind of horseshit was reserved for old westerns where the hero in the white outfit rides into the sunset with the heroine perched on the pommel of his saddle. Still, he had to give her hope that everything would turn out all right.

"We'll make this happen," he said. "If his attorney doesn't want to run with it, we'll go to the news—*60 Minutes*, the newspaper, something."

"And if that fails," she said, her voice cracking, "what then? Dad rots away and dies in an eight by ten cell."

When he reached across the tabletop and gripped her hand, she didn't tense or pull away.

"We're dealing with a system designed by people for people," he said. "No way can it be perfect. Never has been. Never will be. But whenever people are involved, there's hope. We'll make them believe he's innocent."

Her lips curled up slightly at the corners in a brave attempt to smile. But then the dam broke and tears rolled down her cheek.

"I'm sorry," she said and sniffled. "I haven't cried this much since the day I found out my mother had been killed and the police were arresting my father for her murder."

He leaned toward her and gave her hand a reassuring squeeze. "You need to cry. It's okay."

Using her other hand, she brushed away the tears.

He pulled a napkin from one of the unused place settings and offered it to her.

"This is so unlike me," she said. "It's just that my parents were stolen from me, and now I have a chance of getting one of them back."

"I understand." He waited.

Finally she was able to collect herself. She wrapped the napkin he'd given her around her index finger, dabbed at the corners of her eyes, and eyed the smear of mascara on the material.

"I can't believe this," she said. "I must look like a raccoon."

He laughed and gave her a reassuring grin. "You look fine."

Katie smiled briefly then turned toward the window and the cars speeding by on the street. Her mind was clearly somewhere else and he quietly watched her stare into the distance. After several long seconds, she shot him a nervous glance, then picked up her fork and poked at her eggs.

Again, he wanted to tell her everything would be all right, that her dad would soon be free from that dreadful prison. But he decided to let the issue lie. A few words of encouragement from him would surely sound nice, but he had a feeling that wasn't what she needed.

She needed that call from her father's attorney.

Chapter 42

JACK ATE HIS scrambled eggs as Katie continued to poke at hers. He was glad to see her manage a few bites in between glances at her watch. Her appetite wasn't there and obviously it was killing her to have to wait for the call.

"What's her name?" he asked.

He wanted to get her talking to get her mind off the time.

"Who?" she asked, looking up from her plate.

"The attorney. When you mentioned calling the attorney you said *her*. What's her name?"

She shot a look at her watch for the fortieth time. He could see he had his work cut out.

"Moira," she said. "Moira Tuscano."

"Is she any good?"

"Supposed to be." She added with a tone of skepticism, "I've heard she's won a lot of cases. But she sure didn't help Dad any."

He nodded at the ring. It hung from a heavy gold chain around her neck. It was not necessarily the best choice. She must have wanted it handy.

He gave her that reassuring smile he'd given her every time he talked about getting her father out of prison. "She will now. Let's go for a drive. You can show me around Henderson."

She shrugged.

They stepped outside and walked toward his rental Mustang. She was a half step ahead of him, eyes facing the sidewalk, lost in thought.

She needed that call.

He followed her into the parking lot. They were two steps into the lot when he heard a vehicle accelerate and speed toward them. He grabbed Katie by the arm and pulled her back.

A black Chevy Tahoe sped by so close that he felt a gush of wind buffet his face as the car passed.

He held her tight and watched the big SUV race out of the parking lot, onto the street, and down the road.

"Asshole," he muttered into the breeze.

He hadn't been able to see through the tinted windows. He didn't know if the driver was male or female. It didn't matter.

He turned his attention on Katie. Her eyes were wide open and staring in the direction of the fleeing car.

"Geez," she said. "I didn't even hear that car coming."

"Good thing I was here," he said.

She nodded and a sheepish grin curled her lips.

"I can't stop thinking about my dad" she said. "The last time I saw him he looked so frail and lost. I don't think he'll last another year in that place."

"Maybe so." He let her arm slip from his grasp. "But you won't do him much good if you're run down by some idiot driver before you have a chance to meet with that attorney of his."

"I suppose you're right."

"No suppose about it." He grinned, and added, "Besides, I'd like you to stick around a while."

His comment brought a smile to her face and that made him feel good. Now if she would just get that call.

They walked to his car. He stayed close at her side and stood at the passenger door while she climbed in. He wasn't taking any chances.

Then he climbed in.

"Where to?" he asked from the driver's seat.

"Take a right when you exit the parking lot," she said.

"Some place in particular, Miss Daisy?"

She gave him a poke in the ribs with her finger and said, "You want to see where I live, don't you?"

He'd arched his body to the side too late to escape her jab. He grinned, and it dawned on him that he was smiling again and that he'd been smiling a lot during the last day and a half. He couldn't help it. She made him want to smile, to laugh. And when she was sad, he wanted to hold her in his arms and comfort her. He wanted to make her smile.

"I was wondering when you were going to invite me over," he said, still wearing his grin.

She poked at his ribs a second time, causing him to scrunch to the side.

"Not over, Jack," she said. "Just *by*."

He kept a wary eye on her lethal finger and turned right onto Warm

Springs Road. Traffic was light and moving along at a respectable 35 miles per hour. Even so, he half expected the cars to come to a halt, blocked by the wreckage of the black Tahoe that had careened out of the restaurant parking lot.

"You told me you like living here?" he said. "Thought about moving?"

She gazed out the passenger's side window in the direction of the passing buildings. Sunlight streaming through the glass caught reddish highlights in her dark brown hair, which he hadn't seen before. The hint of auburn made her good looks even more spectacular.

"I don't know that I've ever thought about living anywhere else," she said. "It's possible, I suppose—when I was little—but I don't think so. Not with my father in prison a few miles outside of town, and my mother buried in a cemetery not far from the house."

"But the desert? Living in Maui, I can't imagine what it would be like not being close to the ocean, or at least a lake or a river."

"I don't know," she said. "The desert has its own beauty."

"So you really do like living here?"

She turned in her seat and looked at him.

"Yeah, I do," she said.

He gave her a sideways glance. Then he gazed through the windshield at the town and the barren calico hills in the distance. He caught a glimpse of a sandy, rock-strewn, sage-covered vacant lot. A parched creek bed. Sand and stone, but no water.

"The change would take some getting used to," he said. "But I guess I could be happy here, with the right job, and the right woman."

At this comment she turned her head and looked the other way.

An awkward silence filled the gap between them. Had he said something that struck her wrong—found another chink in her armor? A tune from her cell phone broke the quiet.

She quickly dug the cellular from her purse, clicked it on and pressed it to her ear. "Hello?"

He listened to her side of the conversation.

"I have the ring, Moira," she said after a moment. "The ring my father said he lost in Maui."

Chapter 43

JACK WATCHED KATIE as he drove. And listened. Saw her knit her brow.

"That's right," she said, "His father's missing West Point class ring. And please call me Katie. Nobody calls me Mary anymore."

More quiet.

He saw her finger the ring on the chain around her neck with the phone pressed to her ear. Her head was bowed slightly, her eyes wide open and fixed on the dash. But clearly she was peering into the past.

She said, "I've got it right here, and the man who found it."

He checked the roadway ahead and slowed to a stop at a red signal light. He saw her nod into the phone, more listening.

"That's right," she said. "I realized that…but…" She frowned. "We need to meet and talk about this, now. We need to get my dad out of that prison." She huffed into the phone, frustrated.

He checked the cars ahead. They weren't moving. He peered back at her.

"Moira," she said, "I know we've been through this before, but we *have* the ring. We have the hard evidence you told me we needed to prove my dad's innocence."

He watched her grip the ring.

She said, "I'm holding it in my hand." Another nod into the phone. "Of course I realize it'll take time. And don't worry, I know there is a chance nothing will come of it. But we need—"

Katie took a deep breath, and exhaled a long sigh of exasperation. She was probably getting the customary *don't-get-your-hopes-up* speech from the attorney. He hoped not.

"I understand, Moira," she said in clear tone frustration. "But we need to talk now. Dad's dying in that place." She lowered the phone a few inches. Then she raised it to her ear again and said, "First thing in the morning—you promise we'll meet first thing in the morning?"

Her lips formed a half smile. A minor triumph.

She said, "Nine o'clock, your office. And you didn't need to remind me that this is going to be expensive. I'll sell the house if I have to. Let's just get my dad out of that dreadful prison."

Katie clicked off the phone and stared out the passenger's door window.

The traffic ahead of them moved. He gave her a moment while he followed the cars through the green light.

"Well?" he asked.

"Moira's in Los Angeles," she said, obviously disappointed. "At a meeting—she won't be home until late tonight. She wants us to meet her in her office tomorrow morning at nine."

The space between his Mustang and the Beamer in front of him widened.

He glanced at her and asked, "What was that talk about selling your house?"

She sighed. She'd been doing a lot of that.

"It costs money to take a murder case back to court," she said. "Lots of money. And Moira Tuscano isn't cheap."

"Money you don't have."

"Not that much," she said. "I can't touch my trust fund, so all I have is that house. But I'll sell my home if that's what it takes to free Dad. I'll sell that place in a heartbeat."

He focused on the Beamer and eased on the brake when the BMW slowed to make a right turn.

Concentrating on the traffic he asked, "What did you mean when you said 'take the case back to court'? Isn't it a simple matter of turning the ring over to your dad's attorney and me giving her a statement?"

"A bit more than that I'm afraid," she said. "On more than one occasion Moira has made a point of telling me how complicated a process it is to get a murder conviction overturned."

He realized again he knew nothing about how to get someone out of prison. Not legally, anyway. The movies he'd seen didn't go there.

"*Ho`oponopono*," he said, "You'd think no one should have to pay a penny to free someone who's wrongly convicted of a crime."

"Ideally," she agreed. "The problem is proving Dad was wrongly convicted. To do that, you need an attorney. And that costs plenty. But I'll sell my house if I have to—whatever it takes to get him out of that horrible place."

He flashed her another reassuring smile like those he'd been passing out to her since his arrival in town.

"Let's pray it doesn't come to that."

She leaned and kissed him on his cheek.

She asked, "Would you mind dropping me off at my car? I think I'd like to be alone for a while."

"Not at all," he said. "But are you going to be all right?"

"I'm fine. I just want to be alone."

He knew she was tough. But she *had* come close to being run over.

He dropped her off at her car in the parking lot outside Denny's and followed her home to make sure she got there in one piece. That was one reason. Another reason was he wanted to see where she lived.

When they arrived at her house, he didn't want to leave her there by herself. But she insisted she was fine. And he knew she was. She'd been taking care of herself for a long time. She didn't need him there with her.

He watched her walk inside and waited until she closed the door. Then he drove straight back to his hotel with only a quick stop for a six-pack. He needed a beer.

Back inside his room, he put the Budweiser cans in his bathroom sink and covered them with ice from the machine down the hall. Then he popped one open, chugged down a third of it, and carried the open can to the bedside table.

He was concerned about Katie. She'd seemed so discouraged by the wait. Every hour was one more hour her father had to spend in prison. There had already been too many years, too many days, too many hours, too many minutes. She had spent more than a decade standing firm in her belief that her father was innocent. And now she had the proof needed to set him free. Having him spend even one more second in confinement had to be inexcusable in her eyes.

And he couldn't agree more.

Back to the headboard, he stretched his legs out on the mattress and moved his computer to his lap. As he opened the lid and reached for the button to turn the laptop on, he found himself thinking about Ellery, no doubt the result of some unconscious guilt trip on his part. He hadn't really given her all that much thought over the past two days.

A smile creased his face. Katie, on the other hand, had been on his mind almost constantly. He had even dreamed about the young lady. He felt a little bad about his fascination with her, but then again, not really. And that kind of bothered him. He was engaged to Ellery. He should be thinking about her.

Why is it so hard for me to do that?

He turned on the computer, half hoping not to see an e-mail message from her. He'd felt them drifting apart and the gap was widening into a chasm of irreconcilable differences.

Once he was connected to the Internet, he went directly to his messages. The joke Robert sent him in San Francisco a week earlier was still there—he had yet to open it—along with a new joke. There was no message from Ellery.

Too busy, he guessed.

And that was fine with him.

He left the first joke from Robert and opened the second one. He noticed it had been sent right after his phone conversation with Robert Sunday night. The joke read:

Don't let Ellery or this thing with her father whittle you down. You'd look like shit with an eye patch.

Subject: War is hell

A pirate walked into a bar and the bartender said, "Hey, I haven't seen you in a while. What happened? You look terrible."

"What do you mean?" said the pirate, "I feel fine."

"What about the wooden leg? You didn't have that before."

"Well, we were in a battle and I got hit with a cannon ball, but I'm fine now."

"Well, ok, but what about that hook? What happened to your hand?"

"We were in another battle. I boarded a ship and got into a sword fight. My hand was cut off. I got fitted with a hook. I'm fine, really."

"What about that eye patch?"

"Oh, one day we were at sea and a flock of birds flew over. I looked up and one of them shit in my eye."

"You're kidding," said the bartender, "I didn't think you could lose an eye just from a bird shitting in it."

"It was my first day with the hook."

Jack smiled at his friend's humor, but realized Robert was worried about him. He had to admit he was a tad concerned himself.

What had he got himself into?

Chapter 44

KATIE WISHED SHE'D invited Jack in.

She read the same sentence for the third time, sighed, and closed the magazine. It was no use. She could have read the article a hundred times and still none of its content would have registered.

On top of everything going on with her father's case, she'd become more and more attracted to Jack. Whenever he stood close to her, he made her nervous and left her wondering if she should throw her arms around his neck and kiss him, or run like hell. She hadn't expected that.

The attraction complicated matters.

She'd only had a couple of serious relationships with men, and none in the last two years. The guy she was currently seeing was more of a friend, though he wanted their relationship to move to the next level. She'd been harboring the feeling that she didn't have room in her life for a man. Now it seemed she did.

When the phone rang at five-thirty, she hoped it was Jack calling, to save her the chore of cooking herself dinner. On the third ring she grabbed the cordless from the coffee table and switched it on.

"Hello?" Her voice betrayed excitement.

"Katie, I was wondering how you're doing?" It was Brian Wesley.

She closed her eyes and took a deep breath to slow her fluttering heart. In the excitement of the moment, she hadn't stopped to think Jack had her cell number, not the house number. She should have known it wasn't him.

"I'm doing okay, Brian."

"Did you meet with Moira today?"

"She's out of town and won't be in until later tonight. We're meeting in her office in the morning."

"Did she believe you?"

"You know Moira, she's cautious." She sighed. "But yes, she believes me."

"So you still have the ring?"

She fingered the loop of gold on the chain around her neck.

"Nobody's getting this ring," she said. "Not even Moira. Not until I know for sure she's going to use it to get Dad out of prison."

"Hold onto it, Katie. And good luck tomorrow. Be sure and let me know how the meeting turns out."

"I'll give you a call as soon as I know where we stand."

She clicked off the phone and laid the handset on the coffee table. For a few beats she stood thinking about the call, still wishing it had been Jack on the line. The frozen Lasagna she planned for dinner was going to be a far cry from their dinner at the steakhouse, but it would have to do.

She wandered into the kitchen for a glass of wine. Brian Wesley was showing an interest in her dad's case. His unexpected change of heart raised her spirits. Perhaps he *had* just needed a little time to let the reality of the situation sink in.

KATIE AWOKE TO the eleven o'clock news. She had dozed off on the couch a few minutes into the 9 o'clock program she'd been watching. The reporter stood at the scene of a three-car pileup ten miles south of Las Vegas on Highway 15. An all too common occurrence that caused her to wince whenever the wreckage appeared on the screen.

She reached for the remote to change the channel. The last thing she wanted was to watch ambulance crews pulling crushed and torn bodies from the twisted metal. Then she thought about Moira Tuscano driving home from Los Angeles. She would have been on that same highway. The news camera zoomed in on the wreckage, and she held her breath.

As the news camera swept over the smashed vehicles, she saw that Moira Tuscano's BMW wasn't one of them.

A flood of relief consumed her, and she realized that she'd been holding her breath the entire time the broadcast was focusing on the collision. She let herself breathe, and switched off the television.

For a couple of minutes she sat on the edge of the couch, thinking. Knowing that Moira could have been killed in that accident, left her with an uneasy feeling. She glanced at her watch and did the math. Moira should have already arrived home.

Unless...

She had to reassure herself that Moira had made it home safely. It was late, and Moira was probably settled in for the night. But too much was on the line. She needed to talk to Moira, or at least see her BMW parked in the driveway in front of her house. She didn't have Moira's personal phone number, but she did know where she lived.

With the traffic accident still on her mind, Katie climbed into her Camry and backed out of the driveway. She wasn't about to wait and pressed on the gas.

The moment her car entered the cul-de-sac where Moira Tuscano lived, she saw flashing blue lights and a half dozen police cruisers parked in the street. She didn't need to be told. A hollowness gutted her and she felt like throwing up.

When a patrolman flagged her down, she braked and lowered the window on the driver's door.

"I've got to get to the lady that lives in that house!"

"Sorry," the officer said. "I can't let you go in there."

"What do you mean? She's my father's attorney. I need to talk to her, now!"

"Wait here. The detective will want to talk to you."

"Detective?" she said. "What are you saying?"

The uniformed officer didn't answer her. He keyed his handheld radio, spoke a few words, and stood there, waiting.

A minute later, a man wearing blue slacks and a rumpled gray sports coat walked over and spoke to the officer.

Katie got out of her car and stood by the driver's door. She didn't want to wait. "You're the detective?"

The man in the suit walked over.

"Why can't I talk to Moira?" she asked before he could say anything to her. "Surely she's not—"

"Officer Scott tells me you're here to see Ms. Tuscano," he said.

"You haven't answered my question."

"I believe you know the answer," he said. "Now why are you here to see her at this time of the night, Ms—?"

"McIntyre," she said. "Katie McIntyre."

She watched him write in a small notebook.

"Moira was in L. A. today," she continued when he looked up. "We have a meeting in her office at nine in the morning, but I wanted to talk to her tonight. Is she all right? Can I speak to her?"

"Do you know what time she got home, Ms. McIntyre?"

"Look detective, she was in L. A. at a meeting. It would depend on when she left there to return home. She called me earlier today, but I haven't talked to her since. Now tell me what's happened?"

The detective closed his notebook.

For a moment he just looked at her.

She swallowed a sour taste rising in her throat.

"I'm afraid she's dead," he finally told her. "We believe she walked in on a burglary."

Moira dead?

All at once the world tilted, the night filled with a cascade of flashing blue and red lights, sounds blurred together into a dull hum. This was not happening!

She slumped against the front fender of her Camry and started to cry. Tears streaked her cheeks. She wiped them away with the sleeve of her sweater and stared at Moira's house. Not Moira! Not now! She wanted to cry, to let the tears flow, but held back.

She had to get away from there. "Can I leave now?" she asked. "Honestly, I don't know any more than what I've told you."

He studied her a breath longer, then fished his business card from his shirt pocket and handed it to her.

"Of course," he said. "First give me your address and phone number. I may have more questions to ask you."

She pulled her driver's license from her purse, handed it to him, and told him all the other details he wanted. It was all she could do to stand there and watch him write it down in his notebook.

Moira dead? She still couldn't believe it.

"Thank you," the detective said. "I'll be in touch."

She nodded, climbed into her car, and drove away. She couldn't hold back any longer. Tears welled in her eyes and broke loose amid great heaving sobs. Tears, because the woman she'd known was dead. And tears for her father, because Moira was his attorney.

She wondered what she would do now.

For the first time in years she felt hopeless and terribly alone. She sniffed back her tears and tried to convince herself all was not lost. But that wasn't enough. She needed someone to help her think things through—someone to hold her and tell her everything would be all right.

She needed Jack.

Chapter 45

KATIE WAS SITTING on a barstool with her legs crossed, half facing the door, when Jack walked in. Her short black skirt had ridden up on her smooth tanned legs, leaving the hook of a garter belt exposed on her left thigh. Just enough of the strap showed to tell him she was wearing red lace. She wore it for him. And that turned him on. *She* turned him on.

He knew this wasn't just some flirtatious game, but that's how it looked from across the room. He would play along.

Her green eyes locked on his when he walked toward her. She shot him a smile over the top of her martini as she raised the glass to her lips. She knew what she was doing and what that red lace garter belt did to him.

All inhibitions were gone. He had to have her, and would have taken her right there on that bar stool had the cocktail lounge not been full of people.

Neither of them said a word. There was no need to. The response was in their eyes—their look. The way her lips parted just a little—moist and ready. His crooked little smile of delight.

He nodded toward the parking lot. She slid off of her stool and they walked outside together.

The trill of his phone on the nightstand next to his bed had jolted him awake. The vision felt so real, he couldn't believe it was only a dream. But that's what it had been.

He blinked his eyes, forcing the dream to the back of his mind, and picked up his phone.

"Hello," he said with irritation in his voice.

"Jack, it's me."

Katie's voice brought him wide-awake. "I was just thinking about you," he said. "Is everything all right?"

"Can you come over?"

He picked up on a quiver in her voice. *Something had happened.*

"What's wrong?" he asked. "You sound upset."

"Moira's dead, Jack."

He bolted upright. "Dead?"

"I drove to her house, and the police were there. She's been murdered."

He'd heard enough. "I'll be there in driving time," he said.

KATIE MCINTYRE WAS wearing a fluffy white terrycloth robe pulled tightly around her when she opened the door to her house. Her shoulder length brown hair stood out from her head in a mass of damp tangles; her eyes were red and swollen. Jack could tell Moira's murder had hit her hard.

He stepped inside and took her in his arms. She met his embrace, and they held each other for a long moment before she eased herself out of his arms.

"What am I going to do?" She turned, took a step, and stopped with her back to him. Clearly she had more to say.

He listened.

"Moira's dead," she said. "I don't want to sound cold, but I can't believe I've gotten this close to getting dad's case overturned only to have everything collapse around me at the last minute."

"We'll come up with something," he said in a soft voice. "You still have the ring. You can hire another attorney."

She turned and met his eyes. "It's not that easy, Jack."

"We can go to the police—try and talk to the investigator who worked your dad's case. Maybe he'll listen. And there's always the District Attorney's office. The DA might want to reopen the case, since freeing an innocent man could only help his career."

She sniffled and buried her face in his chest. He put his arms around her and held her.

"People care, Katie. No one wants to see an innocent person stuck in prison."

"Do they, Jack? Do any of them *really* care?"

"Moira did. Other people do, too."

She pushed away and peered up at him.

He didn't try to hold her.

"I'm not so sure about that," she said. "And even if Moira did care, she's dead."

"You're not alone in this," he said. "I'm in it with you. And I'm not going anywhere until we find someone who believes in your Dad's innocence and is willing to do what it takes to get him out of prison."

She peered into his eyes, and after a moment leaned forward and kissed him gently on the mouth.

"You really are wonderful," she said.

He knew the kiss had been an innocent gesture. Even so, her lips had been soft and moist on his. He wanted to kiss her back, but knew it wouldn't be right. "Perhaps I'm not as wonderful as you think?" he said.

She gave a thin and shaky smile. "Nonsense," she said. "You've been absolutely wonderful. Your support means a lot to me."

He thought about the promises he'd made to her: he wasn't going anywhere until they had found someone willing to do whatever was necessary to set her father free. But could he deliver?

Good intentions. He recalled hearing the road to hell is paved with good intentions and hoped that didn't apply here. He wasn't ready for hell, even if he were bound for there in the end.

"Like I told you," he said. "We'll work this out. I promise." He took her hand in his and led her to the sofa. She didn't resist.

"Relax," he said. "I'll make us some tea, if you have some?"

"I'd rather have a glass of wine if you don't mind."

"Just point me to the bar."

"There's a bottle of Merlot on the kitchen counter."

"And an opener?"

"In the drawer below. But the bottle's already open. I had some earlier this evening. You'll find some glasses in the cupboard above."

He returned a minute later with the bottle of wine and two glasses. She sat hugging her knees on the sofa. He poured each of them a half glass of Merlot and handed her one.

"This should do the trick," he said.

She took a sip, then another. She patted the seat cushion. "Sit next to me."

Chapter 46

JACK GLANCED AT the cushion, then at Katie wrapped in her fluffy white robe. He looked directly at her then had to avert his eyes. He took in the coffee table, the end tables, the walls and the pictures hanging there—then her. The room was filled with her scent. Her kiss—however innocent—still lingered on his lips. He saw her emerald green eyes watching him.

Those marvelous eyebrows!

The night didn't start out an intimate one. But it was rapidly moving that direction even though he hadn't driven there with the intention of sharing a romantic evening alone with her. Now he didn't know what to think or do. Maybe he should just go.

But she had asked him to join her on the sofa.

He took a seat on the cushion close to her.

She snuggled tightly against his shoulder and he hooked his arm around her. She felt so good that he took a sip of wine and stared into his glass, trying to keep control of his thoughts.

"Perhaps it would be better if we talked about something else for a while," he said.

"If only we could," she answered in a wistful tone.

"But you can't stop thinking about your dad?"

"He's the one suffering."

"Seems to me you're doing a fair amount of that, yourself."

"Maybe so," she said.

He thought, *you're not the only one.* He was all too aware of her body pressing against him. He could feel her breasts rise and fall with each breath, the warmth of her skin through that fluffy white robe. All he could think about was touching her, kissing her, making love to her.

He casually slid his arm from around her shoulder, eased himself to his feet, and stepped to the window. His blood needed to cool and he needed to focus on something else.

He parted the mini-blinds with his hand and peered through the glass at the dimly lit neighborhood. A Chevy Tahoe passed by on the street in front of the house. The big SUV stood out black in the night. He thought about the incident at the restaurant and how close Katie had come to being seriously hurt or killed. He couldn't imagine how he would have felt if she had.

"Have you told your father about the ring yet?" he asked, bringing his mind back on track.

He heard the clink of Katie's glass as she set it on the coffee table.

"I haven't wanted to get his hopes up," she said.

"Knowing he's aware of what's going on here might help—help you, I mean."

"Sorry, I'm not following—"

He faced her. "If he knew you had the ring he lost in Maui, and that you were working on getting him out of that place, he'd have something positive to hold onto—some hope. Wouldn't that make *you* feel better?"

"I hadn't thought of it that way," she said.

He walked around to the back of the sofa and stood massaging her shoulders. A comforting gesture on his part.

She could use it and it certainly didn't hurt him, any.

"We can drive to the prison first thing in the morning," he said. "If you want to."

She leaned her head over and rested her cheek on his hand. "I've never known anyone like you. You make me feel—I don't know, safe."

The collar of her robe slipped. He could see the fullness of one breast and imagine cupping the mound of soft skin in his hand, kissing it.

He knew he had to go. "I think I should go so you can get some sleep."

She stroked his hand with the soft skin of her cheek and he couldn't bring himself to pull away.

"You really don't have to go," she said.

He felt his legs go weak. He couldn't believe he was passing up a night with her! But that's exactly what he was going to do. He gently slid his hand away from her grasp. His breath caught in his throat and he coughed.

"I think I should," he said. "We have a big day tomorrow, and we'll both need our sleep."

He gulped down the last of the wine and set his glass on the coffee table. As he walked toward the front door, she followed. And when he opened the door to leave, she leaned forward and gave him another innocent kiss on the lips. She certainly wasn't helping the situation.

"See you around eight-thirty," he said, fighting off the urge to kiss her back. "If that's all right with you?"

She pulled her robe tight around her. "I'll see you then."

He had to turn and walk away. If he didn't, he'd never get out of there with his morals intact.

He climbed into his rental Mustang and drove away.

After driving barely two blocks he pounded the steering wheel with the heel of his palm. She'd asked him to stay, so why hadn't he? Already he wished he had.

He cranked up the volume on the stereo. The loud music didn't help get her touch out of his mind.

He glanced at the back of his hand where she had caressed it with the soft smooth skin of her cheek. He raised his hand and rubbed the back of it against his own cheek. He closed his eyes. Her scent was there, and on his clothes. He could still taste that innocent kiss. Or was it?

What an idiot!

He suddenly understood that he would never have questioned his decision to leave Katie's house if he truly loved Ellery. He didn't love her, he knew that now. And that for some time he'd kidded himself thinking he did.

He steered to the curb and made a U-turn.

Now that he'd been honest with himself about his feelings for Ellery, he could see no good reason why he should feel bound by a self-righteous code of honor conjured up to save a young woman from herself. Katie was a big girl more than capable of making big-girl decisions. Who in the hell was he to step forward and interject some high-minded morality into the equation?

He was going back to her house. Hopefully her offer still stood.

No more than five minutes had elapsed since he left her house. When he pulled into her driveway he noticed a Chevy Tahoe, similar to the one he'd seen cruise the street earlier, parked at the curb two doors down. Strangely, the SUV sat facing the wrong direction.

He opened the driver's door and had one foot on the ground when he heard a scream reverberate from somewhere inside her house. Then came the crash of something heavy being knocked over, glass breaking, a loud thud.

Katie!

Before he could get both feet out of the car, the front door to the house flew open.

She sprinted toward him without any attempt to clutch the fluffy white robe tight around her.

The top of her housecoat flew open exposing her right breast, and he yelled to her to get in as he fumbled for passenger's door latch.

A man who could've been King Kong's double appeared in the doorway of the house. The hulk had his hand pressed against his bloody forehead. He paused, peered towards her and the car, and staggered after her at a half run.

Jack finally got his hand on the latch and opened the passenger's door.

Katie scrambled inside and slammed the door shut in the big man's face.

Jack hit the automatic door locks just as King Kong made a grab for the passenger's door handle.

The man tugged on it, then slammed his huge knee against the door, rocking the car.

Katie screamed at Jack to drive, but he didn't need urging.

He jammed the key into the ignition and the engine roared to life on the first crank, as he shoved the gearshift into reverse. The car shot backwards at the same time a huge hairy fist tore through the fabric of the convertible top.

Jack mashed the accelerator against the floorboard, and the Mustang careened onto the street.

He hit the brakes hard and shoved the transmission into drive. He floored the accelerator and the tires squealed in a cloud of burning rubber.

A glance into the rearview mirror told him the man was running toward the Tahoe.

They weren't out of trouble yet.

Chapter 47

JACK TOOK A hard right at the first corner, and a hard left at the next. Half-way down the block, he glanced into the rearview mirror on the windshield. No one was following them.

He eased off on the gas. "What the fuck was that all about?" he yelled.

"I don't know!" Katie yelled back.

He saw tears streaming down her cheek and sighed. "Are you all right?"

She clutched the collar of her robe tightly around her neck with one hand and wiped her eyes with the other. "I'm okay," she said. "Just scared."

There were no big black SUVs on the street in front of them, or behind. He took a deep breath and let it out. "Me too," he said. "Me too."

Now that he had a calm moment to think, he put his mind to work on a plan. His first thought was to call 911. And he would have, if he'd had his cell phone with him. But in his rush to get to Katie's house he had left it in his hotel room. His next thought was to use Katie's, even though the likeli-hood she had fled the house with hers was slim. It was worth asking.

He said, "I don't suppose you have your cell phone?"

She shot him a wide-eyed look from the passenger seat. "You're kidding, right?"

Her tears had stopped, but he could see by the size of her eyes she was still very frightened.

He said, "I forgot mine and was hoping you'd grabbed yours. We could call the police."

"Just drive," she said. "Before that asshole catches us."

He glanced into the rearview mirror and checked the roadway in front of them. No big black SUV. He gave the engine a little more gas.

He asked again, "What in the hell happened back there?"

"That big ape wanted the ring," she said. "He must've gotten into the house through the back door. When you drove away, I turned around and he was there standing in the middle of the living room grinning at me."

He saw her eyes open wide.

She gripped his forearm, "He tried to kill me," she said.

Jack felt her fingernails dig into his skin. "Yeah, but why?"

"I don't know why. All he told me was he'd been sent to get the ring."

Jack glanced from her to the road and back at her. "*Sent?* You didn't give it to him, did you?"

She jerked her hand from his arm. "Are you fucking kidding?"

"You could have," he said. "But then I guess not."

"Never," she said. "I told him I'd turned the ring over to my attorney."

"I take it he didn't believe you?"

She shivered and looked away. "The asshole just smiled and called me a lying bitch," she said. "Then the creepy bastard got this crazed kind of sicko look on his face and told me he had plenty of time to find it…once he'd had his fun with me."

He cringed at the thought of what could have happened to her. "And where's the ring now?"

She pulled the chain from under her robe and said, "Around my neck where it's going to stay until I find someone I trust to help me use it to get Dad out of that prison."

"Good," Jack said, nodding. "And the glass I heard breaking when I drove up, what in the hell was that?"

"I hit him with a vase."

Jack gave her a sideways look. He said, "Remind me to never piss you off."

"I was scared, that's all."

He rolled his eyes. "Yeah, right."

They roared up to another corner where he made a hard left. Once again his eyes darted from the roadway to the rearview mirror. He was staying with the flow of the few cars on the road, but kept a lookout for headlights coming up fast behind them.

He couldn't help thinking about what he'd do if the guy in the Tahoe caught up with them. He grew up a fisherman not a hunter. And he'd never been in the military, which limited his firearm experience to the army surplus M1 Garand they kept on the boat for shooting sharks when the need called for it.

Which wasn't often.

Lately the only shots he'd taken were on a golf course. He regarded himself as reasonably good with his clubs. And since he didn't own a gun, he thought that if he had his three iron with him he might have a fighting chance. But then again, he wasn't Tiger Woods and this wasn't the Mercedes Open.

He considered their position. The ape-of-a-man who'd broken into Katie's house had intended to kill her and take the ring, which left little doubt he now meant to kill them both and take the ring.

Jack was good with his knuckles, and considered himself uncommonly strong for his size. But he doubted he could take King Kong down in a fist fight—the guy might even be armed. That meant their best chance was to drive fast and get out of the area before the big ape caught up with them.

"Scared or not," he said to Katie, "you did what you had to do."

Her eyes told him how she felt.

"Good," he said. "Now let's get as far away from your place as we can, and fast. I'm certain Neanderthal man won't give up that easily."

"Do you have any idea where you're going?" she asked.

He saw a street sign coming up and glanced at it as they sped by. "Dinkledorf Road," he said. "What-in-the-hell kind of name is that for a street?"

"Who cares," she said. "Do you know where you're going?"

He made a quick jog off the frontage road and put them on East Lake Mead Drive heading east. Again he checked the mirrors. No SUV that he could see.

"Is this better?" he said.

"If you plan on driving us to Lake Mead."

"Not a bad idea," he said. "That's the last place he'll think to look for us."

Chapter 48

JACK WENT RIGID in his seat. He had no sooner gotten the words out of his mouth when he noticed a pair of high beams appear in the rearview mirror. A car was speeding up behind them, fast.

Having zigzagged their way out of Katie's neighborhood, he couldn't believe the guy in the Tahoe had found them that quickly. He checked his speed. They were doing almost fifty, now, and overtaking cars. He figured the vehicle racing after them had to be a traffic cop.

Good, he thought.

"I think we've got a cop on our tail," he said. "I'm going to pull over so you can report what happened. They'll find that asshole in the Tahoe and put a stop to this shit."

Katie turned in her seat and peered through the back window. "I don't think that's a cop car," she said.

He changed lanes. The bright headlights followed.

No red and blue strobes.

If it was a cop, the officer would have put on his overhead lights to stop them.

Again, his gaze shot to the rearview mirror. His eyes narrowed.

"Shit!" he said and mashed the gas pedal to the floor. "How in the hell did he find us?"

She turned her head back and forth between the rear window and the traffic on the roadway in front of them. "Faster! He's catching us."

"What do you think I'm doing?"

His attention darted from the rearview mirror mounted on the top center of the windshield to the side mirror on the driver's door. They sped past a streetlight. He checked once more. The Tahoe was there behind them, but didn't appear to be gaining asphalt.

When he looked again, a heartbeat later, the gap between them had widened. Breathing room, but not enough.

He fought the urge to bury the car's accelerator in the carpet. There was no doubt in his mind the lighter, sleeker, V-8 powered Mustang GT could outrun the heavier more wind resistant Tahoe, but not unless he got a long stretch of empty highway where he could really open her up.

"Hold on," he said. "And pray this traffic clears."

Even though the traffic had thinned somewhat, there were still enough cars on the road to keep him from taking the Mustang to top speed. Again he checked the mirrors.

Fortunately for them the driver of the Tahoe appeared to have the same problem. But the vehicle was still on their ass.

He couldn't believe they hadn't come across a single city cop or highway patrolman. Any other time police cruisers would have been all over the place.

So much for the movies.

They passed another dozen cars. The highway cleared and he floored it.

The high-powered Mustang did its stuff and a minute later the speedometer pegged the 140-miles-per-hour mark.

The car held the road.

He chanced a glance at Katie. In the light from the dash, he could see her seat belt pulled tightly and her feet planted against the floorboard. Her right hand was clamped on her door's armrest, while her left had a deathgrip on the center console.

A futile gesture at best. They would never survive a crash at this speed.

He forced the fiery image from his mind.

Again, his eyes yo-yoed between the roadway and the rearview mirror. The Tahoe had fallen back several car lengths. But it was still behind them in relentless pursuit.

Jack turned the Mustang's headlights on bright, and the high beams lit up the black ribbon of asphalt ahead of them. To the side of them, the desert's bleak landscape shot by in a blur. A quarter of a mile ahead of the car, a coyote trotted onto the roadway. He let off on the gas pedal long enough to be sure the animal would make it across.

He checked his mirrors.

The Tahoe didn't slow a bit and gained some ground. Another few seconds and he'd be on their bumper.

Jack didn't falter.

The coyote safely disappeared into the darkness on the opposite side of the roadway, and he mashed the gas pedal to the floor again. The car shot ahead, widening the gap between them and the Tahoe.

As the Mustang rocketed along the highway, he kept an eye peeled for any other misguided furry critters taking a notion to cross the blacktop in front of their speeding car. Far in the distance there were two sets of headlights coming at them. Other than that the roadway appeared deserted.

All he could do now was drive, and pray.

Except for a series of long gradual curves, the roadway was relatively straight and he was able to hold the Mustang at a respectable top speed of 140 miles per hour. The Tahoe's big V-8 appeared to keep the SUV in the game, but it never got closer than a half mile behind them.

He checked his rental's gas gauge. When he left his room to drive to Katie's, he hadn't planned on a high-speed chase. With the accelerator wide open, the big high-performance V-8 engine had to be sucking gas.

He was right. The needle on the gauge was approaching empty. Now he wished he'd thought to fill the tank after his long drive on Sunday.

"I think we're fucked unless we can find some way to ditch this crazy bastard," he said.

"What do you mean?" she asked, confused. "We're out running him by a mile."

"The gas gauge. Car's on empty."

"That's not funny," she said, craning her neck to see the gauge. "Didn't you just rent this thing?"

"Yesterday morning. But I went for a long drive. I didn't think I'd end up in a car chase."

"I don't believe this!" She twisted in her seat and peered through the rear window at the Tahoe's headlights. The SUV wasn't backing off.

"Don't ask me what to do," she said. "But whatever you decide on, you'd better do it, and do it fast."

At the farthest reach of the car's high beams, Jack noticed a dirt road leading off to the left. Gravel at best, and rough. He'd take the chance.

"Hold on," he said and jammed on the brakes to make the turn.

"What are you doing?" she screamed.

"We'll lose him in the desert."

"We'll what?"

He took the turn with a little too much speed and the Mustang fishtailed in the loose soil. He got the car back under control and bounced and thumped along the dirt road. Dust filtered through the hole in the convertible top.

As soon as he dared, he glanced into the rearview mirror and saw the Tahoe make the turn. The big SUV was coming fast, and at once he felt foolish for even considering heading off road.

They crossed a dry creek bed. The car's springs bottomed out going up the other side.

His attention cut to the rearview mirror. The Tahoe's headlights bounced as it roared through the same dusty creek bed.

Shit! The SUV was gaining on them.

He realized how stupid it was thinking he could ditch the SUV in the desert. He decided to return to the highway and try to make it back to town and people.

Now he hoped there was enough gas left in the tank to get there.

He looked for a spot to make a hard one-eighty. He knew a U-turn like that wasn't going to be easy, but it was the only chance they had. In another minute the big SUV would ram them from behind.

He spied an area void of vegetation that looked like an abandoned building site. The Tahoe was only a half-dozen car lengths behind them, now. He figured this was his one opportunity to make his move.

"Hold on!" he yelled.

He hit the brakes and cranked the steering wheel. The Mustang slid into a wild turn, and the Tahoe shot past them. He mashed the gas peddle to the floor and the convertible fishtailed onto the dirt track they'd driven in on. His plan had worked.

He guessed they were a mile from the highway. He could see headlights in the distance. All he had to do was get them back to town, where they'd have at least a chance.

Chapter 49

HEADLIGHTS APPEARED IN the convertible's rearview mirror. Jack glanced at their reflection. The Tahoe had made the turn, too, and was once again in pursuit, but appeared to be hanging back amid a spray of gravel kicked up by the Mustang's tires.

He goosed the engine a few times, adding an extra dose of rock to the buckshot-like onslaught.

The gap between the vehicles widened, but only for a few seconds.

Peering into the gloom at the farthest reach of the Mustang's headlights, he saw where the roadway cut the edge of the dry creek bed. He'd have to back off the gas to keep their car from going airborne.

He waited until the last possible second then hit the brakes. The car bounced into the wash and when he checked the mirror, he saw the Tahoe bearing down on them.

He goosed the throttle again, but too late. The Tahoe rammed the Mustang's rear bumper and the impact sent the Mustang skidding sideways into the creek bed.

He fought the steering wheel to keep the convertible under control as the car slid to a stop in a cloud of dust.

The Tahoe continued on through the dry wash and up the other side. Jack didn't wait to see what the driver was going to do next. He jammed his foot down on the gas pedal.

The car didn't move and he could hear the hum of the rear tires spinning in the soft sand.

As the Tahoe's brake lights lit up the darkness, he knew at once that they had to abandon the Mustang. He shoved the car's transmission into park and switched off the engine.

"Come on!" he shouted, throwing open his door.

He didn't wait to see what Katie was doing. He was out of the car and pulling open the passenger's door before she could get out of her seat. They had to move fast.

The door opened and she swung her legs out.

He grabbed her hand and pulled her from the car. The instant she was on her feet, he took off running, taking her with him. They ran in the soft sand for about fifty yards, then up the bank and into the harsh desert landscape.

Keeping hold of her hand, he pushed himself hard to put as much ground as possible between them and the driver of the SUV. And though the night air was quite cool, he sweated profusely.

A half moon and a blanket of stars provided enough light for them to see by, but it was still awkward going. The gnarly exposed root of a bush snagged his foot, and he fell. A loose rock rolled like a ball bearing under his shoe and he went down again. He swallowed his pain and scrambled to his feet.

A minute later, Katie cried out and fell to the ground, holding her foot. He stopped to help her up.

"We have to rest a minute," she said, gasping for breath. "I can't keep going like this."

The soles of her flimsy house slippers offered little protection from the rocky soil.

He peered in the direction of where he figured the cars were. He couldn't see the Mustang or the Tahoe. But he could see a flashlight beam sweep the desert a hundred yards away. King Kong wasn't giving up.

After a few breaths, she gripped his hand. He pulled her to her feet and waited while she slowly put weight on her injured foot.

He held onto her. "Can you stand?"

She worked her ankle, leaned over and massaged it, then straightened. "I'm all right," she said. "Let's go."

"Just a second." Jack focused on the flashlight beam. "Listen."

She peered into the darkness, then looked at Jack. Her eyes told him she'd heard it too: a man's voice.

"It's no use running," the man in the distance called out. "Give me the ring, and I'll let you go."

"Like hell," Jack muttered to Katie. "He wants that ring, and he doesn't want witnesses."

She said, "Even with my sore foot I can outrun that hairy ape."

He peered down at her scratched and bloodied feet and her feeble slippers. Not much in the way of foot coverings. He admired her spunk.

He asked, "You sure?"

She tugged on his arm. "Let's go."

They took off running, and kept running, and falling. When his breathing turned to labored huffs, he stopped. Katie had to be out of breath, too.

She rested her hands on her knees, breathed in and out, and asked, "Is our friend still there?"

He scanned the desert landscape behind them and spotted the flashlight beam. They'd managed to widen the gap, but they hadn't lost him.

"Guy's determined," he said. "I'll give him that much."

She looked. "I didn't figure fatty would make it this far."

"Or even be able to follow us." Then he noticed just how much her white robe stood out against the dark countryside. "Take off your robe and give it to me," he said. "That thing has to be sticking out like a beacon in the night."

"All I have on underneath is a pair of panties."

He unbuttoned his aloha shirt, stripped it off, and handed it to her. "Wear this."

She turned her back, shrugged off the housecoat, covered her breasts with her left arm, and handed the robe to him with her right. She turned her back again and slipped into his shirt.

"I take it you have a plan," she said, buttoning the top button.

"See those rocks sticking up over there?" he said, pointing at the silhouette framed by the lighter night sky. "Hide there while I put the slink on this asshole. I'll join up with you once I've led him off in the other direction."

"But—"

He didn't wait for her protest. He shoved his arms into the robe that was way too tight, and took off running in the direction of the goon.

"Jack!" she called out just loud enough for him to hear.

He didn't stop.

Chapter 50

KATIE RAN STRAIGHT for the dark shape against the night sky. It took her less than five minutes to reach the rocks: two monoliths protruding from the earth like pillars, with a jumble of smaller boulders scattered close by. She sagged against the boulder closest to her, breathed in, and peered into the expanse of desert gloom.

Jack had to be okay.

She couldn't see him anywhere, only the flashlight beam sweeping back and forth in the desolate wasteland far in the distance. She had to trust he would be all right. To think otherwise would drive her crazy.

There were enough other things for her to worry about. Like hypothermia.

She glanced around. A blanket of stars overhead and a slab of rising moon lit up the rocks enough for her to see them. A bleak, black and white moonscape, with no color. She dusted off a chair-sized boulder and sat down to wait. The surface of the stone was cold and rough against her bare skin. She shivered from the chill and hugged herself to keep warm.

Inhospitably hot in the daytime and bleak and cold at night, the wasteland of scrub, rock and sand went from one extreme to another. She'd grown up with the desert and appreciated its rugged beauty. Still, it frightened her to sit there in the middle of the night, alone.

A coyote yipped in the distance, then another, and another.

She stared toward the sounds. The hungry pack was after a rabbit or a mouse most likely, but she envisioned them chasing Jack back to her hiding spot in the rocks.

She peered up at the two stone pillars behind her, wondering if she should try and climb to higher ground. Then she dismissed the idea when she realized how ridiculous it was. The man who'd attacked her in her living room was chasing them—he was likely armed and ready to kill.

There were worse things to be afraid of than a few scrawny coyotes.

She stood up and scanned the area. Jack would be there any minute and they would need a place to hide. She picked her way around the outcropping and noticed how the rocks trailed off into a ravine on the opposite side. The coyotes were quiet, they'd made their kill. She stood still and listened to see if she could hear Jack coming.

Nothing.

She started down the slope.

At the bottom of the incline, about forty feet down from the top, she found a man-sized gap amid the rocks. Two tall boulders, three feet apart at the base, angled together at the top to form the opening. She peered into the void: dark nothingness, like staring into a deep well.

She pulled back and looked around. The darkened entrance was more than just a shadow, but on the outside it was similar to a hundred others in the jumble of rock.

Nature could have made the cave in the beginning, but someone had dug there. She could see tailings. But the debris was old and blended in with the rocky soil, making it difficult to recognize unless someone knew what they were looking at, especially at night.

She had no idea how far into the hillside the tunnel went, and wasn't about to go in there alone. But the mineshaft would make a good hiding place. She would have never noticed the opening in the dark if she hadn't stumbled onto it.

She climbed to the top of the ravine, skirted the rock monoliths, and hurried back to her place on the chair-sized boulder. Jack was out there in the darkness running for his life, their lives. He'd return any minute.

She wanted to be waiting for him when he did.

Chapter 51

JACK SUCKED IN lungfuls of air and stood looking at the rock outcropping. Beads of sweat trickled into his eyes. He wiped the perspiration away with the flat of his hand and blinked back the sting from the salt pouring out of his system. His legs knotted. Naked from his waist up, he should have been cold, and would be if he didn't keep moving.

But he'd run about as far as he could.

At first he didn't see Katie. Then he spied her silhouette atop a boulder about fifty feet away. A dark shape, not much detail, like the rock around her. But enough that he knew she hadn't heard him coming because she had yet to turn her head and look in his direction.

"Katie!" he called out in a hushed voice, as he closed the final few feet between them.

She jerked her head around and peered in his direction.

He waved to make it easier for her to see him.

"Jack!" she said in a hushed tone. "You scared the shit out of me. For a second I thought you were that big goon."

"Sorry," he said. "I wasn't trying to frighten you."

She stood and stepped toward him. "I'm just glad you're safe."

"Me, too." He looked into the darkness behind him. "Sorry about your robe."

"What happened to it?"

"Buried it so that I wouldn't be seen circling back here."

"Glad you did. I'll tell my aunt you put her Christmas present to good use."

"Worked like a charm, too," he said, facing her. "King Kong followed me like a lost puppy."

She narrowed her eyes at the distant gloom.

He pointed and said, "He's about a mile that direction."

"Good!" she said. "The big goon can stumble around out there all he wants. As long as he stays away from here."

"You like that word, don't you?"

"What word is that?"

"Goon."

"Yeah, I do. The name fits, doesn't it?"

"Sure does."

"The point is, they both fit. Goon or King Kong, he's one big, persistent sonofabitch. Let's get out of sight."

"I found a place," she said. "On the other side."

"Good. I'll follow you, this time."

She led him around the jumble of boulders and into the ravine. When they reached the bottom, she pointed and said, "Over there, that opening in the rocks. I think it's the entrance to a mineshaft."

He looked in the direction of her pointing finger. The opening stood out more like a shadow in the moonlight, not a hole in the ground. If you weren't right on top of it, you'd never know it was there.

"Give me a minute to make sure it's safe," he said.

She shot him a glance. "I'm going with you."

He smiled. "Not until I know it's safe."

She gripped his hand and held it. He could tell she was worried about him.

"All right," she said. "But whatever you do, be careful."

He was two steps ahead of her when he reached the opening to the tunnel. He took a cautious step inside.

Once he was out of the moonlight, he paused to let his eyes adjust to the darkness. He looked behind him. She stood at the opening, framed by the night sky.

Brave enough to smash a vase over King Kong's head. And daring enough to face the big bad boogieman in the cave.

She was a trooper.

He took another step. A spider web latched onto his face and chest. What he had been afraid of. He slapped the sticky strands away and shivered. He hated spiders.

After what felt like a long time, his eyes adjusted to the bit of nightlight that managed to find its way into the shaft. He looked around. In the gloom beside and behind him, he could make out shoring timbers, rough–hewn earthen walls, bits and pieces of derelict supplies once vital to the mine's operation—some of it identifiable and some not. In front of him, the tunnel was a ghostly shadow that quickly faded into pitch-black.

He stood a moment, peering into the black maw. The mine could continue on for ten feet or a mile, but there was no way for him to tell in the dark. And the air smelled earthy and foul. Something lay dead in the depths of the shaft.

Chapter 52

JACK HEARD KATIE call his name. A hushed tentative voice; she was definitely worried.

He turned and faced her. Keeping his voice down, he said, "It's some sort of mine all right. There's some stuff stacked along one of the walls but I can't tell what it is."

"Don't go too far," she whispered back. "It might not be safe."

"Trust me, I'm no James Rollins."

"Don't you mean Indiana Jones?"

"He might as well be. You saw the movie *Indiana Jones and the Kingdom Of The Crystal Skull?* Rollins wrote the novelization and loves crawling around in caves. But I don't think it'll be necessary for *us* to venture very far inside. We can stay right here near the opening, unless King Kong shows up. Then we'll have to play it by ear."

"Let's hope he's had enough of the desert."

"Should have, after the run I gave him."

He'd led their pursuer so far in the opposite direction that he really didn't believe the man would find them there. But that didn't mean it couldn't happen. He studied the outline of the shapes stacked along the wall and spied one that looked familiar. He took hold of the handle and raised the business end close to his face. The shovel was jagged and no doubt rusty. Its sharp edges would surely cut deeply. But in order to use such a weapon he'd have to get close to the big ape.

Too close.

He returned the shovel to its place against the wall and picked up a wooden box sitting next to it. He couldn't make out the items stacked inside and carried the carton to the entrance of the mine, under the light from the stars and the moon. Katie stepped close to his side, and he shifted over so she could get a look at what he'd found.

According to the writing stenciled on the outside panels, the box had held dynamite. And there were a couple of sticks left. That sent a nervous shiver dancing up his spine.

He fought back an urge to gently set the box aside and get far away from it.

Instead, he looked more closely.

The sticks of explosive were actually two dust-covered candles. He breathed a silent sigh of relief.

"Had me going there for a minute," he said.

"Me too," she said.

He reached inside and pawed the items: a tattered cardboard box of wooden kitchen matches and a can of what he guessed were beans. The label on the can had deteriorated and he was sure the food inside had too. But the matches were dry and even though their cardboard container was rotting and falling apart, he figured they would still light.

He scanned the landscape around them, and listened. Only rocks and desert scrub.

He looked at Katie. She surveyed the countryside as well: she'd picked up on his thoughts.

She met his eyes and shook her head. He shrugged. Even if they couldn't see the goon, he was sure they would have heard the big man huffing from effort if he were close.

"If I can get one of these candles lit," he said, "I'll take a look around inside. That way I can make sure we're not sitting on a snake or scorpion, or any of the other nasties crawling around out here in the desert."

"I'm going with you." She reached for his arm.

He removed a candle and a match and set the wooden box on the gravel floor just inside the tunnel. He handed her the candle and kept the match.

She held the wax torch steadily in front of her, with the wick pointed outward. She knew what he needed.

He struck the match against a rock and the tip flared. He cupped his hand around the flame and held the fire to the wick. The candle started to burn and she handed it back to him. He cupped his hand around the flame and faced the tunnel.

They took a step inside and both jerked backwards.

She threw a hand to her mouth and muffled a scream.

"Shit!" he gasped.

She clutched the front of the aloha shirt Jack had lent her. "Looks like a man standing there doesn't it?"

"I'm not sure it isn't."

"If it moves, I'm outta here!"

"And I'll be right behind you, but I don't think that will be necessary. It's just a pair of overalls hanging from that wooden beam. No body."

"Unless it's a ghost."

"In that case, I'll be out of here for sure."

He unhooked the overalls and held them up in front of him. They were filthy. And the heavy fabric was well worn and a little rotten. Other than that, they were wearable.

He asked, "Would you like a pair of pants to go with that shirt?"

She pointed at the overalls and said, "Those?"

He smiled. "I'll put these on. You can wear my Dockers."

She rubbed her arms, and glanced down at herself, shivering. He could see the tails from his aloha shirt covered her panties, but just barely. Her legs had broken out in gooseflesh from the night air, not ghostly apparitions.

"You bet," she said. "But let me have the overalls. You take your shirt back."

"Nonsense."

He stepped deeper into the mine and used the flame to light up the floor of the shaft. No crawly creatures to bite them. He dripped some wax onto a rock, stuck the candle there. Then he removed his shoes, stripped off his pants, and tossed them to her. He gave the overalls a good shake and slipped them on. By the time he had his second shoe tied, she had his pants pulled on and was cinching the belt around her waist.

"How do I look?" he asked, holding his hands out to the side.

She snickered and said, "Like a farmer, or a miner in this case."

"The eighth dwarf?"

"Not hardly."

He smiled and retrieved the candle. The tunnel continued beyond the reach of the light from the single flame. He took a few steps and stopped. He couldn't think of any reason to venture farther, yet. He made a visual sweep of their portion of the cave. No ghosts, just a couple of spiders hovering on webs high in the shoring timbers.

"Now we sit and wait for daylight," he said.

They cleared a few rocks from the floor of the shaft and sat down next to each other with their backs to the wall.

"Cozy," he said.

She snuggled close. "Very."

He slid his arm around her shoulders, blew out the candle, and stared through the mouth of the tunnel at the wedge of moonlit desert beyond. She was right; it did possess an undeniable beauty, and certain death.

Chapter 53

JACK WAS GLAD to have Katie snuggled tightly against him. The mineshaft provided some protection from the night chill, but not much.

Ellery, he was sure, would be complaining by now. He huffed to himself. Ellery wasn't anything like Katie.

"It sure seems someone doesn't want that ring to find its way into court," he said.

When Katie didn't answer, he figured she'd fallen asleep. Sitting there in the dark, he couldn't see whether her eyes were closed or not. Like him, she could be staring into the night, thinking about the events over the last couple of days. Or she could have finally given in to exhaustion. He leaned his head back and closed his eyes.

"Brian Wesley is behind this, you know," she said after another moment of silence passed.

He opened his eyes and said, "I thought you'd fallen asleep."

"No, just thinking about what you said."

"What I said?"

"That someone doesn't want the ring in court," she said.

"And you think Brian Wesley's that person—your father's former business partner?"

"I do."

"That's bold thinking. Why him?"

"The alarm being shut off at the house—I know I set it that night. He has the combination. Also, besides Moira and possibly her secretary, he's the only other person who knew about the ring."

"And when he couldn't find the ring in the house, he sent King Kong to get it from you?"

"Not just get," she said, "Take! And something tells me he wanted me dead, too."

"If he *is* after that ring, it makes sense he wouldn't want you around as a witness."

"Or you," she said. "You can bet Brian Wesley wanted us both dead."

Jack hadn't considered that possibility: she could very well be right. "So what you're saying is, that once Brian Wesley had the ring and you out of the picture, he'd send that big goon to take care of me. Which means he wants to make sure your father stays in prison?"

"Right. And without any loose ends."

"You and me."

"Right," she said.

"And your father's attorney."

She didn't answer.

He asked, "Why would he want to do that?"

"I don't know," she said. "But we have to get the ring to someone who can help Dad."

"You did well, you know?"

"How do you mean?"

"Hitting King Kong over the head and running out of the house like you did. And out there in the desert, the way you kept going even when you couldn't. And not being afraid to help me check out this mine. You've got guts. No doubt about that."

"Thank my Grandpa Charles. He's the one who taught me to be a fighter."

"He seems like a tough old bird. I like him. The way he talked about the battle of Saipan...man that was a nasty fight."

"Did he tell you he was shot in the leg during that battle, and that he killed over a dozen Japanese in their final attack?"

"No he didn't," he said. "Your grandfather told me Lee Marvin had been shot in the butt there. But he didn't say a thing about himself."

She smiled. "Grandpa gets a chuckle out of that story. But I don't believe he thinks it's at all funny."

"Maybe it's his way of coping with the horror of war."

A few beats of silence passed then she said, "Can you believe Grandpa taught me to shoot a gun? Right out here in the desert—bottles and cans for targets, that sort of thing. Thought I should learn how to use one. You know, just in case."

"In case King Kong attacks you in your house?"

"Exactly," she said. "And there I was without a gun."

"Would've been nice if you'd had one," he said. "But you didn't need to pump that goon full of lead; you did just fine with the vase."

"Jack," she said, "that was leaded crystal."

They both chuckled.

He didn't need to be a trained investigator to know Brian Wesley was behind the attack on Katie at her house earlier in the night—and probably even Moira's death. What didn't make any sense was why Brian Wesley would go to such lengths to keep Katie's father locked away.

"I don't know," he said. "Why would your father's former partner care if your father was released from prison?"

"It doesn't make sense, unless—"

He felt her straighten next to him.

She said, "He killed my mother and let Dad take the fall for it, that's why."

It seemed to Jack she was reaching for answers. "And Wesley did that because—?"

"Because he was the one having an affair with her."

"How can you say that for sure?"

"You're kidding," she said. "We're out here in this fricking cold-assed desert in the middle of the night, half naked and freezing our butts off inside an old mineshaft because Brian Wesley sent that big goon to get the ring, and kill me. Isn't that enough?"

"It means Wesley wanted the ring," he said. "Which tells me he wants your father rotting in prison. It doesn't mean he murdered your mother, or even that they were having an affair."

"No?" she said. "Why else would he kill to make sure blame didn't shift from dad to someone else? The police might figure out he was the one who murdered Mom, that's why."

He could see the logic in her thinking. She had taken a giant mental leap in her deduction, but she had the benefit of eleven years of supposition to help her piece together the puzzle.

"You're right," he said. "I'm sorry—sorry for what he did."

Katie sighed and said, "Me too."

"Jack," she said a moment later, "it's not just that Brian Wesley wants to see Dad stay in prison that makes me think he and Mom were having an affair. And that he killed her. There's more. A lot of little things that don't necessarily mean much by themselves, but when you stack them all together—"

He waited for her to finish, but she had fallen silent. Finally he said, "Tell me what happened, Katie. Can you do that? I mean, would it bother you too much to talk about it?"

"You deserve to know everything that happened," she said. "I told you mom was found dead inside the houseboat. The investigation revealed she had been beaten to death with a cast-iron frying pan. Can you believe it, a fucking frying pan from her own stove? The cops found it in the sink—her blood and hair were all over it."

"How'd she come to be up there on the lake in your family's houseboat that night—in February?"

"I don't really know. The night before, Mom got a phone call at home. It was a few minutes before eight o'clock. I remember because I was in my room doing homework while I waited for a show I liked to come on TV. When I asked her who called, she told me Dad had. And that he told her not to worry." Katie exhaled a loud breath. "I still remember hoping it was him on the phone. In my heart I knew he was going to walk into the house any minute and we'd be a happy family again."

"But he didn't?"

"No," she said. "Not that day. Mom seemed edgy and upset after getting the call from Dad. She paced the house until about 10 o'clock that night, then she told me she going out for a while and that everything was okay, that she was going to make things right with Dad." She huffed and added, "I told the stupid detectives what she'd said to me, and the lousy prosecutor used my statement against Dad during his trial."

"But that doesn't mean he killed your mother."

"I never thought so either. But that's the way the prosecutor made it look."

"So what happened after your mother left the house?"

"I stayed up about an hour watching TV and then went to bed. When I got up that next morning Mom wasn't home, and her bed hadn't been slept in. At first, I had my hopes up that she had spent the night with Dad. But when she didn't call that morning, I got worried and stayed home from school to wait for her."

He searched out her hand in the gloom and gave it a reassuring squeeze.

She paused a moment at his touch. "Around noon, I called Uncle Brian. Jesus, I can't believe I grew up calling him Uncle Brian. Anyway, he tells me he hadn't seen my mother and that he was starting to worry. I always thought it was strange Brian hadn't called the house to check on Mom since he knew my dad and her had argued and that she hadn't shown up for work."

"One more straw on the camel's back, huh?"

"What's that?"

"One more mark against Brian Wesley. You said it was a culmination of little things that led you to believe he murdered your mom."

"That's right," she said, "another straw."

"So, then what?"

"Later that same afternoon, the detective working my mother's case came to the house. That's when I found out Mom was dead. The detective had traced the houseboat to High Desert Security—Dad must have been writing it off through the business. Good old Uncle Brian had been only too happy to tell the cop about the argument between Mom and Dad. And that was something else I thought was strange: Brian not calling to let me know the police had been to the office; and *him* not personally giving me the horrid news about my mother."

"More straws."

"More straws," she said.

"And your dad?"

"He came home four days later. I was still in protective custody at the time. But I found out from Moira the police arrested him at the front door. I can't believe they had been sitting there the whole time just waiting for him to come home."

"If I was to guess, I'd say Brian Wesley knew and probably tipped the cops off that your dad was back in town."

"Dad did say he had called Brian to tell him he was on his way home from the airport."

"Let's add another straw."

"That fucker," she said. "Brian is going to pay. I'm going to make sure of that."

Chapter 54

JACK FELT HER anger and listened to her say *I*. But she wasn't alone, now. He was in it with her. All the way.

"*We*," he said.

"We," she agreed. "Sorry."

"You've had a tough time of it," he said. "I have to admire your grit."

"Yeah, well, as I told you, I had help—my aunt and Grandpa. I couldn't have made it without them."

"From what I've seen of your grandpa, he's a real character. If your aunt is anything like him it's no wonder you've turned out to be the strong, determined woman you are."

"With Mom dead and Dad in prison, Aunt Regina was the closest thing I had to a mother; and Grandpa McIntyre the closest thing I had to a father. I love both of them to death. They put their lives on hold so they could help me keep my life on track during some—I hate to admit—very difficult and impressionable high-school years. And Grandpa was the one who paid my way through dental hygiene school."

"Do you like being a dental hygienist—putting your hands in people's mouths and scraping their teeth? Sounds about as much fun as stripping barnacles off the bottom of a boat."

"Well, I enjoy making my patients want to smile. And I like meeting people. It's nice to know not everyone in the world is bad. So what do you do? Work, I mean. You never have told me what you do for a living?"

"I didn't think you'd be interested. And since it doesn't matter—"

"Of course I'm interested," she said, interrupting. "It's just that, well—"

Jack smiled to himself. "I know."

He waited for her to say more, but she didn't.

He continued, "Right now I'm not sure. Mostly I captain a fishing boat. Not that interesting a job, really."

What he wanted to tell her was that he was engaged to a rich drop-dead gorgeous blonde and that he was her father's *yes-sir* man. But he couldn't quite bring himself to say the words.

She said, "But you like doing it, right?"

"My father runs a commercial salmon boat out of Fields Landing near Eureka in Northern California—or I should say my younger brother does now. I grew up fishing."

"You sound as though you're tired of that kind of life?"

"I like boats; and I like fishing—when that's what I feel like doing. I just don't want to do it for a living."

"Then do something different."

He paused a second "I just might."

A pack of coyotes yipped in the distance.

They both listened to the eerie sound.

"What about boyfriends?" he asked, when the yipping stopped. "Surely there's a man in your life?"

"Not really," she said. "There's a guy I see on occasion, but we have our own priorities. I don't think either of us feels strongly enough about the relationship to give up our freedom for the sake of a commitment."

"How does he feel about what's happened in your life?"

He could almost see her shrug.

"Richard's supportive, or at least he tries to be."

"Must be that freedom thing," Jack said.

"And you?" she asked. "You're not married, what about girlfriends?"

She had him. He had to be honest with her.

"I'm engaged," he said. "But I don't know. Things don't seem to be working out."

"You miss her?"

"I thought I would, but no, not really."

"And you're engaged?"

"I have a feeling I might not make the wedding."

"That'd be too bad."

"I'm not so sure," he said.

She didn't answer.

He waited.

She said, "Thank you for being honest. That kind of sincerity is rare in a man."

He said, "So this Richard guy—no commitments there?"

"None."

"But if the right guy came along, you'd commit?"

She snuggled closer.

"I suppose I would," she said.

He slipped into thought and she didn't say more. Sitting in silence, his back to the earthen wall, the cold of the desert night settled in. He wished they still had her fuzzy white robe for a blanket.

He crossed his arms over his chest and pulled his knees up tightly against them to ward off the chill seeping into his bones. The quiet solitude reminded him of the long, lonely hours he had spent salmon fishing on the ocean.

He'd always used that time to ponder what was and what could be. And sitting there in the darkened cave, in the middle of a vast wasteland waiting for daylight, was much the same as sitting in a boat waiting for a fish to strike.

The cold kept him from falling asleep, but the chill didn't stop his mind from working. An hour later, he was still thinking about his future with Ellery.

All at once he noticed a circle of light sweep over the rocks outside.

The beam came from above.

King Kong.

He figured the lughead had to be peering down the slope from the rock pile above.

The best possible angle for them to not be noticed.

He pulled the shovel close and gripped the handle. Holding his breath, he waited.

Katie stirred next to him and settled again as she resumed her peaceful cooing.

He decided not to wake her.

Not yet.

The circle of light swept back over the rocks, then moved farther out into the rugged landscape.

He slowly exhaled and listened.

All he could hear was the pounding of his heart and the yipping of coyotes in the distance.

He maintained his vigil for a good half-hour. The flashlight beam did not reappear and no ghostly shape materialized at the mouth of the tunnel.

He allowed himself to relax, figuring Wesley's thug must have tired of his search and moved on. That's what he hoped.

He set the shovel aside, and once again drew his knees up in front of him. The cold crept in on him more than before. He shivered and hugged himself. Perhaps the bitter air that threatened to freeze them had driven their pursuer to cover.

An ally in Mother Nature.

He was beginning to doze when something startled him wide awake. Maybe one or two of the coyotes had wandered nearby. Or perhaps it was just the lonely desert night playing games with his imagination.

He watched and listened.

The moon hung low in the sky beyond the mouth of the mineshaft, filling the tunnel with its cool light. Katie was sleeping soundly, and as far as he could see, nothing but a gentle breeze stirred the scraggly brush outside.

He dismissed whatever it was that had alerted him and shut his eyes.

But they popped back open.

He couldn't sleep until he knew they were safe.

Chapter 55

JACK BLINKED SEVERAL times and peered through the opening of the mine-shaft. The sky was starting to lighten with the rising sun. He must have dozed off, and checked his watch: a few minutes before six.

He could see Katie more clearly now. She was still asleep and he hated to wake her. But with it getting light outside, they needed to try and get back to town. They couldn't hide in the cave indefinitely.

"We need to get going," he said, nudging her awake.

"What?" she said and blinked.

"Time to go," he said.

She stretched and yawned, then cringed. "Jesus, my feet are sore. Hope I can walk."

"Me too." He nodded at her tattered slippers. "The next time you're chased out of the house in the middle of the night by some goon, wear your hiking boots."

She narrowed her eyes and her expression hardened. But just as quickly, a minute upward curl of her lips betrayed her appreciation of his humor. "Next time? You talk like this is the sort of thing I do for fun."

He shrugged. "I don't know what you do on Saturday nights. You could dance naked for all I know."

"Not in the desert," she said.

He extended his hand. "Let me help you up."

She gripped his fingers and heaved.

"I'll admit I do like to skinny dip whenever possible," she said as he pulled her to her feet. "But I only dance naked on Fridays. And this little episode, I assure you, is one experience I never want to repeat."

He grinned. "What do you think…can you walk?"

She tried a couple of careful steps.

He watched. Her feet had to hurt.

She said, "I'm not up for any marathons, but I'm sure I'll be all right once I get moving."

"I hope so. I'd hate to have to carry you out of here."

"You're full of compliments this morning."

"That'll improve once I've had my coffee," he said. "Wait here while I see if our pal King Kong is still around."

He took a quick peek from the entrance.

No one.

He stepped outside, looked around, and climbed the slope to the top of the rocky drop off.

No one.

The cruel, unforgiving landscape looked different in the early morning light: still bleak and desolate, but not so foreboding. The desert was tranquil and possessed a unique beauty. The beauty Katie had talked about. Peering far into the distance, he could see his rental Mustang, but not the Tahoe. King Kong had apparently given up and left.

For now.

He scanned the route he had taken on foot the night before to lead the brute away from Katie and the stone outcropping. In the daylight it didn't look as if he'd run far, but it had seemed like forever in the dark. A couple of miles away small specks moved in both directions along the highway.

"Is he gone?" Katie asked from behind him.

He cocked an ear in the direction of her voice, but kept his focus on the horizon in front of him. "I thought I asked you to wait in the mine?" There was a hint of irritation in his voice.

"You did," she said. "But if it's safe for you to be out here, then it's safe for me."

"And if he'd been out here waiting for us?"

"Then I would have hit him with this."

He glanced back at her with an involuntary smile. She stood holding the shovel in both hands like a crude battleaxe.

His Viking-girl warrior.

"I bet you would," he said. "But I don't believe that's going to be necessary. I think he's gone."

She stepped to his side and peered in the direction of the highway. She looked a mess after their night in the mineshaft. And beautiful.

"What's the plan?" she asked. "I'm sure you've come up with one by now."

"You think so, huh?"

"I do."

"It so happens you're right," he said. "I think we ought to hide that ring here in the mine where it'll be safe. That will at least give us some bargaining power if things go to shit on us. If need be, we could tell Wesley we left the ring and a note with a friend, explaining everything along with instructions to turn both the ring and the note over to the police if anything happened to us."

"I think I saw that in a movie once."

"I'm sure you did. I never said I was original."

"Okay. And then?"

"Then we take that shovel you are so partial to back to the car and see if we can dig a path out of the sand. I'd rather drive to town than walk."

She handed him the shovel and said, "Time's a wastin'."

That was all Jack needed to hear. He led her back to the mineshaft and found a suitable hiding place for the ring: a rusty bean can wedged into a narrow gap behind a shoring timber five feet inside the entrance.

"I don't think anyone will find it there, unless we want them to," he said.

She nodded. "Let's get out of here."

He led her back up the hill, helping her across the rocks when he needed to, taking his time so as to not rush her. It was obvious her feet hurt.

When they were a hundred or so yards away from the rock outcropping, he looked behind him. The rocks that had been dark shapes in the night, now stood out as two monoliths extending at a slight angle to each other forming a sort of V.

For victory.

But only a partial triumph. Even so, that was enough. He was sure they'd be able to find their way back to those rock pillars—their Stonehenge in the middle of the Nevada wasteland.

In daylight it didn't take long for them to reach the Mustang. Another victory of sorts, he figured. Then not.

Even though their ride sat where they abandoned it, with its rear wheels buried in the sand, the car wasn't as they had left it. He rushed forward the last few feet and stopped. The convertible roof was ripped to shreds, the windows were shattered, tires flattened, and there were at least a half-dozen bullet holes in the hood.

Now he knew what had startled him awake when he'd dozed off that first time: gunshots. He dropped the shovel and stepped to the passenger's door. He peered through the hole where the window had been.

"We can forget about the car," he said. "King Kong took the keys."

Katie managed a laugh. "We were about out of gas anyway."

He looked her up and down, then glanced at his own ratty overalls. The two of them were a sorry sight, indeed. She looked like a bag lady and he looked like something that had blown in off the desert.

Which—in a way—he had. They both had.

He stroked the thick stubble on his chin. "We're not exactly dressed for a trip to the big city, Ethel. And I sure didn't want to have to walk there. But it looks like that's what we're gonna be doin'."

Chapter 56

JACK AND KATIE walked along the dirt road to the highway. She bet him they wouldn't catch a ride with anyone, not the way they looked. He assured her they would. An old guy with weathered features and a white beard, driving a Dodge pickup truck nearly as old as he was, pulled over and let them climb in the back.

"I win," Jack said to Katie when they were seated in the bed of the truck.

"I'm glad you did," she said. "But technically you didn't bet. You only told me we would. So, no prize."

"No?"

"That's right."

"We'll see," he said.

The old guy dropped them off at the first mini mart he came to in town. Jack thanked him and waved him off.

"Now we call a cab," he said.

"Tell me again why we're not calling 911?"

"Because they'd send a patrolman. You need to talk directly with a detective, today. Not wait around for one to contact you it in a day or two."

"So we go straight to the police department?"

"After we go to your house."

"After?"

"Look at us." He motioned with his hand at her and then himself. "And I stink."

"All right," she agreed. "We go to the house first."

He took a step, but stopped when she gently gripped the back of his arm above the elbow as if to hold him there.

He straightened and joked, "What, Ethel? Now I'm not good enough to be seen with you?"

She planted her hands on her hips and said, "Don't be that way, Fred. You know you can take the man out of the desert, but you can't take the desert out of the man."

"I had no idea you were so sensitive about what people think."

She chuckled. "When we go inside the store, let me do the talking. At least I won't scare the clerk."

He grinned. "Be my guest."

The cab arrived fifteen minutes later, with a Sikh driver dressed much better than them. They rode in the taxi to within a block of her house. He asked Katie to pull his wallet from the rear pocket of his pants, since she was wearing them, and paid the driver with cash.

"We'll walk from here," he said. "Someone might be watching the house, waiting for us to show up. I want to check the neighborhood out before we got too close."

"The neighborhood looks normal to me," she said. "I don't see the Tahoe anywhere"

"Don't be so sure."

"Do you really think King Kong would chance hanging around here, knowing we'd come back with the police?"

"We're not coming back with the police."

"He doesn't know that."

"I'm not sure that big lughead knows much of anything. He didn't look that smart to me. More muscle and bone than brain matter. But Brian Wesley *is*. And I'm betting he'll hang tight until he sees if any of this is going to come back on him. But, you never know."

"Brian's smart all right. And he doesn't give up easily. Let's get inside the house before my neighbors see us."

They jogged across the street and up the sidewalk. The front door to her house was still ajar.

They paused.

"Are you sure you're willing to go in there?" he asked.

She furrowed her brow. "This was your idea, remember?"

"Maybe it wasn't such a good one."

"*Now* you say that!"

They both eyed the door.

She said, "We're here. Let's go."

Chapter 57

HE CHUCKLED, HURRYING to catch up to her as she rushed into the house ahead of him.

"At least take it slowly," he said.

She stopped a few feet inside the door and glanced around the living room. He stood next to her. The glass from the broken vase was on the floor where it had fallen after she smashed it over King Kong's head. The coffee table in front of the sofa was knocked over, but the place didn't look ransacked. Which meant no one had raided the house after the attack on Katie.

Even so, that didn't mean no one was hiding inside, waiting for her return.

He glanced at her. She appeared to be listening and he did the same.

Nothing.

He watched her tiptoe over the glass shards and step to the kitchen counter. He stayed put. Returning to the house without the police had not been one of his better ideas. If no one were there now, he was sure it was only a matter of time before King Kong or another one of Brian Wesley's goons came back to finish the job. The thought of that made him nervous.

"What are you doing?" he asked. "Get your clothes and let's go! I don't want to be here when one of Wesley's enforcers comes back."

She tossed him an apple and took a small bite of one, herself. She chewed and swallowed. "Relax," she said. "No one's here. Besides, goons only come out at night."

"A known fact, huh?"

"Sure is."

He didn't share her confidence.

She took another bite of her apple and padded over to the refrigerator.

He walked to the kitchen counter where he could keep a close eye on her.

She handed him a bottle of water and winked. "Be back in a few minutes," she said. "I want to take a hot shower and change into my own clothes before we go to the police. And it wouldn't hurt you a bit to at least wash your face. You look as though you spent the night in a cave."

"Me?"

She grinned.

He watched her walk away, down the hallway leading to what he assumed were the bedrooms. For half a second, he debated following her: she might not be safe. But she needed her privacy. A full minute later he heard a door close and a shower come on.

He couldn't believe she was so calm.

The hum of running water raised a vision of her standing naked in the hot spray.

He took a deep breath and let it out. He couldn't believe he was thinking about those things now, not after what had just gone on!

He took a bite of his apple and peered down at the grungy overalls he was wearing. They were filthy, and he no doubt smelled as bad as whatever it was that had died, deep in that mineshaft.

Maybe she wouldn't mind if he joined her? Just open the door and step into the shower as if he had been invited.

The sound of the water being turned off saved him from fantasizing further. Then he thought about toweling her dry.

He had to get his mind back on track.

Outside he heard a brief crunch of tires on gravel followed by a thump-thump, a slight screech of brakes and a car door slamming.

He crept to the window. His stomach tied itself into a knot as he separated the blinds to take a look.

Across the street a neighbor was lifting grocery bags from the back seat of a blue 4-door Volvo sedan.

He exhaled his held breath and swallowed.

At the sounds of Katie moving around in a back room he returned to his vantage point near the hallway entrance and peered down the corridor. The door to a bedroom at the far end was open, and in plain view, at the foot of a bed, was a rumpled bath towel. She was in there, but around the corner and out of sight.

He chewed on another bite of apple and watched. If only she would walk by the door without any clothes on, just once! Maybe then he could let go of the fantasy building inside him. But that was wishful thinking. It would take more than a mere glance at Katie's naked body to make him forget about her.

"Perhaps you should hurry?" he said.

She appeared in the doorway to the bedroom as if on cue, dressed in jeans and a lightweight sweater. In her left hand she held a small overnight bag, in her right his shirt and pants.

She smiled and tossed him his clothes as she walked toward him. "Your turn, big boy!" She nodded at the half-open door to her right. "There's an extra bar of soap in the cabinet under the sink if you need it. I think you do. And a clean towel on the counter."

For sure she had caught him trying to peek into her room, and he only hoped his face wasn't as red as it felt. He took a step toward the bathroom, and she pushed open the door for him.

"Enjoy," she said, pinching her nose with her fingers.

From the grin on her face when she let go of her nose, he knew she was toying with him.

She seemed to have a knack for not making it easy for him and that made him even more nervous. Just being in the house made him apprehensive, and controlling his ever-growing fantasy about her was making it worse. This was definitely not the time for flirtatious games.

"I'll be out in a minute," he said, edging past her.

As he stepped into the bathroom, he undid one overall strap and let the corner of the bib fall away, exposing the matted hair on chest. When he turned to close the door, he saw Katie lingering in the hallway, looking at him.

Damn those beautiful emerald green eyes! And those wonderfully thick eyebrows!

He wondered if she was having the same thoughts about seeing him in the shower as he'd had about seeing her. Even in the filthy overalls he was confident about his body. Women liked the way he looked, liked his muscles. But this just wasn't the time.

Damn!

"We do need to get going," he said with a hint of regret.

"I'll get the car warmed up."

He watched her walk away, then closed the door.

Ten minutes later he walked into the living room, scrubbed clean. But his Dockers and Aloha shirt were still dirty and wrinkled from the night in the desert.

Katie stood at the kitchen counter waiting for him. She smiled. "Better," she said. "Can't change the looks but you at least smell good."

"The improved me," he said. "Let's get going. The sooner we get the police solving this mess, the sooner I can get into a change of clothes."

She led the way into her garage where they took their seats in her Camry and buckled themselves in. She started the engine and looked at him.

He nodded.

She said, "Here we go," and pressed the garage door opener.

Chapter 58

JACK TURNED SIDEWAYS in his seat and scanned the neighborhood as Katie backed her Camry onto the roadway. Before the car had even come to a full stop, she had slipped the transmission into drive. The car lurched forward with a chirp of the tires.

"Are you in a hurry?" he asked.

"I want this over with," she said.

"Getting into a wreck on the way won't help matters."

"I'm a good driver," she said. "Hold on."

They made it to the police station in record time. He pointed out an open parking space close to the building, and she whipped her car into it.

He said, "Since you're the one who was attacked, you probably should do the talking. Besides, you know more about what is going on than I do."

"I planned on it," she said. "But feel free to jump in any time."

"No problem."

He glanced at her clean clothes, then at his shirt, and said, "I still look the part, too. That might help some."

She glanced at him, nodded, and arched a thick brow. "But you smell better. And I'm glad for that."

"Me too," he replied, and climbed out of the car.

He held open the door to the police station and followed her inside the lobby. She stepped directly to the reception counter and told the female officer on duty that she wanted to speak to a detective in the Crimes Against Persons Unit. The officer told her to have a seat and wait.

Jack liked Katie's bold style. "Where'd you pick up that fancy lingo?" he asked when they were sitting down.

"My father is in jail for murder, remember? It's amazing what you can learn if you listen."

Less than two minutes later, the female officer called them to the counter. She then buzzed them through a door leading to a long corridor, to which she pointed with an accompanying nod of her head.

"Lieutenant Voyles' office is through the door on the right and across the room," she said. "You can't miss it."

"Thank you," Jack said.

They walked down the corridor, opened the indicated door, and stepped into a large room with desks arranged nose to nose. A detective stood hunched over one of the desks, talking on the phone. There was only one private office, and it was glassed in against the far wall. Wide vertical blinds hung from the ceiling on the other side of the glass to offer privacy. They were open. An impeccably dressed man in his late forties sat behind the desk inside.

Katie led the way. Jack followed.

He made a note of the name painted on the door: Lieutenant Harvey Voyles.

She knocked on the metal doorframe, and they waited.

The lieutenant looked up from his work and straight at Katie. He smiled and rose from his chair.

Jack noticed the lieutenant's gaze wander up and down Katie's body.

"I'm Lieutenant Voyles," he said. "What can I do for you?"

Jack didn't usually make snap judgments about people, but there was something about the way Lieutenant Voyles looked at Katie that told him he was not going to like the guy.

And there was something else that didn't sit right with him. The lieutenant was a bit too fashionable. Not at all what Jack considered appropriate for an over-worked, underpaid cop. He was tall, fit, well tanned, and dressed in a designer-label suit. His salt and pepper hair looked as if it had just been styled in a posh salon on the Strip.

That's what irked Jack. The lieutenant appeared more concerned with how he'd look standing next to Catherine Willows on the set of CSI, than solving real cases and arresting criminals.

Jack and Katie stepped inside the office, but remained standing.

Katie stiffened. "A big goon attacked me at my house last night," she said. "The guy meant to kill me, and I know who put him up to it, and why."

Lieutenant Voyles motioned toward the two straight-backed chairs directly across from his desk. "Please, have a seat," he said. "Tell me what happened."

She chose to stand and spent the next fifteen minutes telling him how she was attacked inside her house. That her assailant was after a West Point class ring, which her grandfather had given her father, and that he had chased them into the desert, where they spent the night in an old mineshaft. She told him they had hidden the ring to keep it safe. But she didn't divulge the location.

Lieutenant Voyles' eyes remained on her. He didn't ask where.

Jack added the part about the Tahoe almost running Katie down at Denny's. Given everything that had happened to them, he thought he should. There was no doubt in his mind the two incidents were connected.

"He meant to have that ring," she added. "And he would have killed me to get his hands on it. Brian Wesley is the only person who could have sent that big goon to my house." She planted her hands on her hips and stood resolute.

Lieutenant Voyles' lips spread into a thin smile.

Jack found none of what she'd said amusing. He really didn't like this guy.

"Interesting," Lieutenant Voyles said. "Why would Brian Wesley want to do that?"

She took a step closer, leaned forward, and rested her hands on the edge of the lieutenants' desk.

Jack liked her style.

She said, "Because he killed my mother and let my father take the fall for her murder, that's why."

The smile slipped from Lieutenant Voyles' face.

Jack figured the man was getting it.

Voyles said, "This ring, you have it with you, now?"

Her eyes fixed on his. "No, I told you, we hid it."

"So you did," he said. "Tell me, what makes this ring so important?"

She took a deep breath, exhaled, and straightened. "The ring proves my father is innocent," she said. "That he wasn't lying when he claimed he was in Maui at the time of my mother's murder."

Chapter 59

JACK WATCHED THE expression change on Lieutenant Voyles' face. If the officer hadn't understood before, he did now.

Voyles asked, "How does this ring you claim to have, do that?"

Katie said, "You're not aware of the case?"

"Refresh my memory."

"My dad traveled to Maui under a false name," she said. "That was dumb, but he did. In court he swore that while he was there he lost the ring while diving in an area called Turtle Town. A couple of weeks ago, Jack was diving on that same reef and found the ring. He returned it to my grandfather. And that's how I got it. I planned to turn the ring over to my dad's attorney Moira Tuscano, but she was murdered before we had a chance to meet with her."

Jack added, "Wesley probably killed her, too."

Lieutenant Voyles gave them a long investigatory look. "I've seen the reports on that case," he said. "Evidence suggests Ms. Tuscano walked in on a burglary. A crackhead ripping her off to get enough money for a fix, probably."

"Or that big goon, looking for the ring," Katie said.

Lieutenant Voyles refrained from comment.

Jack could almost hear the wheels squeaking inside the man's head.

After a pause, Voyles said, "For a moment let's play like I don't know what's going on here. Why in God's name would Brian Wesley have murdered your mother? And why would he send someone to kill Ms. Tuscano?"

"Because he's a pig," Katie said. "He and my mother were having an affair, and she tried to break it off. Moira Tuscano was my father's attorney, and I told Wesley I was going to turn the ring over to her. Use your imagination. You're the cop."

The Lieutenant leaned back in his chair, his narrow lips curled in a contemptuous smile.

Jack was getting fed up with the guy's smugness.

Voyles said, "Just because Brian Wesley was screwing your mother, doesn't mean he killed her. As for Ms. Tuscano, I sure as hell can't think of any reason he'd want that bitch attorney dead."

Katie winced and Jack's jaw muscles tightened.

He could have hit the guy, cop or not. "Show some respect, Lieutenant. You're talking about the lady's mother. And you can keep your opinions of Ms. Tuscano to yourself."

Lieutenant Voyles rocked forward in his chair. "Don't tell me how to talk ,or what to think or say," he said. "The two of you are making accusations without anything to back them up, except a daughter's love for her cheating mother and dirtbag father."

Jack tensed.

Katie grabbed his arm. He stayed put.

"Screw you, Lieutenant!" she said. "That big lummox attacked me in my house. I hit him with a vase and the broken glass is on the floor, if you care to take a look. His blood and hair are probably on it."

"Watch how you talk to me," Lieutenant Voyles warned. "I'll send a patrolman by for a look. But that still doesn't prove Brian Wesley had anything to do with it."

She sighed, clearly frustrated. "Lieutenant, my father claimed he was in Maui at the time of my mother's murder. The ring proves it. And Jack here is the man who found it. Besides Moira Tuscano, I've only told one person about him having found the ring. And that's Brian Wesley. Who else could it be?"

Lieutenant Voyles shook his head. "It might look that way to you, but it's also possible Brian Wesley mentioned the ring to someone who mentioned it to someone else. Or maybe the wrong person overheard the two of *you* talking—gold prices being what they are. Word gets around. What you're saying doesn't prove a thing."

She glanced away. Then she took a deep breath and faced Lieutenant Voyles. "My God, how many times do I have to tell you my dad said he went to Maui? That's exactly what he did. The ring proves he was there."

"It proves the ring was in Maui," he said. "Not that your father was there when the murder was committed."

"Honestly, Lieutenant, how else would the ring get there? Everyone who knew him testified he never took that ring off. It meant too much to him."

"Maybe staying out of prison meant more to him than some silly old ring."

"There's nothing silly about that ring," she said. "It was Grandpa Charlie's. He earned it."

"Just an expression," he said.

She said, "Dad had a sunburn, in *February*. What'd he do, sit in a tanning booth somewhere?"

"Possibly. He could've done a lot of things. A desperate man does whatever necessary to vindicate himself when he's facing a murder charge."

Again she exhaled a deep breath and glanced to the side. When she faced him again, a tear hung in the corner of her eye. She brushed it away with the tips of her fingers. "I don't understand. Why are you refusing to believe Brian Wesley is responsible for what's happened to me, to my family?"

He didn't answer.

"Can't you see what's going on here? It all adds up. Besides myself and Jack, two people knew Jack had found the ring: my father's attorney Moira Tuscano and his ex-partner Brian Wesley. Moira's dead. Brian's not. The man wants that ring. And he wants my dad in prison. Why? Because Brian killed my mother, that's why."

Lieutenant Voyles rocked forward, planted his forearms firmly on his desk, and eyed them both. "Let me put it to you this way," he said. "I know Brian Wesley, personally. Brian and I meet and play golf at least once a month. We even get together for dinner from time to time. He donates money to the police fund, local youth groups, all sorts of community projects. I assure you, Brian isn't a man who goes around killing people."

Katie glared at him.

He stared back at her and added, "Or threatening young ladies."

She nodded almost imperceptibly, turned her head, and gave Jack a tiny smile of resolve, not pleasure. "You ready? I think we're done."

He said, "I am."

She faced the lieutenant without smiling. "Don't bother sending a car to my house," she said. "It was a mistake for us to come here."

Lieutenant Voyles didn't comment.

Jack had nothing to add. He waited for Katie to lead the way out and when she stepped past him, he followed. But at the doorway to the office, he paused and turned.

There *was* something he wanted to add.

Chapter 60

JACK FACED THE lieutenant, opened his mouth, and closed it. He wanted to tell Voyles to go fuck himself. And would have, if not for Katie.

He reconsidered and said, "Nice hair."

He turned and followed Katie.

She didn't say a word on their way out of the building and he let her simmer. She had a right to be mad. He was, too.

Voyles' apathy toward the attack on her, when someone clearly wanted her out of the way, permanently, was inexcusable. The man's judgment was clouded by his friendship with Wesley. He shouldn't have let that get in the way of doing his job.

Politics, and possibly a box or two of Cuban cigars at Christmas.

The thought of Lieutenant Voyles and Brian Wesley playing political footsies turned his stomach.

He climbed into the car and watched Katie climb in on the driver's side. She jammed the key in the ignition, started the engine, and pulled into traffic. She had yet to comment.

He said, "Can you believe that guy?"

"Fucking asshole," she said. "That's what he is. And a prick. That's another good name for him."

He gave her a sideways look and started laughing. Swearing just didn't fit her character. Not earlier, not now.

He'd heard her use foul language several times over the past few days. Each time it had seemed appropriate given the circumstances. But even so, the words sounded almost comical coming out of her mouth and now he couldn't help laughing.

She shot him a hard look.

He swallowed his laughter, mostly.

"What's so funny?" she asked.

"I don't know," he said. "You, me, that pompous prick Lieutenant Voyles, Brian Wesley, that big ape. There's not a damn thing funny about any of it, but for some reason I feel like laughing."

She focused on the road ahead, quiet. Then she started to laugh.

He looked at her: she looked at him.

They both laughed.

He had needed to laugh, and so had she. The tea kettle inside him had been simmering, about to explode. He figured it had been the same for her. The release helped keep him from coming apart at the seams, but he was not a happy camper, by any stretch of his imagination.

When he'd set out to return the ring to its rightful owner, he never imagined the quest would land him smack in the middle of a deadly game of hide and seek with a murderer. But it had, and he didn't have a choice in the matter, at least not one he was going to allow himself. He knew he could turn tail and run back to Maui any time he wanted to, but to do so would leave Katie to face Brian Wesley and his big goon alone. That was unacceptable.

Where would that leave me?

He thought about that for a moment. He'd never run out on Katie, but he didn't want to be served up like a turkey on a platter, either. Which was exactly the way he had felt more than once, and especially now that the police didn't seem all that concerned for Katie's safety or his. He might have expected that kind of questionable law enforcement from some backwoods small town, but he hadn't expected a response like that from the police department of a fast-growing Las Vegas suburb.

Jack was more than capable of coming up with several ideas of how they should proceed, but he wasn't calling the shots, Katie was. Which was fine with him. Since she was the real victim in everything that had happened so far, he was content to let her take the lead—at least for now. He'd just have to trust her to make the right decisions for both of them.

"Okay mighty leader," he said, "where to from here?"

"We're going to see my dad."

"So you decided it's time to tell him about the ring?"

"And talk some things over with him."

"Are you going to tell him about Brian Wesley?"

She nodded. "You bet."

"And you think that's wise?"

She shot him a wry smile. "I'll let you decide," she said, "once we've talked to my dad."

The gears in his mind started to grind.

What would prison do to an innocent man?

He leaned his head against the seat and closed his eyes. They'd been on the run since dawn. The morning was going by fast, and they had yet to resolve a thing. Moira was dead, and thanks to Lieutenant Voyles, Brian Wesley was free to continue his deadly I-want-that-ring game unless something happened that directly implicated him in a crime.

By then, Jack feared, it would be too late.

"We have to hurry," Katie said. "We need to be signed in before 10:00 to make morning visitation."

He'd gotten used to her driving. With his eyes closed, he said, "Just don't get us killed before we get there."

"And cheat Brian Wesley out of the pleasure?" she said. "Not a chance."

She pressed on the accelerator.

Chapter 61

THEY ARRIVED AT High Desert State Prison, forty miles northwest of Las Vegas, a few minutes before ten. The correctional facility was a sprawling complex of modern housing units, lethal electrical fencing, and gun towers.

Katie still didn't slow down.

The visitor lot was nearly full. She flew into the first available space, parked, and took off in a dead run toward the reception center. Jack followed closely behind her.

Cutoff time was only seconds away.

Jack and Katie both breathed a sigh of relief as they reached the counter with moments to spare.

"We're here to visit Michael Sean McIntyre," Katie said to the clerk.

Twenty minutes later, they walked into the dining hall. Her father, dressed in an orange jumpsuit, sat at a metal table waiting for them.

Jack immediately noticed that the man had Katie's dark brown hair, only his was graying on the sides and top. His thick mustache and a short beard were streaked with gray. His green eyes sat deep under a prominent brow, but at his temples the corners were heavily creased, making him appear years older than fifty-four.

But even from ten feet away, Jack could see the fire of life still burned.

Her father stood as they approached and gave them a big smile.

Katie stopped and gripped Jack's arm and for a second he wondered if something were wrong. Then he noticed that the sullen look she had worn, since their encounter with Lieutenant Voyles, had been replaced with a broad grin. Coming there had definitely been the right decision.

"If you wouldn't mind," she said, "I'd like to have a few minutes alone with my father before I introduce you to him."

"Take all the time you want," Jack said. "I'll wait right here."

He tried his best to look earnest and forthright in his dirty, wrinkled clothes, and watched Katie rush to her father.

While they talked quietly, Jack examined the sterile room. Inmates and their female visitors occupied several of the other metal tables. All were under the watchful eyes of a guard posted in a cage high on a wall. He'd seen scenes like this in movies. There was nothing intimate or cozy about these visitations. In person, they were even more cold and impersonal than they appeared on film.

"Jack," Katie said, waving him over, "I'd like you to meet my dad."

Jack stepped quickly to the table and extended his hand. "Glad to meet you, sir."

"Call me Sean."

Jack watched Katie and her father. Eleven years of prison hadn't dampened their love for each other.

He smiled. "Katie hasn't stopped talking about you since the two of us met."

Her father arched an eyebrow. "Is that right? Katie and I've been talking for five minutes, and all she's done is talk about you." He winked at Katie and added, "My daughter's everything to me. I want to thank you for all you've done, and especially for looking after her these past couple of days."

"I'm not sure who's been looking after whom," Jack said. "If you'll excuse me for saying so, your daughter is a beautiful lady."

Katie's gaze fixed on Jack.

He gave her a sly look. "And quite resourceful at times."

She blushed slightly.

"And determined," he added.

Sean McIntyre laid his hand on top of Katie's and said, "Katie hated me at first. Did you know that? She blamed me for her mother's death and hated me for it. But deep down she's always believed I was innocent. I love my daughter, and I'm relieved she was able to learn the truth."

Katie beamed at her father. "Jack, I told Dad that you found his ring in Maui and traced it to Grandpa at the retirement home in Boise." Her voice was bristling with excitement. "And that we plan to present the ring as evidence to get him out of this dreadful place."

"Did you tell him the other stuff?" Jack asked.

Her smile disappeared "I told him Moira was killed."

"And?"

"I told him everything," she said.

That brought a determined look from her father. "It flat pisses me off to know someone tried to hurt my daughter," Sean McIntyre said, between clenched teeth. "Which makes my being locked up in here that much worse. If I were out, I could protect her."

Katie reached across the table and gripped her Dad's hand. They looked at each other and there was no mistaking the love between them.

"How about our conversation with Lieutenant Voyles? Jack asked. "Did you run that past your dad?"

"That, too," she said. "Everything."

Sean McIntyre spoke up. "For some time, I've suspected Brian Wesley was responsible for my wife's murder. One thing about prison, you have a lot of time to think. I've spent many a long night in my bunk mulling over everything that happened, looking for answers. The long lunches away from the office, a sudden rash of unexplained absences, awkward glances between him and Angela."

His voice trailed off into silence.

Jack waited.

Sean McIntyre balled his hands into fists. "Brian Wesley was having an affair with my wife," he said. "And the rotten sonofabitch killed her. I'm sure of it."

Katie shot her father a wide-eyed look.

Jack was almost as surprised to hear it as she was.

She said, "That possibility never entered my mind until last night. Why didn't you tell me?"

"I didn't want to say anything to you without proof. I'd say this proves my suspicions."

"The burglary, Moira's murder, the attack on me and being chased into the desert by that gorilla," she added. "I'd say everything that's happened since that ring surfaced pretty much proves it."

Sean McIntyre glanced down at his fingers, pursed his lips and nodded.

Jack was content to listen.

Sean McIntyre said, "You know, Brian Wesley all but stole the security systems business from me."

"What do you mean?" she asked. "The trust fund, and Moira's bill? You said he bought you out."

"Brian did. And he paid me a sizable chunk of money. But nowhere near what the business was worth. Under the circumstances there was little I could do but take what Wesley offered. I'm not sure if that was part of some grand scheme on his part, or whether it just worked out that way, but I have to wonder."

"Grand scheme or not," she said, "the ring is a definite threat to his lifestyle. I know he likes to party, and according to Lieutenant Voyles he's gone out of his way to buy friends in the police department. I'm sure he's not going to stop until he gets his slimy hands on that ring. We have to do something to make sure that doesn't happen, and quickly."

"We all believe that Wesley murdered your wife," Jack exclaimed. "That's the only reason he would want the ring bad enough to kill for it. The question is, how do we stop him? Lieutenant Voyles made it clear he wasn't going to do anything. That means Katie and I are still targets for King Kong or anyone Brian Wesley sends after us to get that ring."

Sean McIntyre's eyes flashed from Jack to Katie. "Where's the ring now?"

She answered, "We stashed it in the old mine where we hid last night. We thought it would give us a bargaining chip if Wesley's thug got his hands on us once we were out of there."

He snorted, approvingly.

"That was probably a wise decision," he said. "It buys you a little time. But that's about all."

He clinched a fist, pounded the tabletop. "I'm sure he wants you dead. By now he has to know you're wise to what he's doing, and he can't afford to leave any witnesses around to make life difficult for him."

"And that's precisely what worries me," Jack muttered.

"Forget Lieutenant Voyles," Sean McIntyre said. "You need to take that ring to Detective Lipke."

"The cop that put you in here?" Katie asked in surprise.

"Lipke may have put me in prison, and I don't particularly like him for that. But in spite of how everything turned out, he seemed like an intelligent and fair man—someone you can trust to do what's right. I think he'll listen."

Chapter 62

JACK HAD TO believe Detective Lipke would be willing to help. Unless Wesley had donated heavily to the man's retirement fund, which at the moment seemed like a definite possibility.

"You okay?" he asked Katie, once they were outside and on their way to the parking lot.

She offered a wry smile and brushed her hand across her eyes. "I'm fine. Really. I've cried every time I walked out of that place, but this is the first time I walked through those doors feeling there's hope."

Her eyes sparkled with confidence. "My father has held onto the belief he would get out of prison someday," she said. "Thanks to you, he has a real chance of being released from here and having his name cleared."

"Don't sell yourself short, Katie. You're the one making this happen."

"Nonsense, Jack. Not many people in this world would have done what you did. You not only found the ring, you had the presence of mind to return it to my grandfather—not to mention your willingness to fly here and help set the record straight."

He took her hand and held it. She was looking at him with those magnificent green eyes of hers, and her lips were parted just right.

He wanted to kiss her more than anything, but settled for the warmth of her skin against his. "Hearing you say that means a lot," he said. "I'm glad I'm here with you."

She looked at him a moment longer. Then she gave him a quick peck on the cheek. "Me too."

They arrived at her Camry, and climbed in. Neither of them said anything as she began the drive back to town.

Not until Jack spotted a McDonalds. "You mind hitting the drive through? I'm starved."

"Now that you mention it," she said, "so am I." She made the turn into the parking lot and fell in line behind a half dozen other cars.

"I was thinking," he said. "Maybe we should call ahead just to make sure Detective Lipke is in his office and not out working a case or something?"

"I think that's a good idea," she said, digging her cell phone out of her purse. "I'll call information and get the number."

Jack reached over and snatched the phone from her hand. "You order, I'll make the call.

"Whatever you say, Fred. A Big Mac value meal okay with you?"

He grinned. "Super-size it."

She edged the car forward as the line moved, and he called information. As soon as he had the number, he made the call and asked to talk to Detective Lipke. He listened, thanked the woman, and switched the phone off.

"What happened?"

"Lipke retired three years ago," he said. "I thought you and I should talk before I asked to be transferred to someone else. I sure didn't want to end up talking to that dickhead Lieutenant Voyles."

She stared straight ahead and chewed the tip of her thumbnail. After a long moment of silence she said, "Dad believes Detective Lipke is the person we should talk to. I think we should try to contact him before we go to someone else with this. Even if he's retired, he's still a cop at heart. If he doesn't want to get involved, perhaps he'll at least steer us in the right direction."

"Okay. But how do we get his phone number? I really doubt he's listed in the phone book."

"Let's get our burgers. Then we'll call back and ask if someone there will pass along a message for him to call us."

Once they had their food orders, Katie parked in a space in the lot.

"Let me make the call this time," she said. "They might have questions."

"No doubt they will," he said, handing her the cell phone. "And we'll know if we're wasting our time or not. If we are, then we need to come up with another plan, and fast. I don't think Wesley is going to sit back and let us run around free to do whatever we want with that ring."

"Let's hope for the best," she said, and made the call.

She pressed the phone tight to her ear and said, "I'd like to speak to someone who could relay a message to Steve Lipke, a detective who retired a few years ago."

She paused. "No, it's an old case. A murder he worked eleven years ago, my mother's murder."

He watched her shake her head into the phone.

"I just need to talk to Detective Lipke," she said after a breath. "Can you get a message to him to call me as soon as possible? It's important that I speak with him."

She bit at her lower lip, started to say something, then listened. She had to be frustrated. Then she smiled. "Thank you," she said. "And I understand you can't promise he'll call. Just please tell him it's urgent."

She switched off the phone. "The receptionist promised she would pass the message along to him. So now we wait."

"Okay, so we wait. Any suggestions?"

"I'm not sure I want to go back to my house. How about your hotel?"

He didn't want to go back to her house any more than she did. But going to his hotel room might not be such a good idea either. For sure Brian Wesley knew where he was staying, and his room number. They were probably safer where they were, but he didn't want to sit in the McDonald's parking lot all afternoon.

"All right," he said. "My hotel it is. And let's just hope Detective Lipke calls soon."

It was twelve-thirty when she backed her car out of the parking space. She'd shifted into drive and was pressing on the gas pedal when her cell phone chirped. She jammed her foot on the brake, bringing the car to a jolting stop.

Jack's head jerked forward then back against the seat.

He recovered as she dug her cellular from her purse, flipped it open, and raised the phone to her ear without checking the number.

"This is Katie," she said. She nodded and listened and nodded some more.

Jack waited. He knew it was Lipke calling.

She told him about the ring, Moira's murder, the attack on her at her house, their being chased into the desert and the conversation they'd had with her father. It had apparently been enough to get the former detective's attention, because she pulled her checkbook out of her purse and scribbled directions down on the back of a deposit slip.

"I can't thank you enough," she said and closed her phone.

Jack figured it was good news. "Well?"

"He wants to talk to us. He gave me directions to his house and his phone number in case we get lost. His place is a bit of a drive from here, but he thinks it would be better for us to go there."

"Well let's get going. I certainly don't want to sit here any longer."

She floored the gas pedal and the car accelerated onto the roadway.

While they sped along, she said, "Lipke lives in a development named White Hills Equestrian Estates, near Boulder City. I've seen advertisements for that place. Five-acre lots offering pristine country living. Last I heard they are on the third phase, but from the pictures they show on TV not many people have built places there."

He thought about the overexpansion that had gone on everywhere. "Just so you know where we're going," he said.

The development where Steve Lipke lived was located south of Lake Mead, about fifty miles southeast of Henderson, just over the Arizona State line. They had to drive across Hoover Dam to get there. Lipke's prefab home sat on the far edge of the third phase, well away from the other homes in the development.

They stopped at the end of a dirt drive and saw a rail-thin man, in his late fifties, sitting in a folding aluminum chair on the porch of a doublewide. They noticed a gun lying across his lap.

"Jesus," Katie gasped. "Is that a rifle?"

"Or a shotgun," Jack answered. "Doesn't matter. Let's get out of here."

"I'm with you."

"Wait," he said, as she dropped the car into gear. "He just waved us up."

They watched the man stand up and lean the long barreled gun against the wall next to the front door.

"What do you think?" she asked.

"I'd say the gun isn't meant for us."

Chapter 63

JACK AND KATIE climbed out of her car and met at the front bumper. She said in a low voice, "That's him. Older and grayer, but just as tall. He's the man who put Dad in prison."

Jack figured the former detective was every bit of six foot five or six, and at least six eight in his cowboy hat. Being rail-thin made him look even taller.

"Well," Jack said. "He's the man who put your dad in that awful place. Let's hope he's the man who'll get your dad out."

"Detective Lipke," Katie said as they approached the steps leading up to the deck. "I'm Katie McIntyre. You remember me?" She nodded at Jack and added, "And this is Jack Ferrell."

"That's *former* detective," Lipke said. "And sure I remember you."

He noticed Jack eyeing the gun leaning against the wall and said, "Don't worry about the shotgun. I've had some problems with coyotes."

"Coyotes?" Jack said, glancing around at the barren subdivision.

Lipke jabbed a finger toward a chicken wire pen at the side of the house and said, "They're after my pheasants. That's what I do now, raise game birds for rich people to hunt. Come on up and have a seat in the shade."

Jack followed Katie up the steps. This was her show and he figured she would want to take the lead. Lipke had put *her* father in prison for all those years, and she was about to tell the man he'd made a mistake.

Katie took a good look around as she stepped onto the large covered deck. Her gaze settled on the front end of a dusty red Bronco backed in on the far side of the house, then shifted to the front window. The blinds were open—no drapes. Jack checked but couldn't see any movement inside.

"You live alone?" she asked.

"My wife passed away a couple of years ago." He didn't elaborate on the cause of her death and she didn't press.

"You like living way out here?" Jack asked, nodding toward the scrub-dotted desert landscape.

"I do. It's quiet, and I'm away from all the reminders in town."

Jack knew what Lipke was getting at. The ghosts from the cases he'd worked would be in every house, alleyway, and vacant lot. "It is pretty here," he conceded.

A light breeze blew across the deck. There was a definite chill in the air. Jack and Katie took a seat on a porch swing hanging from the rafter at the end of the deck and huddled closely together.

Lipke slid his chair over and sat down facing them. "On the phone, you told me you found the ring your father claimed he lost in Maui at the time of your mother's murder." Lipke said. "Let's start there."

"Jack's the one who found the ring," Katie looked at Jack. "I think he should be the one to explain how that happened."

"All right," Lipke said. "I'm listening."

Jack planted his elbows on his knees. "It's quite amazing, really. I live on Maui—have been for a little over six months. My friend Robert Foster and I were diving on a reef known as Turtle Town. Robert can verify everything I'm telling you. The ring was in a depression in the coral ten or fifteen feet under water. The sun's rays must have struck the gold band just right, because it kind of winked at me. Just a glimmer of gold, but enough to catch my eye. I almost drowned getting that ring."

Lipke's stare held firm. He asked, "If you had no prior knowledge of who lost the ring, how did you meet up with Ms. McIntyre?"

"That's a stroke of luck in itself. Because the ring was over sixty years old and from the time of WW II, I decided it would be interesting to locate the owner, and if he were still alive, return the ring. Through West Point's web site I traced the ring to Katie's grandfather, Charles McIntyre—his initials are on the ring. He's living in a retirement home in Boise. Since I was in San Francisco on business, I drove there and returned the ring."

Lipke folded his arms across his chest and held them there. "And?"

Jack continued. "Charles McIntyre is a nice old guy and quite interesting to talk to. But apparently he has problems with his memory, because he phased out on me and never did tell how the ring had become lost on the reef. I didn't know if he'd even remember me and that I'd returned his ring, so I left him a brief note of explanation along with my name and phone number. I guess I was hoping he'd call. Anyway, Katie here—" he glanced at her "—did call about a week later, and that's when I found out what was going on."

Lipke's dark deep-set eyes focused on Jack's.

That's all it would have taken for Jack to confess if he'd been lying. But he wasn't. He stared back.

"And out of the goodness of your heart," Lipke said, "you jumped on a plane and flew to Vegas to help this young lady clear her father's name?"

"A man's life is important, Mr. Lipke," Jack said. "I didn't come here just to help Katie clear her father's name. I came here to free a man who's been locked up for a crime he didn't commit."

"As I said on the phone," Katie interrupted, "we planned on turning the ring over to my father's attorney. Jack was going to tell Ms. Tuscano how and where he found it. But she was murdered the night before we were supposed to meet with her at her office. Her death might have been coincidental to the ring showing up, but we find that hard to believe. Other things have happened, too. My house was burglarized Sunday evening while I was out having dinner with Jack, and we think the person responsible for that was looking for the ring."

"And you think Brian Wesley is behind it all?"

"Damn right we do! Dad's convinced Brian was having the affair with Mom. So am I. And we both believe he killed her. Why, we don't know. But he killed her. Other than Moira Tuscano, Brian was the only person I'd talked to about the ring."

"You told me you were chased into the desert."

"Last night a big man I've never seen before attacked me inside my house. Fortunately for me, Jack drove up as I was running out of the front door. I was able to jump into his car, and he drove us the hell away from there. But the thug chased us into the desert. That's where we lost him. Thanks to that asshole, we spent all last night hiding out in an old mineshaft. This morning we walked to the highway and caught a ride back to town."

"Tell the detective what King Kong said to you in the house," Jack urged.

Lipke looked at Jack then back at Katie.

She said, "Right before I broke a vase over the hairy ape's head, he told me he wanted the ring and that he'd come there to get it. The only way it makes sense is if Brian Wesley sent him."

"I don't want to tell you your business," Jack said. "But you have to agree that everything points to Brian Wesley. The man doesn't want Katie's dad released from prison and the case reopened, because there's a good chance he'd end up on the hot seat."

Lipke studied them for a long moment. Finally he unlaced his arms and said, "If I remember right, a lieutenant by the name of Voyles is in charge of Homicide. Why aren't you talking to him about this? Ms. Tuscano's murder and the assault on you, they're his responsibility."

"We did," she said. "He refused to believe Brian Wesley had anything to do with what happened to me. Seems Wesley donates a lot of money to the police fund. He and the lieutenant are friends."

"That's unfortunate, but not surprising. I know Wesley. He never impressed me, but he's made a point of ingratiating himself with law enforcement. Over the years he's donated heavily to the police fund."

"My father is the one who suggested we come to you for help. In spite of the way his trial turned out, Dad believes you're an honest and fair man whom we can trust to do what's right. Is that true, Mr. Lipke? Can we trust you?"

"If you're asking if I'm trustworthy, yes."

"So you'll help?"

"I didn't say that."

"What are you saying?"

"You need to understand I'm not on the force anymore."

"So what you're telling us is you won't help?"

"I'm saying let me think about it."

"You had me drive all the way out here so you could tell us you'd think about it?"

"I had you drive out here so I could see whom I was talking to. You can tell a lot by looking into a person's eyes."

"And what did my eyes tell you?" she asked.

Lipke stood up, an obvious sign they'd been dismissed.

"I told you," he said. "I'll think about it."

Chapter 64

JACK LISTENED TO the disappointment in Katie's voice as they drove away. She had expected Lipke to be more willing to get involved and perhaps he had, too. But it did make sense for the former detective to balk at going after Brian Wesley.

After all, the man *was* retired. And Wesley was connected.

"You really think talking to him was a complete waste of time?" he asked.

"Don't you?" she said.

"He did say he'd think about it."

"Right. The man's more interested in guarding his pheasants. All he's going to think about is being ready with his gun when those poor coyotes show up for dinner."

"Want to stop and get something cold to drink? We can talk over our options."

"What options are those? No one wants to get involved. Dad's in jail. It's easier to leave him there."

"There are always options," he said.

He doubted she was giving up, even though she made it sound that way. She was stronger than that and just needed to vent.

He'd help her past it. "We just have to figure out the next step."

"And a beer will help?"

"Doesn't have to be a beer. But now that you mentioned it, I'll buy."

"Maybe we should stick to iced tea."

"If that's what you want."

"How about the café up ahead?"

He let her question hang in the air a moment and said, "I won't let you give up. You know that?"

Her expression softened. "Maybe I will have that beer."

"There you go."

"You've got me figured out, haven't you?"

"How's that?"

"I won't give up, ever."

WHEN JACK AND Katie stepped out of the roadside diner half an hour later, they saw Lipke leaning against the hood of his dusty red Bronco, next to her Camry. Neither of them spoke as they walked up to him.

"You asked if you could trust me," Lipke said. "I'll let you be the judge of that."

Jack and Katie shrugged and nodded at each other. Jack motioned a hand toward Katie in a clear sign for her to take the lead.

She said, "I guess you wouldn't have followed us here if we couldn't."

Lipke looked at her for a long moment, tipped his cowboy hat back on his head and said, "Where's the ring now?"

She glanced at Jack.

"Tell him," Jack said.

She scanned the lot as if checking to see who might overhear her. Obviously satisfied, she faced Lipke and said, "We hid it in the desert last night. We didn't want to chance getting caught with the ring on us."

Lipke gave them a long look, but didn't press for more.

"Any ideas?" Jack asked. It was obvious Lipke had mulled over everything they'd told him or he wouldn't be there. He was no doubt running it all over in his mind again.

"It makes sense that Wesley was behind the attack on you last night. The fact that the goon—as you called him—said he was after the ring would tend to prove that. Primarily because Wesley was the only person you'd told about the ring—your father's attorney excepted. And since Ms. Tuscano was murdered, my money's on him."

"Okay, so you agree," she said. "What do we do now?"

"First, you need to know the case against your father has always bothered me. Everything pointed to his guilt. But his alibi was so outlandish, I found myself wanting to believe him. If he hadn't been so stupid as to fly to Maui under a false name and pay cash for everything, we could have substantiated his whereabouts at the time of your mother's death."

"So you put him in prison anyway."

"Not just me. There were other people involved who were less convinced."

"You were the investigator."

"And I did my job. But there were aspects of the investigation that bothered me, especially now that it appears Wesley has some reason to want your father in prison and the case left closed. Right from the beginning Wesley seemed awfully eager to point us in the direction of your father. He was even the one who called to tell us your dad was back in town.

"And during the trial, he fed the prosecutor stuff about your father and mother having marital problems. At the time, I thought he was just an honest businessman doing his civic duty. Given what's happened, I think he just wanted to keep the investigation focused on your father."

"I told you, we believe he killed Mom," she said. "Dad does too."

"Let's suppose I agree with you," Lipke said. "What motive did Wesley have to kill your mother?"

"Dad's positive Wesley is the man Mom was involved with, and feels he killed her because she was ending the affair. He also told us that Wesley all but stole the security business from him, because he only paid a fraction of the company's worth. Maybe that had something to do with what happened as well."

"Your accusations are still a lot of supposition by both of you. But I can honestly say, I've never much liked Brian Wesley—even back when I was working your mother's case—and I'd love to nail the bastard if he's guilty. The problem is, we need more than suspicion and a little circumstantial evidence to convict him of murder."

"What about my finding the ring, right where Katie's dad claimed he lost it?" Jack asked. "Doesn't that prove anything?"

Lipke said, "I believe you found that ring on the reef just like you said, and it certainly tends to prove Katie's father's alibi that he was on Maui. But then again, a jury might be led to believe the ring had been planted there after the fact. I'm afraid we need more."

"So what do we do?" Jack asked. "The police aren't going to get involved. Do we take the information to some other agency? Or is that out of the question since Wesley's such a pillar of the community?"

"Old-timers like me are dinosaurs. The officers today are cut from a different bolt of cloth. I'm afraid they won't go after Wesley the way I would have if I were still working Homicide."

"So what you're really saying is—" Jack smiled, "—this is personal, and you want to be the one who takes Wesley down?"

Lipke's eyes narrowed. "Damn right it's personal! I helped put a man in prison who didn't belong there. Wouldn't you feel the same way if you were in my shoes?"

Jack gave a slight nod. "Guess I would."

Katie huffed. "You said we need more. Circumstantial evidence was all it took to convict my father. Why isn't that enough, now?"

Lipke held his answer for a moment, then said, "Just understand, that's how it is."

"Because the man makes a few donations and puts on a good party?" she scoffed.

"Wesley has powerful people on his side," Lipke explained. "I'm not saying it's right that political influence should affect law enforcement one way or the other, but that's the way the game is played. We have to accept that."

Katie and Lipke were suffering greatly from the wrong done to Michael Sean McIntyre. Jack knew there was only one way to heal their wounds. Wesley had to go down hard, and they both had to be there when he took the fall.

He said, "When I operated my father's salmon boat, there were days when we would catch a load of salmon, and there were times when we hooked the wrong fish—a bonito or something. Whenever that happened, we rigged another bait, threw the line back in the water, and tried again. It's time to try again. And this time, we make sure the right bait is used. Tell me, Mr. Lipke, just how serious were you when you said you'd love to nail Brian Wesley?"

Chapter 65

JACK POSITIONED HIMSELF in front of Katie's couch, and Katie stood next to him. He scanned the layout of her living room, then peered toward the hallway, where Lipke was concealed. The former detective had said they needed more. What could be better than a confession?

That was the best they could hope for.

Still, Jack wasn't totally convinced they were pursuing the best course of action. But this was the plan they had agreed on. And Katie had been quite clear that she was all for it.

It was time to bring Brian Wesley down.

"As long as Wesley stays in the living room, he won't be able to see you," he said, loudly enough for Lipke to hear.

"Relax, Jack—" Katie touched his arm, "—it'll work."

He glanced at her and forced a wry smile. He'd seen movies where detectives who lacked the evidence needed to bring down a killer, used a witness—usually a pretty woman—to lure the killer to a late night meeting in a remote place, where the psychopath was then tricked into confessing. The confession was taped via a hidden microphone, so that the statement could be used against the killer in court. It seemed something always went wrong.

"I'm worried you'll get hurt," he told her.

"You're acting like a nervous ninny. This'll work. Besides, you know there's only one way we're going to get Wesley to admit to killing my mother. Wesley has to think he's holding the winning hand."

"The plan sounded better when we were standing next to Lipke's old Bronco talking about it. Now I can't help but think there's a better way to do this."

"There isn't," Lipke said. He stood in the opening to the hallway, arms casually crossed in front of him.

"This is too dangerous! Katie could be hurt. Or even—" Jack couldn't bring himself to say the word *killed*.

"Trust me," Lipke said. "I won't let anything happen to her."

Jack wasn't convinced. Lipke had told them he missed the hunt. And that with his wife gone, there was little for him to get excited about. He'd even resorted to shooting at coyotes. He hoped Lipke wasn't using their case to resurrect the juices that had dried up in retirement.

"Famous last words," Jack said.

"And true, none the less," Lipke assured him.

He stepped over to the couch where Jack and Katie were standing and retrieved the digital micro recorder sitting on the sofa table. He pressed the *record* button, and then the *pause* button. That done, he parted the leaves on the plant sitting in the center of the table and positioned the recorder where it couldn't be seen.

"There you go," he said. "When Wesley knocks on the door, press and release the *pause* button. That'll start it recording. This machine has a great microphone and it'll pick up every word that's said, once he steps into the living room."

"You're sure about that?" Katie asked. "We only get one shot at this."

"It'll work." Lipke pressed and released the *pause* button and walked to the front door.

Jack watched.

There was too much that could go wrong. He hoped their plan worked.

"Test one, two, three, test," Lipke said in a normal tone of voice.

Jack noticed Katie's lips tighten in concern. She shared his uncertainty. They both looked at the tape recorder.

Lipke walked back to the mini device and pressed the *play* button. His voice came across a bit faint, but they could make out every word.

A glimmer of gold drew Jack's attention to the big West Point ring hanging from the chain around Katie's neck. It had been Lipke's suggestion that they make a detour on the way to her house and retrieve the ring from its hiding place in the old mine.

The bait.

One person had already died. He couldn't help but wonder if they could ever truly be ready to do what they were doing.

He dismissed his doubts. He'd see this through. And he wouldn't let anything happen to Katie.

Lipke readied the recorder and glanced from Jack to Katie. He nodded. "If you're good to make that call, we're all set here."

Katie picked up the cordless phone and dialed Brian Wesley's number. Then she took a seat on the couch and leaned back with the phone pressed tightly to her ear.

Jack and Lipke watched and listened.

"Brian," she said into the phone a moment later, her voice shaky, "a man attacked me in my house last night."

There was a pause.

"No—" she slowly shook her head from side to side "—I'm all right. A friend drove up to the house just in time for me to jump into his car, and we got away."

Another pause. Another nod of her head.

"That's right. But the guy followed us and chased us into the desert. We wrecked our car and had to hide from him all night. We walked out late this afternoon." She shook her head, again. "No, we haven't called the police yet. We planned to, but I wanted to talk to you, first. I'm scared. Can you come over?"

Lipke gave Katie a thumbs-up signal as she nodded into the handset. "Don't worry," she said. "I'm not going anywhere. Just hurry! I'm really scared!" She switched off the phone and set it on the coffee table.

"That was perfect," Lipke told her. "Now we wait."

Jack felt his stomach doing flip-flops. He wondered if Katie's stomach was doing the same.

"Are you sure you're all right with this?" he asked her.

She offered a thin smile. "Don't worry. I'm fine."

The former detective walked over to the window and was peeking through the blinds at the street. His face was devoid of emotion, but Jack could tell that the man was looking forward to the confrontation with Brian Wesley. Seeing the veteran officer peer out at the street like that made Jack wonder how a person could ever get used to something like this—the adrenaline flow—all that juice.

He felt Katie's hand on his arm. He turned at her touch and peered into her amazing green eyes. There was something he wanted to say but couldn't find the words. He gripped her hand and offered her the same thin smile she had given him.

"You're worried, aren't you?" she said, her voice calm.

He thought about what she'd said. "Just promise me you'll be careful."

"I promise."

He didn't want to admit it, but he was afraid of what Wesley would do. In movies the situation always got nasty before it got better. And the Cavalry never showed up in time to save the day, if they were called at all. He wanted to make sure that didn't happen with them. He paced the floor thinking.

Then an idea popped into his head.

He asked Katie for her cell phone. He flipped it open and dialed 911 but didn't hit the send button. He was sure that if he could keep the phone concealed from Wesley, he could quickly press *send* and summon the police. The idea wasn't all that extraordinary, but he figured any plan that could get them help in a hurry was a good one.

He placed the cell phone behind the throw pillow at the end of Katie's couch. He'd just have to make sure he sat on that end.

The three of them fell quiet. Looking about the room he saw things he hadn't noticed before: an 8 x 10 framed picture of Katie's father with a woman, who looked so much like Katie she had to be Katie's mother. And two other framed photos: 3 x 5s, one on each side of the photo of Katie's parents. Aunt Regina, he suspected, and Katie's Grandpa Charlie. Seeing Charles McIntyre's face brought a smile. He really liked the old guy. Then his eyes focused on a Ping putter leaning against the credenza, butted up to the wall next to the hallway.

"You're a golfer?" he asked, turning to face Katie.

She looked at him, and he nodded toward the credenza. "I noticed the putter."

She glanced toward the golf club. "When I have the time," she said. "I'm not very good."

He shot her a toothy grin and said, "Maybe I can help you shave a few strokes off your score?"

"Maybe," she said. "If we get the chance."

They both fell quiet again, and he thought about her choice of words. *What have I gotten myself into?*

"He's here," Lipke said, a minute later. He pulled the Colt Detective Special from his ankle holster and took his place in the hallway.

A moment later there was a loud knock. Jack took a deep breath and let it out before pressing and releasing the *pause* button on the micro recorder.

Then he nodded at Katie.

She flashed a thin nervous smile and walked over to let Brian Wesley in.

Chapter 66

JACK STOOD AT the end of the couch with the cell phone hidden behind the pillow. Katie was visibly trembling when she reached for the doorknob. Her display of fear on the phone had been a convincing touch. Her hands shaking like that was no act.

"Uncle Brian, I'm glad you're here," Katie said when Wesley stepped inside. She put her arms around his neck and hugged him as a frightened child would a parent. Then she peeled her arms away and nodded toward Jack.

"This is Jack. He's the man who found the ring."

Wesley glanced around the interior of the house. His eyes moved back and forth as he turned his head, taking in the entire room.

"It was good of you to return her father's ring," he said, looking at Jack. "Not many people would go to the trouble." He furrowed his brow at Katie. "You still have the ring, I hope?"

Katie walked over to the coffee table and turned to face Wesley. She pulled the chain from inside her blouse and showed him the ring.

Wesley stepped to within a yard and a half of her and stopped. Jack realized she had chummed the man in the way a fisherman does fish. Wesley was now no more than four feet away from the recorder. Everything he said would be picked up with total clarity.

Brian Wesley was dressed in a black long-sleeved button-up sport shirt, tan Dockers, brown cowboy boots, a big silver and gold rodeo-style belt buckle. To Jack's amazement, the man was almost exactly as he'd pictured him.

He was six feet tall, with neatly trimmed, light brown hair, a square jaw, a few extra pounds around the middle, but not many. Around 200 pounds, maybe 205—about ten pounds heavier than he was. And a golden brown tan that suggested Wesley—like his bosom buddy Lieutenant Voyles—spent a lot of time in a tanning booth.

Jack wasn't impressed.

"Ever since last night," he said, "Katie has been scared sick. She was sure you'd help."

"That's why I'm here," Wesley said, and held out his hand to Katie. "Give me the ring and I'll keep it safe until we figure out what we are going to do."

Katie gripped the ring.

"I'm sorry," she said. "No one is getting this ring until I'm sure they are going to use it to set Dad free."

"Come on, Katie, give me the ring."

"I'm sorry, Brian, no."

In one quick motion, Wesley pulled a small flat semi-automatic pistol from his pants' pocket and pointed the muzzle at her head. "Give me the ring. Now!"

She took a step back. Her fingers tightened around the ring.

Jack tensed, ready to lunge at Wesley. But not yet.

"So it was you all along!" she said. "Wasn't it?"

"As if you didn't know," Wesley said, his lips curling into a wry smile. "Now give me the ring!"

"For God's sake, Brian, why?" A tear welled and broke loose. "You murdered my mother; I want to know why!"

"The thing about murder, Katie, once you've killed someone, the killing gets easier. And after a few times, it's no big thing at all." He motioned the barrel of the gun toward the couch. "Both of you, on the sofa, now!"

Jack took a seat close to the pillow concealing the cell phone. He slowly slid his hand underneath, visualized the phone's buttons and ran his finger over them like Braille. Then he pressed *send*. Now all they had to do was stay alive long enough for the Cavalry to arrive.

Katie stood her ground.

"You haven't answered my question," she said.

Wesley shoved her backwards onto the couch.

Jack started up. He wanted to get his hands on Wesley's throat.

Wesley motioned him back down with a jab of the gun's barrel.

Jack settled onto the cushion.

Wesley said, "Not that it will do you or your father any good, but yes, I killed your mother. And I must say, I'm surprised. I really didn't think it would be that difficult for you to figure out."

"That wasn't a problem," Katie said. "Not once I realized you were after the ring." Her eyes narrowed into angry slits. "But why did you kill her? You're my Uncle Brian. You'd always been there for me."

Wesley's lips curled up in a sick grin. "And for your mother."

The muscles in the corners of her jaw visibly tightened. "So you *were* the one she was having the affair with," she said.

Wesley made a snorting sound. "That's right."

"You've done a lot to destroy this woman's life," Jack interrupted. "I think you should at least tell her why."

That brought another snort from Wesley. "First, give me the ring."

Katie glanced from Wesley to Jack and back at Wesley. She had yet to let go of the ring.

Wesley held out his left hand while holding the gun firmly in his right. The muzzle was pointed at her face.

She lifted the chain over her head and handed it to him. "You've got the ring," she said. "Now tell me what happened."

Jack watched Wesley hold the West Point signet up in front of his face for a closer scrutiny. The man had to be sure. Or was it for a final look, as if to say 'I won'?

Wesley slid the gold ring and chain into his pants' pocket and said, "Your mother's death was an accident. She called and insisted I meet her at the houseboat. I'm not sure why she chose the houseboat instead of a bar in town, but she did. Maybe she wanted one last fling."

"Fling?" Katie's voice choked with anger.

"You didn't know? Ha," he said. "Your mother loved to fuck. She was a real hose monster. She liked it hard and deep and in all three holes."

Katie glared at him. "Fucking asshole!"

Wesley chuckled.

"Why, Katie," he said. "I thought you wanted to hear the truth?"

She didn't respond.

The smirk slipped from his face. "That's what I thought," he said.

After a moment, he continued, "As I was about to say, when I got to the boat she unloaded on me, saying she planned to break off the affair. And then she threatened to tell your dad I'd been skimming cash from the company. How she knew, I don't know. But she insisted I put the money back. That made me mad, and I grabbed the first thing I saw. Unfortunately for your mother, it was a frying pan. By the time I realized what I'd done she was dead. All I could do then was try to point the investigation away from me. Your dad made that easy. He really did some stupid things."

"That was no fucking accident." Katie's expression hardened as she practically spat the words from her mouth. "You killed my mother and made sure my father—your friend—went to prison for a murder you committed. And it was all about money."

Wesley shrugged. His smirk returned. "Better him than me. But you'll never get me to admit any of this to anyone. And without that fucking ring to back up your story, you'll be the same old pathetic Mary Kate McIntyre going to any lengths to prove your murdering father innocent. And your boyfriend, here—" he looked at Jack "—he's just a willing accomplice, eager to say anything to get into your pants."

"Did you kill her father's attorney, too?" Jack's anger was clear in his voice.

"Let's just say I was buying myself a little time."

"You bought more than a little time," Lipke said from the hallway. "Now, drop the gun before I take extreme pleasure in putting a rather large hole in your suntanned hide."

Wesley slowly turned his head and peered over his shoulder at Lipke. The retired detective's two-inch barreled .38 was pointed at his face.

Jack breathed a sigh of relief as Wesley let the gun slip from his fingers.

Before it hit the floor he said, "My compliments, Katie. I suppose you're wearing a wire?"

Katie pushed herself off the couch and slapped Wesley's face.

"Feel better?" he asked.

"Fuck you!" She reached into the plant on the coffee table, retrieved the micro recorder, and held it in front of her where Wesley could see it. "We got your entire confession on tape," she said, "I'm sure it'll make for interesting listening."

"Enough," Lipke ordered. "Put your hands behind your head and face the wall."

Wesley did as he was told. With his back turned, he said over his shoulder, "I guess it's only fitting you are the one to take me in. I just didn't think you were that smart."

Lipke didn't answer. He looped a finger through the nickel-plated handcuffs he'd carried during his years as a cop, pulled them from his belt, and stepped forward. He reached to snap the cuffs on Wesley's wrists.

Without warning, the front door burst open.

The thug who had chased Katie and Jack into the desert filled the opening. He was holding a large-bored handgun, and it was pointed directly at Jack.

Chapter 67

FOR A MOMENT, everyone inside the living room, except Brian Wesley, stood in stunned silence, staring at the big man waving the chrome plated .45 semi-automatic pistol.

"He's a cop!" Wesley yelled as he scrambled to grab his gun off the floor.

Lipke made his move, no doubt spurred by his years of law enforcement training and a sheer will to survive.

Jack was moving too, driven by his own survival instinct. So was Katie.

Gunshots boomed inside the house as Lipke and the big man fired their weapons.

Lipke went down on the carpet, clawing to pull himself into the hallway for cover. Blood soaked his right pant leg; his Detective Special lay on the floor.

The big man was still standing inside the front door with a small circle of blood staining his left shoulder. Undaunted by the bullet wound from Lipke's .38, he stood searching out his next target.

Jack dived for Lipke's revolver.

A bullet from the goon's .45 nicked Jack's ear as he hit the floor.

His hand found the wooden grips of the snub nose .38, and he came up with the gun. He pulled the trigger twice with the short barrel pointed at King Kong's chest.

The revolver bucked in his hand.

He wondered for a split second if he had missed.

The big man stood unmoving. His .45 was aimed at Jack's head.

It seemed to Jack as if the world around him were frozen in time. Even though he knew he was about to die, he couldn't move. Nor could he close his eyes. He waited.

All at once, the thug's determined expression morphed into one of confusion.

He lowered his gun an inch and looked at his chest. A circular red stain formed on his shirt, slightly to the left of his breast pocket, then another red blot appeared. The two bloody splotches grew and joined together into one.

But he didn't go down.

And he still held the gun. The barrel of the .45 came up.

Jack squeezed the trigger of the .38 again and again.

On boom followed by a click and another click.

The shiny semi-automatic fell from the massive hand as the big man gripped his throat. Blood gushed from between his fingers.

His mouth opened as if to talk.

Jack waited, the muzzle of the .38 raised, still pointing.

What he heard was a sick gagging sound that bubbled from of the man's mouth in a thick red slurry of tissue and cartilage, and more blood. A lot of blood.

A beat later, King Kong toppled to the floor.

Jack breathed in, then he heard Katie scream.

He had forgotten about Brian Wesley. He turned to see her sprawled on the carpet. She was bleeding from the mouth. Wesley stood over her with his little semi-automatic pistol pointed down at her.

Out of bullets, Jack threw the snub nosed .38 at Wesley.

The revolver struck Wesley's hip.

Wesley scrunched to the side and turned the pistol on Jack.

Jack lunged and grabbed the Ping putter leaning against the credenza.

Wesley fired a quick shot, then three more.

All four bullets struck the wall behind Jack.

His fingers tightened around the rubber grip of the golf club as he swung it at Wesley's head.

Wesley threw up his left arm to ward off the blow.

The bone in Wesley's wrist snapped and he went down. His gun bounced on the floor and landed a couple of feet away.

The coffee table was between them. Jack couldn't get to the gun.

Wesley spied it.

Jack threw the coffee table aside at the same time Wesley reached for the little semi-automatic.

Katie got there first and made a grab for the handgun.

Wesley slapped her arm aside, and the gun slid away a few inches.

She reached, wrapped her hand around the gun's grips, and turned the muzzle on Wesley.

She fired twice.

Wesley was a foot away from the end of the gun when it went off. The first bullet exploded his right eyeball. The second shot punched a small round hole in the center of his forehead a fraction of an inch below the scalp line.

Wesley stared at her with his good eye and extended his right hand, fingers groping the air. A bloody goo oozed from his ruined eye socket.

Jack knew the man was dead. His mind just hadn't realized it yet. He watched, strangely fascinated by the sight.

So did Katie. She inched back, making him reach. A final act of defiance.

Wesley slumped to the floor dead.

She let the gun slip from her fingers and sat on her heels, staring wide-eyed at Brian Wesley's lifeless body.

The odor of burnt gunpowder hung heavily in the air and its pungent smell filled Jack's nostrils. He looked first at Katie, then peered down at Wesley's corpse and at the bloody carcass of the giant on the floor by the front door.

This isn't real!

The room fell eerily quiet. A couple of long seconds later, Jack heard sirens wailing in the distance.

He checked the sofa for the cell phone, and noticed it on the cushion. The sirens were getting louder, and he realized the 911 operator must have traced the call to Katie's address. He sighed.

Too late…just like in the movies.

He picked up the phone and heard a woman's voice asking if anyone was there.

"People have been shot," he told her in an unwavering voice. "Send an ambulance."

Again, he looked at Wesley's body and then the body of Mighty Kong lying just inside the front doorway. He was surprised by his own calmness.

He said, "And tell the police no one inside the house is armed, that the men who tried to kill us are dead."

He switched off the phone with the woman still talking on the other end of the line, and laid the cellular on the arm of the couch. Katie was still sitting on her heels.

He helped her to her feet. "Are you all right?"

She dabbed at her split lip with the back of her hand. When she checked for blood, her hand was shaking. "I guess. But I don't know how I'll be once reality sets in."

"You did what you had to do," he said, as he slipped his arms around her. "If you hadn't shot Wesley, he'd have killed us for sure."

She eased herself out of his arms and looked down at Wesley. "I'm glad he's dead," she said. "And I'm glad I shot him. I'm probably wrong for feeling good about killing him, but that's how I feel."

"I think you have a right to feel that way. Besides, you were only defending yourself." Jack glanced at the body of the big man he'd shot, and added, "I know I sure don't have any regrets about taking down King Kong over there."

"Can someone give me a hand here?" Lipke asked. He was sitting with his back against the wall, next to the entrance to the hallway. His hand was pressed against the wound in his leg.

Jack and Katie moved at the same time.

Katie rushed to Lipke's side, and Jack headed into the bathroom. He was back in the living room seconds later with a wad of clean towels. He gently pulled Lipke's bloody hand away from the bullet hole and pressed a folded towel over the oozing wound.

He was not unfamiliar with serious injury.

Once, on his father's salmon boat, a deck hand had accidentally slashed the artery in his leg with a razor sharp fillet knife. Jack remembered how the blood had pumped from the gash. They had saved the deckhand's life by probing the wound with their fingers and pinching the artery off. Lipke's bleeding wasn't as profuse as that. He placed the palm of his hand on the towel and applied pressure.

"I don't think the bullet hit the artery," Jack said, doing his best to sound optimistic.

Lipke slumped against the wall. He winced and took a couple of deep breaths. He filled his lungs, pressed his hands to the floor, and repositioned himself with help from Katie.

He sighed. "Now I know why I retired when I did," he said. "I'm definitely getting too old for this shit."

Jack chuckled. "That chair on your front porch looking better, is it?"

"Yeah," Lipke said. "And maybe those pesky coyotes aren't so bad after all."

Jack grinned. "You did well, detective. And our plan worked."

Lipke winced. "Too well I'm afraid."

Half a minute later, two uniformed patrol officers appeared in the open front door, guns drawn. Jack was on his knees next to Lipke's injured leg, keeping pressure on the wound with the towel. Katie was sitting on her heels next to the former detective holding his hand.

"I'm a retired cop," Lipke groaned the words. "We're not armed."

Chapter 68

JACK STARED AT the bare walls of the interrogation room. The detective who'd been questioning him had left him sitting there alone. He wondered what was happening. The detective walked back in five minutes later.

"You're free to go," he said.

Jack eyed him a moment, then stood up. "What about Katie?"

"She's being released as well," the detective replied. "You can wait for her in the lobby."

"And then what?"

"As far as we're concerned, nothing."

"I'm talking about Katie's father," Jack said. "He's going to be released, right?"

"The case will be turned over to the District Attorney. It might be a week or two before his release gets pushed through the court, but I think you can plan on setting a plate for him at the Thanksgiving table."

"And Detective Lipke?"

"I understand the wound isn't serious. He'll pull through fine."

"Glad to hear he's going to be okay. Thanks."

"He was lucky, you all were."

Jack nodded and exited the interview room. He had plenty on his mind but had nothing more to say to the police. He glanced around the detective squad room. The place seemed different somehow; not quite as alien as it had seemed the morning before, when Katie and he had talked to Lieutenant Voyles. But he realized the room felt that way to him only because he had spent so many hours there, too many. This was definitely a place he didn't want to set foot in again.

Ever.

He walked out of the squad room and followed the hallway to the lobby. He realized he was too wound up to take a seat.

And Katie hadn't walked out yet.

After a couple of minutes of pacing the floor, he checked the large round clock on the wall: it was almost five in the morning. He and Katie had been held in separate interview rooms for over six hours.

He was anxious to find out how she was doing.

When she stepped into the lobby five minutes later, he reached her in three long strides. For a few long seconds, they stood looking at each other. His heart raced and the corners of his mouth shot up in a toothy smile. Her eyes were bloodshot and droopy, and her hair hung in limp strands.

She was beautiful.

He took her hand in his and held it.

"Are you okay?" he asked.

"I'm hanging in there."

"They took your clothes for evidence, too, huh? At least the detectives were considerate enough to have you bring an outfit to change into."

"It felt good to finally be able to get out of those bloody things and wash up. Too bad you ended up with another pair of old overalls. Hope they're clean."

"They are. And they almost fit."

"Let's get out of here."

He could hear apprehension in her voice. He grinned, hoping to hide his own feelings of uneasiness.

"I know a great Denny's restaurant if you're interested," he said. "Breakfast is on me."

She met his grin with a shaky one of her own. "I *could* use a cup of coffee," she said. "Only I should be the one buying."

"You?" He asked.

She pointed at his bandaged ear and said, "I feel like I owe you."

"Nonsense," he said. "The bullet barely nicked me." He opened the door for her and they walked outside.

The air had never smelled so good. He inhaled and let it out. It would smell even sweeter to her father.

He had told his version of events, four times: once to one team of detectives, then three times to another. His story had been the same each time. He wondered how the questioning had gone for Katie.

"Did they give you a hard time?" he asked her.

"Not really. You?"

"I'm sure the experience could have been a lot worse," he told her.

"When you have nothing to hide, it's easy to be honest."

"Don't forget about Lipke," he said. "It had to help having his statement in the mix, especially since he was the detective who worked your mother's case and put your father in prison."

"I guess we can all rest easy now."

"Especially your dad," he added.

His comment brought a smile to her face. "I passed Lieutenant Voyles in the hallway on my way to the lobby," she said, standing on the sidewalk in front of the building. "He didn't have anything to say to me."

"The crow he had for breakfast probably didn't sit well."

"Yeah, I'm sure it didn't."

Jack chuckled. "He'll probably need a new golf partner, too. Maybe I ought to ask him if he wants to play a round or two?"

"I think he's going to be busy for a while," she said. "I'm sure he'll have some explaining to do when his captain reads what I had to say about the man."

"You blasted him too, huh?"

She grinned. "Couldn't resist."

A uniformed officer walked up to them. "I'm Officer Lee," she said. "Karen Lee. I'll be giving you a ride back to your house."

Jack eyed the female officer a moment. She was of Asian ancestry, pretty, petite, and maybe all of twenty-two years old. He couldn't quite picture her in a life and death situation like the shootout they had just survived. She wore a gun high on her hip and he hoped she knew how to use it.

"That's nice of you," he said.

Officer Lee escorted them to her patrol car and opened the rear passenger's door. Jack started to get in, then stopped. He noticed the seat was molded hard plastic exactly like the one in the car he had been brought to the station in. And there was that same wire mesh screen separating the front and rear seats.

A cage for animals.

He straightened and faced the officer. He was sure he could speak for Katie when he said, "Thanks. But I think we'll take a cab."

Katie didn't argue.

They rode in relative silence to her house. Jack paid the driver. When he turned around, Katie was standing in her driveway, looking at her place. The crime lab personnel were gone and the police officers securing the area had left. Even so, she did not appear to want to go any farther.

"Would you like to check your house and clean up a little before we go?" Jack asked.

Katie's eyes told him what she was thinking. "I'm not in any hurry to go inside."

He knew the scene in the living room was too fresh. There was nothing he needed to say.

She used the electronic opener in her purse to raise the garage door. They climbed into her Camry, and she drove.

He gazed out of the window and felt different, deep inside.

The sky was beginning to lighten when they arrived at the restaurant. He got out of the car, inhaled a lungful of morning air, and looked around as if he were seeing the world for the first time. The mountains to the east stood out against a ribbon of pale yellow and blue. There wasn't a cloud in the sky. He rubbed his arms against the chill. It promised to be a beautiful fall day.

They walked inside without talking and eased themselves into a back booth as far from the other customers as possible. Their waitress walked up to the table.

"Just coffee," Katie said.

Jack placed his order.

"I've waited eleven years for this moment," Katie said, once their waitress walked away. "It feels good to have all that pain and uncertainty behind me."

"So what are you going to do now?" Jack asked.

"After my Dad is released, you mean?" She looked at her hands and began fidgeting with her fingers. She shrugged. "Don't really know," she said. "Get on with my life, I suppose."

He wondered what *get on with my life* meant to her. He could feel the void in his own life now that the final chapters of his ring quest had played out. He couldn't imagine how he'd have felt if he'd carried the eleven-year burden Katie had.

"And you?" she looked up at him.

"Call Avis and tell them the police have their car in the impound yard."

"Seriously, Jack, what are you going to do now that we don't have to run around town trying to prove my dad's innocence?"

"Good question" he said, staring into his coffee. "I've got some business to take care of. Then, well, like you, get on with life, I expect."

"In Maui?"

"Seems so."

"The desert really is pretty." She was looking directly at him. "And it's not all that different from the ocean—a vast unforgiving emptiness that appears void of life until you look closer and see it's full of God's creatures."

Jack arched a brow at Katie. Had he heard her right? Or had it been wishful thinking on his part? "Are you saying you wouldn't mind if I hung around Vegas awhile?"

She smiled. "I've sort of gotten used to you being here."

He returned her smile. She *did* have feelings for him. "Interesting," he said. "I've kinda gotten used to being here."

"But you have to go?"

He held her in his gaze, not liking the answer to her question. "Yes. But I wish I didn't."

Chapter 69

A FEW MINUTES after eight, Katie drove into the parking lot of Jack's hotel.

They sat in silence for a long, awkward moment and Jack realized Katie was waiting for him to make a move.

He didn't know what to say. "That shower is going to feel mighty good."

She looked straight at him. "I'm really not ready to go into my house. Maybe I can get a room here?" Her answer held a hint of expectancy.

He understood her perfectly.

Damn those eyebrows, anyway!

Not all that long ago he would have jumped at the chance of getting her into bed. But not now. He couldn't do that to her. It just wouldn't be right—to her, or Ellery.

"The room next to mine is empty," he said. "Or at least it was."

She peered deeply into his eyes.

Green, alluring—she wasn't making it easy for him.

"With any luck it still is," she said, and laid her hand on his. "We can get together for dinner if you'd like."

He couldn't stop looking at her eyes, and those wonderful eyebrows.

"I'd like that," he said.

He stood next to her while she registered. Number 209 was still vacant. He felt a tinge of regret for not inviting her up to his room, but thought better of himself for the decision.

No guilt, no regrets...

He led the way upstairs and along the walkway leading to their rooms. They came to her room first and she inserted her key card. As the light on the lock turned green, a part of him wished it hadn't. But mostly he was glad.

He waited.

She gripped the handle and pushed open the door. Then she turned, leaned up to him, and kissed him on the corner of the mouth.

Just an innocent kiss between friends.

She didn't linger. She stepped inside her room and closed the door.

He stood a moment, and watched the door close. Perhaps he was being foolish.

But then maybe not.

Once inside his room, he didn't make it any farther than his bathroom doorway. He stripped right there and walked inside to shower. He could hear the water running in the bathroom next door. For the second time in as many days, he pictured the silhouette of Katie's body behind the fogged shower door. But it didn't quite feel right. And he regretted having pictured her as a photo in a girlie magazine. Still, he couldn't lie to himself.

Those eyebrows are intriguing.

He let the hot water run on his head, shoulders, and back for a full fifteen minutes. When he finally turned off the water and stepped out of the shower, he noticed the water wasn't running in Katie's room.

Had the shower left her wide awake like he was, too wound up to sleep?

Or was she sound asleep, dreaming big-girl dreams?

The man who murdered her mother and did so much to destroy her life was dead. Soon, she would see her father walk out of prison a free man. And watch his face light up at the sight of her, knowing a daughter's unconditional love for her father had made it happen. There was much for her to dream about.

She deserves a life of sweet dreams.

When he walked over to his bed to stretch out, he noticed the blinking message light on his phone and found himself hoping Katie had called while he was in the shower.

He snatched up the phone's receiver and listened to the message. The smile slipped from his face at the sound of Ellery's voice, asking him why he hadn't called. And when she started in on him about not caring for her and voiced doubts about the wedding, he sighed and dropped the receiver on its cradle.

His cellular was sitting on the bedside table next to the room phone. He'd left it there, plugged into its charger, when he rushed to Katie's side the night Moira was found murdered. He picked it up and flipped it open. There were at least twenty missed calls from Ellery over the past day and a half.

She was furious.

He guessed she had a right to be. But he was in no mood to get into it with her on the phone, not now anyway. He'd call her back, later.

He stepped to the desk and took a seat in front of his laptop. He knew there would be a couple of dozen messages from Ellery waiting for him there, as well. But he also knew Robert might have sent him something. After listening to Ellery's scathing rebuke, he was in the mood for something funny, and Robert always managed to make him laugh.

The computer screen lit up and a few seconds later he was viewing his list of e-mails. Ellery hadn't disappointed him. He didn't bother counting her messages: there were at least the two dozen he'd figured on, along with two from Robert. One was the joke Robert had sent to him in San Francisco a week earlier. The second e-mail was a day old. The subject line read "Russell Carter."

He moved the cursor straight to Robert's joke and clicked on it. It read:

NUFF SAID! WOMEN ARE SMARTER THAN WE POOR MEN.
A Story with a Moral

> *A woman and a man are involved in a car accident on a snowy, cold Monday morning; it's a bad one. Both of their cars are totally demolished but amazingly neither of them is hurt. God works in mysterious ways.*
>
> *After they crawl out of their cars, the woman says, "So you're a man. That's interesting. I'm a woman. Wow, just look at our cars! There's nothing left, but we're unhurt. This must be a sign from God that we should meet and be friends and live together in peace for the rest of our days."*
>
> *Flattered, the man replies, "Oh yes, I agree with you completely, this must be a sign from God!"*
>
> *The woman continues, "And look at this, here's another miracle. My car is completely demolished but this bottle of wine didn't break. Surely God wants us to drink this wine and celebrate our good fortune." Then she hands the bottle to the man.*
>
> *The man nods his head in agreement, opens it and drinks half the bottle and then hands it back to the woman. The woman takes the bottle and immediately puts the cap back on, and hands it back to the man.*
>
> *The man asks, "Aren't you having any?"*
>
> *The woman replies, "No. I think I'll just wait for the police to get here."*

MORAL OF THE STORY:
Women are clever and evil. Don't mess with them.

Not all women, Jack assured himself. There was no doubt in his mind that Robert was referring to Ellery—his friend had been right about her from day one. She wasn't the woman for him, and he should have run away from her, the instant they started seeing life differently. He pitied the next poor sap she enticed into her spider web.

He closed the joke and opened Robert's other message: it had attachments. He read the first part of the message. Robert's girlfriend Kazuko had gotten Kimo Holowai a job on a research boat owned by the Pacific Whale Foundation. He was to begin work immediately.

Jack smiled.

In the second part of his message, Robert informed him that a coworker at the Hyatt knew Russell Carter, personally. And that employee had told Robert secrets about Carter only a select few people on the island knew.

That got Jack's attention.

When he'd read the remainder of the message—detailing what Robert had been told about Carter—and viewed the attachments, he had to laugh. The information Robert had given him was no joke, but considering Carter's hard-ass image, it was far funnier than all of Robert's jokes put together.

A winning hand.

Chapter 70

WHEN KATIE EASED her Camry to a stop at the curb, in front of the airport terminal the next morning, the awkwardness of having to say good-bye hung heavily in the air between them.

Jack turned in his seat to face her. "I'm only on standby. I could easily fly out tomorrow or the next day. Let me help you get your house back in order."

"You've done enough," she told him. "Workers are coming in to replace the living room carpet and repair the bullet holes. I'll probably have them paint the entire house before they're finished. Either way, it's being taken care of. And while the work's being done, I'm going to drive up to Boise and tell Grandpa the good news about Dad."

"Say hi to him for me."

"I will. And, Jack—"

She looked away.

He took her hand in his and held it.

"I know," he said. "It's hard for me to say good-bye."

Moisture welled in the corners of her wonderful green eyes. He wanted to reach and brush the teardrops away.

She said, "I don't like good-byes, Jack."

He grinned and said, "How about: 'Here's looking at you, kid'?"

"Didn't Bogie say that?"

"I never said I was original."

"Maybe not your sayings, but you're one of a kind, Jack. And I'll never forget you."

"I'm counting on that," he said. "Give my regards to your dad and remember to say 'hi' to your grandfather for me."

JACK DIDN'T BOTHER calling Ellery to pick him up at the airport. The short e-mail he had sent her that morning, letting her know he was on his way back to Maui, was enough. He hadn't known what flight he would get or what time he would arrive. He figured he'd just show up.

He grabbed a cab and arrived at the *ohana* in Wailea shortly after three in the afternoon. He'd spent the entire flight deciding what he was going to do about his life. He obviously didn't love Ellery. She was the right person for someone, he was sure. But he wasn't that man. When he'd thought she was the answer to his dreams, he'd only been kidding himself.

People—he told himself—will do all sorts of crazy mixed-up things when they think they love someone. And he *had* thought he loved her.

Now he was sure that he was definitely not suited for the lifestyle Ellery demanded. And no way could he work for a man like her father.

He would like to have been able to point an accusatory finger at Ellery, but he'd come to understand it wasn't Ellery's fault their engagement wasn't working out. She knew exactly who she was and made no attempt to hide it. The problem was he hadn't been totally honest, not with himself, not with her. And when their relationship began to fall apart, he had been looking for someone to blame for his unhappiness—with her, and for the half-dozen years he'd sacrificed for his family.

It had been easy to blame his father for those six lost years, and it was easy to blame Ellery for his failed romance. He was going to make sure he didn't repeat those mistakes.

He stepped inside the *ohana* and found Ellery sitting on the couch. She was furious with him. That was obvious by the way she glared at him from across the living room. He didn't blame her for being upset. Maybe her anger would make what he was about to do easier.

"I'm waiting, Jack," she said. "You have a lot of explaining to do."

He said, "Explaining, yes. But I'm not going to make excuses for anything I've done. For some time I've sensed our relationship wasn't what it should be. I seem to do a lot of things that piss you off, and I find myself getting irritated at many of the things you do. We're different people, Ellery. We want different things. You can't help who you are, and I can't help who I am."

Ellery stood up and put her hands on her hips. The fire had not left her eyes. "And you are just now realizing that?" she said. "I suppose that slut in Las Vegas had something to do with this nonsense you're telling me. What'd she do, flash her tits at you? That's about all it'd take."

"That was a nasty thing to say—even for you."

She scowled and added, "If the shoe fits, wear it."

He didn't want to buy into her game. "Just so you know, Katie had little to do with my decision to break our engagement. But what happened there did. We'll leave it at that."

"Do you really expect me to believe you?"

"Believe whatever you want."

"The wedding, all the planning—this past year? None of that means anything to you, does it?"

He shrugged. "We had some good times, I won't deny that. And I am sorry for how things turned out between us. At least we don't have a bunch of presents to return."

"So it's over then?"

"The Hawaiians have a word for what I'm doing: *ho`oponopono*. It means doing what's right."

"Right?" she asked. "Right for whom?"

He gave her a long look. He couldn't change who she was or how she lived her life. And maybe he had no right to. But he wasn't going to play a part in her version of *Father Knows Best*.

"Ellery," he said in a soft, easy tone of voice, "there's something you need to know about your father. From what I've seen of the man, he isn't fair or honest when it comes to doing business. He ordered me to fire Kimo Holowai for no good reason other than seeing if I would do it. That made me sick to my stomach. But I went against my beliefs and did it for you.

"And then I found out your father has been bribing local politicians to get his development projects pushed through. That makes me ill, as well. You, on the other hand, believe that's how people get what they want in this world. And that's why you and I could never have a life together. I'm done, Ellery, with you and your father. And keep in mind, your dad could dump you as easily as anyone else if it suits his needs."

Ellery's eyes narrowed.

He waited.

"I love my father," she said. "Nothing you've told me changes that. And he'll never disown me, because I'm his daughter."

"But of course."

"Are you done?"

"I'm only telling you these things, because I did love you. I don't any more, but I don't hate you either."

"Screw you, Jack!"

He removed the Rolex she had given him and handed it to her. "Enjoy your life I don't think it's right for me to keep this."

She grabbed the watch from his hand. "You're a fucking asshole! I'll give it to someone who appreciates me."

Jack grinned. She was exactly who he'd thought. "Go right ahead. Frankly, I don't care what you do from now on. I'm out of here."

He was sure Ellery had plenty to say to him. She'd probably thought up names to call him that he had never heard of. But he couldn't see any sense in standing exchanging insults. To do so might make her feel better, but no amount of vulgarity would change how he felt. He turned and headed for the bedroom to pack his clothes and the few personal items that meant something to him.

His back had been turned no more than a second or two when he heard the front door to the *ohana* slam shut. A couple of beats later, he heard a car motor start and the car roar off. She had saved him the pain of saying good-bye, but he still felt the prick of the thorn.

He and Ellery had shared some fun times—especially in the beginning, before life got in the way. He'd remember her for how she had once brought a smile to his face. But he would also remember there was an ugliness that went along with her physical beauty. And that taught him a very important lesson that reminded him of something his mother used to say: *The best looking peach in the basket wasn't always the sweetest.*

Finally, he understood what she meant.

Chapter 71

ELLERY'S BMW CONVERTIBLE was still gone when Jack carried his bags to his Jeep. He had no idea where she'd run off to, and he didn't care. He didn't harbor any ill will toward her, but she was no longer his responsibility. He didn't figure she would have any problem finding a man eager to take his place. He wished her luck.

Once his bags were sitting in the back of his Jeep, he picked up the manila envelope he'd brought with him and walked into the main house unannounced. Thomas Seaport's Escalade and Russell Carter's black Mercedes were parked in the driveway. He knew they'd be in Seaport's office.

Seaport was sitting behind his desk. Carter sat in a padded chair a few feet in front of him. They both eyeballed Jack when he marched into the room.

"You've got some explaining to do, Jack," Seaport told him.

"That's the second time I've been told that."

"Second time?" he asked. He furrowed his brow. "You might be engaged to my daughter but don't get smart with me."

"That's exactly what I'm doing," Jack said. "For once I'm getting smart. First of all, I'm not engaged to your daughter any longer. Second of all, I know about Gordon Kaeha and the payoff you made to him. I'm not sure what effect this will have on your casino deal, but I've composed an e-mail exposing your bribery scheme and sent a copy to the Governor, the Attorney General, the Department of Land and Natural Resources, the Kahoolawe Island Reserve Commission, and the *Maui Times*. And I may send the information to a half dozen other people before I'm done."

"Empty gestures, Jack," Seaport said. He leaned back in his chair, laced his fingers behind his head and added, "You can't prove a thing."

"Hard evidence, no," Jack admitted. "Only information, I'm sorry to say. Letting everyone on the island know what you're up to might not stop you from taking advantage of people and raping this land of all that's beautiful, but at least everyone will know how you do business."

Seaport rocked forward and gave Carter a nod.

Carter got up from his seat and closed the door to the office. Having done that, he took up a position a few feet to the side and behind Jack.

Jack caught the movement out of the corner of his eye and heard the door close. He knew what was coming. "So now what? Carter here beats me into a bloody mess and uses my body for shark chum on that fancy boat of yours?"

Seaport smiled. "I don't kill people, Jack. I ruin them."

Jack couldn't resist a grin of his own. "Fire your best shot, asshole. I've just seen the dark side of hell and trust me when I say you're just a piss-ant in the game." He threw a nod over his shoulder at Carter and added, "And keep in mind, Tinkerbell here isn't fooling anyone."

Jack opened the manila envelope and removed a dozen 8x10 color printouts of photographs Robert had e-mailed him in Henderson.

His ace in the hole.

"Get a load of this shit," he said and tossed the copies onto Seaport's desk. "If I were you, I'd be looking for another goon—one who wears boxers, instead of panties."

The pictures spread out in front of Thomas Seaport like a hastily dealt poker hand. Three of them showed Russell Carter wearing a bra and panties. A couple showed him wearing a lace garter belt. The others showed him wearing a metal studded leather collar and black crotchless panties revealing an abnormally small penis that stood out in contradiction to the big man's large feet and hands.

Seaport pulled his hands away from the desk as if it had been infected with a highly contagious disease. His eyes narrowed, and he shot Russell Carter a disconcerting look. Then he focused on Jack. "Get out of here! Needless to say, I don't ever want to see you again."

"My pleasure." Jack turned to leave and stopped.

Russell Carter brushed past and peered down at the pictures. His face swelled beet-red. "You fucker! I'll break you in half for this!"

Jack raised his right palm, extending it in front of him in a gesture to stay back, and took a couple of steps toward the door. He'd had his fun. Enough was enough.

"Relax, dickhead," he said. "Your wife hasn't seen those pictures yet, or at least I haven't shown them to her. And I won't as long as you stay the hell away from me and my life. I have no predisposed prejudice toward gays or lesbians. People should embrace who they are. You're the exception. You're an asshole. Needless to say, I don't ever want to see you again." He shot Seaport a look and threw in, "Sorry for borrowing your line, but I thought it fit."

Thomas Seaport rose from his seat, pointed to the door, and said, "Get out of here, Jack, now!"

Jack walked out of the house still wearing the same grin he had when he left the two men standing in Seaport's office. Ellery's car was parked where it had been earlier. She was back, but he had nothing more to say to her. And he doubted she had anything to say that he wanted to hear.

He took one last look at the Zodiac and climbed into his Jeep. The toys Ellery had bought for him meant nothing. He was leaving them behind. They'd be missed—at least until he replaced them—but he'd have his self-respect.

He cranked up the vintage flathead four-banger and listened to the sixty-five-year-old engine roar to life. While he waited a few seconds to let the motor warm up, he got the feeling Ellery was watching him.

He saw her glaring at him from the doorway of the main house, her mother standing behind her. He gave the women, the place, and all that it stood for, a perfunctory salute and drove out of the gate.

Chapter 72

JACK SPENT THANKSGIVING evening in the Kahului airport, and that night on a plane. The next morning he steered his rental car into the parking lot of the Doubletree Riverside Hotel in Boise, Idaho, at nine thirty on the dot. His red-eye flight had landed on time and he went straight to the car-rental agency. But this time he was driving a silver Pontiac. He passed on the offer of a Mustang.

He parked near the hotel entrance, and fifteen minutes later he was opening the door to his room. He dropped his luggage on the floor and for a second, just stood there looking at the furnishings. This room was no different from the one he'd stayed in before: same layout, same bedspread, same furniture. But there was something different about the way it felt. The far-from-home feeling of the hotel room on his first visit to Boise wasn't there.

This time, he was in no rush to leave.

And he knew exactly where he was going.

He smiled at the thought and stepped to the window. The sun's rays felt warm on his face, and he soaked them up with his eyes closed. He remembered the woman he'd seen in the room across the way the night before he met Charles William McIntyre. He tried to pick out the room where the woman had stayed. He couldn't, but it didn't matter. Surely she was long gone, getting on with her life, just as he was?

He was eager to see Katie. He considered calling ahead just to make sure she was at the retirement home, but quickly dismissed the idea. He didn't want to chance spoiling the surprise. He couldn't wait to see the look on her face when he showed up at the home unannounced.

When he had called her the week before to see how she was doing, she'd told him her father had been released from prison and that they were going to Boise to spend Thanksgiving with Grandpa Charlie.

Just how it should be.

Jack was sorry he hadn't arrived there in time to share the holiday with them. He counted on Katie and her father still being in town.

Thirty minutes later he walked into the Ridgeview retirement home. This time he carried a box of Krispy Kremes in with him. He didn't recognize the woman behind the counter.

"Good morning," he said as he set the box on the counter.

"Can I help you?" she asked.

He leaned slightly forward and squinted at the name badge pinned to her uniform. "You sure can, Helen," he said. "These doughnuts are for you and the rest of the staff. As for me, I'm here to see Mr. McIntyre. And could you tell me if his son and granddaughter are here visiting him?"

Helen's eyes beamed at the box of doughnuts.

"I saw them come in about half an hour ago," she said. "But I had to step away from the desk for a few minutes and don't know if they left or not. I'll check and see if they're in his room."

He watched her pick up the receiver to the phone on her desk, mumble a string of words, listen, nod her head, mumble some more, and return the receiver to its cradle. She was at the counter a second later.

"His nurse informed me Mr. McIntyre is down by the river. His son and granddaughter are with him."

"Perfect. How do I get there?"

Helen pointed to a side door and said, "Out through there and follow the walkway. You can't miss it."

"Thanks. Enjoy the doughnuts."

The walkway outside led to a large grassy area, not unlike a small park. Tables and chairs sat under several large trees, which provided ample shade in the summer time for anyone wishing to escape the heat, and a couple were placed out in the open for those who didn't. Most of the leaves had fallen from the branches with the first chill of fall, but the sun was out. The families visiting their parents and grandparents welcomed its warmth.

He walked straight to the river.

Charles McIntyre was on a bench facing the water. Sean McIntyre sat on one side of him. Katie sat on the other, facing her grandfather. She was smiling and talking and her dark brown hair glistened in the morning sun.

"Pardon the intrusion," Jack said, when the three generations of McIntyres turned their heads at the sound of his approach. "I thought I'd drop in and say 'hi.'"

Katie's cheeks crinkled into a gigantic smile. "Jack!" she cried, rising to her feet. She nodded at his heavy jacket. "Where's your aloha shirt?"

He grinned and unzipped his down parka, so that she could see he had on the same lime green aloha shirt he was wearing the day he first met her. "It's still my favorite."

Katie's father stood up, motioned toward a vacant table on the lawn ten feet away, and said, "Let's grab that table so that we can sit down together and talk. There's plenty I want to say."

"I'd rather stand if you don't mind," Jack said. "It was a long flight." He nodded at the river. "And it's quite nice down here by the water."

"Of course," Sean McIntyre said, and extended his hand. "I really can't thank you enough for all you did. There has to be something I can do for you."

Jack noticed that he was wearing the West Point class ring. He doubted the man would ever take it off. He gave the man's hand a firm shake. "Your thanks is enough."

He shot Katie a big smile and winked.

Out of the corner of his eye, he noticed Katie's father and grandfather glance from him to her. They both smiled.

Chapter 73

JACK DID HIS best to keep from staring at Katie's wonderfully thick eyebrows. They had decided on the restaurant at his hotel for drinks and dinner. Sitting across from her, he was trying to keep his eyes directed at the list of entrees even though he already knew what he planned to order.

He set his menu aside and gazed at her over the top of the candle burning in the center of their table.

"Run that by me again."

"We were talking about my dad," she said.

He forced himself to focus on her beautiful green eyes. They sparkled like emeralds in the candlelight.

"Freedom agrees with him," he said. "Your dad looks ten years younger than he did that day I saw him in the prison."

"He does at that."

"So what's the latest? How's Detective Lipke doing?"

"I visited him at the hospital the day you left. He was looking forward to the chair on his porch. He said he was sorry for what happened to my dad, but says he can rest easy knowing Wesley finally got what was coming to him."

"And your father, does he have any idea what he's going to do now that he's a free man?"

"Brian Wesley wasn't married—a playboy to the end. Dad's suing his estate for civil rights violations. He'll probably own High Desert Security again by the time it's settled. But I'm not sure he wants any part of that business, even if he does end up with it."

"I can understand how he could feel that way. I suppose you're going to stay in the house with him?"

"For a while, just until he adjusts to the free life. Then I'll probably buy a small house or a condo. I'll most likely be staying in Henderson."

"Like you said, the desert has a beauty all its own."

"How about you, Jack? You told me you broke off your engagement. Are you going to stay on Maui?"

"Nothing there for me but lots of sun, salt water, sand, and scantily-clad suntanned women," he said, and flashed her his best grin. "The truth is, I've grown rather fond of the desert now that a beautiful woman has pointed out its charm. I might even take up prospecting. It just so happens there's a mine I know of not too far from Henderson."

"Can't you be serious even for a moment?" Katie huffed.

Jack let the smile slip from his lips as he looked deeply into those lovely green eyes. "Of course I can," he said. "I'm not drawing any assumptions on where any of this is headed, but I *can* tell you there is only one woman I truly care about. That's you."

Her peered down her hands and fidgeted with her fingers.

After a moment, she said, "I hoped you'd come back. I even thought about taking a vacation on Maui and looking you up."

He took her hands in his and held them. Her skin was warm and soft—inviting to his touch.

"We've been through some tense moments together," he said. "And there's nothing like a gunfight to put us in touch with our feelings. But there is a lot we don't know about each other. The best part about it is, now we have time to find out how we really feel."

She looked directly at him. "So what do we do?"

"For now, we get to know one another."

"For now?"

The smile returned to his face. "I talked to my former biology professor, at the college I attended in Oregon, when I gave up my scholarship and left school to help my dad work his salmon boat. Professor Payne actually remembered me. Anyway, he told me the college couldn't reinstate my scholarship. Not that I expected them to. But he did say he'd write a letter of recommendation to the Dean. And he offered me a job in his lab. I'm really doing it, Katie. I'm going to get my Bachelors degree in Marine Biology. I'm going back to college and finish what I started."

"That's wonderful!" she said. "When do you start?"

"The spring quarter if everything goes according to plan. Until then I thought I'd find a place to stay in Henderson—maybe park cars at a casino or something. I want to spend time really getting to know you—your likes, dislikes, the good and the bad. And I want you to know those same things about me. Then...well...we'll see how we feel about each other. You mean a lot to me, Katie. I don't want to screw things up for either of us."

He leaned forward and tenderly kissed her on the corner of her mouth. Then he slowly settled back in his seat, and for a long moment they looked at each other.

He touched his lip and thought about the kiss she had given him that night at her house, and again outside his room at the Holiday Inn.

But her expression told him she wanted more.

He got up from his seat, stepped to her side of the table, and extended his hand.

She laid her fingers in his palm.

A silent understanding.

He gently lifted her to her feet, took her into his arms, and held her close.

They kissed, and this time there was no mistake.

It was more than an innocent kiss between friends.

About the Author

WILLIAM NIKKEL IS the author of *Cave Dweller*, the first book published in his Jack Ferrell series. A former homicide detective and S.W.A.T. team member for the Kern County Sheriff's Department in Southern California, William is an amateur scuba enthusiast, gold prospector, and artist who can be found just about anywhere. He and his wife Karen divide their time between California and Maui, Hawaii.

Visit William Nikkel online at Facebook and williamnikkel.com.

14427179R00134

Made in the USA
Charleston, SC
10 September 2012